ONCE
UPON
A MURDER

ONCE UPON A MURDER

A LADY LIBRARIAN MYSTERY

Samantha Larsen

CROOKED
LANE

NEW YORK

Published in the United States by Crooked Lane Books, an imprint of The Quick Brown Fox & Company LLC.

Crooked Lane Books and its logo are trademarks of The Quick Brown Fox & Company LLC.

Library of Congress Catalog-in-Publication data available upon request.

ISBN (hardcover): 978-1-63910-621-9
ISBN (ebook): 978-1-63910-622-6

Cover illustration by Sarah Horgan

Printed in the United States.

www.crookedlanebooks.com

Crooked Lane Books
34 West 27th St., 10th Floor
New York, NY 10001

First Edition: February 2024

10 9 8 7 6 5 4 3 2 1

To Keith Larsen

The Wolf, I say, for Wolves too sure there are
Of every sort, and every character.
Some of them mild and gentle-humour'd be,
Of noise and gall, and rancour wholly free;
Who tame, familiar, full of complaisance
Ogle and leer, languish, cajole and glance;
With luring tongues, and language wond'rous sweet,
Follow young ladies as they walk the street,
Ev'n to their very houses, nay, bedside,
And, artful, tho' their true designs they hide;
Yet ah! these simpering Wolves! Who does not see
Most dangerous of Wolves indeed they be?
       —"Little Red Riding Hood," by Charles Perrault

CHAPTER 1

Miss Tiffany Woodall was forty years old, and she had never been a mother. Since she was a spinster, this was probably for the best. However, it didn't take the pain away from the monthly reminder that she had no children of her own. This morning, she'd already bled through one rag, and her wretched stomach was cramping more than usual.

"Are you sure you don't want any bread, Miss Woodall?" Mary asked. The pretty young maid that lived with her had bright blue eyes and glossy brown hair.

Tiffany opened her mouth to speak, but had to close it quickly and cover her lips with her fingers. Just being in the kitchen with all the smells rather overwhelmed her. After a few moments, she was able to regain her composure. "Just weak tea, dear Mary. I am afraid that I do not have an appetite this morning."

Mary brought her a porcelain cup of tea and shook her head before taking her own seat at the table across from Tiffany. Her own plate was full of toast and eggs. "You need to eat more, Miss Woodall, or we'll have to take in all of your dresses, you're gettin' so thin."

"I am sure my appetite will be back soon."

Her maid pointed at her with a fork. "Mrs. Day says that yer pinin' over the bookseller."

Mr. Samir Lathrop.

Tiffany choked on her tea. Coughing, she brought the napkin up to her mouth to cover it. "When did you speak to her?"

Shrugging a shoulder, Mary sniffed. "Just about the town. I'm friends with her daughter Jessica."

Tiffany took another sip of tea and wished for the thousandth time that she had not stopped Samir from speaking last September, the night before her trial. He'd said, *"Tiffany, there's something that I need to tell you—"*

Tiffany had stopped him from continuing because she didn't know if she would have to go to prison or be hanged for masquerading as her half brother Uriah last year in a foolish attempt to keep her cottage. Little had she expected that the Duchess of Beaufort would come to her aid the following day and convince the assizes judge to throw out her case. If only she had let Samir speak that night. She had filled in the rest of his sentence so many times in her own mind:

I love you.
Will you marry me?
I want to be the father to your children.
Let's start a family library together.

Samir, however, had never brought the topic up again. Nor had they been alone together since. Mary was always underfoot, and Tiffany's reputation was a bit wobbly after having disguised herself as her brother. Besides, Samir had to be careful of his position as the constable in Mapledown. Yet, how she wished he would ask her to marry him. Tiffany loved him utterly and wanted nothing more than to be his wife.

She pulled her brother's pocket watch out and saw the time. "Oh dear. I am running late. I am sorry to leave you with the dishes again. I shall do them myself after dinner."

Half of Mary's mouth quirked up in a smile. "You do realize, Miss Woodall, that I am your servant?"

Tiffany found her own lips curling up. Five months ago, Mary would have kept her eyes lowered to the table and never dreamed of teasing her mistress. She liked this bold young woman much better.

She got to her feet, and her stomach cramped again. "I do, but we are more than mistress and servant. We are friends, and I shouldn't wish you to think that I am taking advantage of you."

Mary laughed. "Since you pay me and educate me, perhaps it is I who is taking advantage of you."

Tiffany patted the young woman on her shoulder. "Never. Don't forget to practice writing your alphabet after your chores. Both lower and uppercase letters."

"I won't."

Covering her mouth with her hand again, she left the kitchen and put on her calash bonnet, cloak, and leather pattens beneath her boots. Then she grabbed her umbrella. It was difficult to prepare for the weather when it was equally likely to snow or rain, and either way there was a great deal of mud on the path to Astwell Palace.

Tiffany took one more sustaining breath before opening the door of Bristle Cottage, her very own home. It appeared that the weather could not decide if it would rain or snow, for the sky was doing a bit of both. Pushing open her umbrella, she lifted it above her head and began to walk down the path to the road. Her eyes were so fixed ahead of her that she didn't see a large object that blocked her way. Tripping over it and landing face-first in the mud and snow, Tiffany dropped her umbrella. It rolled a few feet away from her.

Her gloves were wet and muddy, as were the skirts of her dress. What in heaven's name had blocked her usual path? Slowly getting to her feet, she turned to see the bulge she had tripped over.

It was a man.

And his body was half covered in snow. Which meant that the corpse was cold and most likely dead. Warm skin melted snow, like the wet on her cheeks that looked like tears. Tiffany stooped down to her knees and saw that the man was very tall. Even face down in the mud, he had to be six feet. Practically a giant. He wore no hat, and the back of his head and hair were covered in blood.

With all of her strength, Tiffany tried to turn the body over. She pushed with her hand and then added her right shoulder until the form slowly turned face up. The legs still tangled stiffly together.

She knew that face.

Even muddy and bloody, she would have recognized Mr. Bernard Coram anywhere.

Tiffany yanked off her wet glove and pressed her hand against his neck. There was no pulse there. His skin was as cold as ice and extremely pale. One of his eyes looked as if it had been blackened. And there were four long scratches on his left cheek. His lips were blue, and snow frosted his eyebrows. He'd been dead for many hours.

While Tiffany had never liked the handsome young former footman, she certainly hadn't wished for his death.

And what was he doing near her home?

Bristle Cottage was at least a mile from the village of Mapledown, and the road in front of her house led to Astwell

Palace. The place from which he had been dismissed five months previous for his terrible treatment of the Duchess of Beaufort's adopted son, Mr. Thomas Montague. She recalled that his parents' farm was somewhere near the village.

Who or what had killed him?

Only last year, Tiffany had helped solve her own half brother's murder and the death of a lady's maid. She glanced around the road and open area. Between the mud and snow, she didn't see a rock large enough to bludgeon a head. Nor any other man-made item that might have been used as a weapon.

The sleet had covered up any tracks that might have been left by an animal or a murderer. The scratches on his face could indicate an unfortunate meeting with a wolf or a bear. She remembered the fairy tale from her childhood, "Little Red Riding Hood." A young girl goes into the forest to visit her grandmother's cottage and is tricked by a wolf disguised as the old woman.

> *"Grandmamma, what great arms you have got!"*
> *"That is the better to hug thee, my dear."*
> *"Grandmamma, what great legs you have got!"*
> *"That is to run the better, my child."*
> *"Grandmamma, what great ears you have got!"*
> *"That is to hear the better, my child."*
> *"Grandmamma, what great eyes you have got!"*
> *"It is to see the better, my child."*
> *"Grandmamma, what great teeth you have got!"*
> *"That is to eat thee up."*

Then the wolf eats the girl. Tiffany's cottage was in the forest; however, there were no Big Bad Wolf's footprints in the mud.

Only the two freshly made ruts from the wheels of a carriage, which led her to believe that Bernard had met his death at the hands of a human.

Taking another breath, Tiffany got back to her feet and entered the cottage. She could hear the clinking of china in water. Mary was washing the breakfast dishes. She hoped her mother's plates could survive the ordeal.

"Mary," she called out, so as to not alarm her maid. "I'm afraid there has been an accident."

The young woman rushed out of the kitchen with her apron on, and her eyes widened at the sight of Tiffany's disheveled figure.

"Oh, dear Miss Woodall! What happened?"

Tiffany pulled off her other muddy glove. "It was not me that suffered from an accident—or at least, not a serious one. There is a body in the road. I was hoping that you could go round the back of the cottage and then to the village to inform Constable Lathrop of it. I would go myself, but I am already unconscionably late for the palace."

Mary nodded. "The little duke will be in a right fit, he will."

Tiffany didn't bother to respond, but took off her pattens and boots before going upstairs and changing her muddy skirt. Luckily, her blouse was not attached to it. In only a few minutes, she was back out the door and on the road to Astwell Palace, carefully circumventing the corpse this time. She took a few steadying breaths and clutched her umbrella tighter. The sleet rain was soaking her new skirt. But she dared not be late for work. The Duchess of Beaufort had already done her a great favor by allowing her to retain her late half brother's position as librarian, employment reserved exclusively for educated males. The duchess, however, had Tiffany to thank for the evidence that saved her adopted son, Thomas, and her own life. Still, Tiffany did not wish to take advantage of the duchess's dubious good nature. The duchess stopped by the library at unexpected intervals to check on Tiffany, and criticized everything from her appearance to her work.

Mr. Ford opened the servant's door near the kitchen for Tiffany. "You're late, Miss Woodall."

The elderly butler had a beaklike nose and a slight limp in his left leg. His countenance was disapproving.

Tiffany exhaled slowly. "I am afraid it has been quite a wretched morning, and it is not entirely my fault. I found a dead body in front of my cottage."

The maids stopped their scrubbing to look at her in surprise. Monsieur Bonne came out of his kitchen, bowl and whisk in hand. Even the gardeners, whose names she didn't know, gazed at her with wide-eyed interest. They leaned forward in their seats.

"Was it a vagrant?" Mr. Ford asked.

Bernard's blackened eye and scratched face reappeared in her mind. Tiffany shook her head.

Mrs. Wheatley, the housekeeper, was a short woman with a trim figure and sharp green eyes. They were now focused on Tiffany. "Who was it, Miss Woodall? Anyone we know?"

She couldn't help but bring her hand back to her mouth as the nausea reared up in her throat at the memory. Tiffany managed a curt nod. "I am afraid so. It was Mr. Bernard Coram, who used to be employed here."

Monsieur Bonne, the chef, spoke very rapidly and animatedly in French, and Tiffany did not understand a word of it. She had already learned that the language she'd been taught at school was not at all similar to the words that servants from that country spoke. Tiffany saw and heard conversations all around the room between maids, grooms, and the gardeners as she took off her muddy pattens, which hadn't quite done their job of keeping her shoes out of the muck; then she removed her cloak and calash, and hung up her umbrella.

Mr. Ford cleared his throat, and as if he were the king, the mutterings ceased instantly. "No more chattering—get back to work," he said, and then turned his beaklike nose to Tiffany. "I assume you have informed the constable of this?"

She nodded. "I sent Mary. I didn't dare be any later than I already am."

The butler took out a handkerchief and handed it to her. "For your right cheek, miss. There is a bit of mud there. When Constable Lathrop arrives, I will send him to the library. I daresay he will want to interview you about the discovery."

Tiffany wiped her cheek with the white cloth and was mortified to see a great deal of brown on it. "The constable will probably want to speak to the members of the staff as well. Mr. Bernard Coram had both friends and enemies on it."

She tried to give him back the handkerchief, but he shook his head infinitesimally. Not a gray hair out of place. Feeling the blood rush to her face in embarrassment, Tiffany pocketed the white cloth.

Mr. Ford cleared his throat once more. "I will inform Her Grace about the murder at once. She will want to know."

Tiffany tucked back an errant curl and bobbed a curtsy before leaving the butler's august presence. But it wasn't until she'd left the servants' quarters and was walking down the main hall that she realized Mr. Ford had used the word *murder*. She'd simply said that she'd found a body in front of her house and had given no description of the state of it.

CHAPTER 2

Opening the door to the library, Tiffany was immediately accosted by a six-year-old ruffian with a wooden sword.

"Surrender, ye bilge rat!" he said in a high, sweet voice. The speaker had angelic golden hair that was almost coppery, and it curled around his narrow face. Brown eyes were the largest feature in his countenance, but he also had a button nose, rosy cheeks, and sharp little white teeth. There was a sash tied around his head, but the rest of his raiment was silks, and it wasn't difficult to recognize the young Duke of Beaufort: Lord Peregrine Francis Alfred David Erskine. Tiffany had nicknamed him "Beau."

He smiled at her with his sharp, perfectly straight teeth, and Tiffany knew exactly why he had every person in the palace around his little finger. Herself included.

Tiffany raised her hand to her forehead and saluted him. "First Mate Woodall, reporting for duty, Captain Beaufort. Sorry to be late—there was an accident that I had to help take care of first."

Beau lowered his wooden sword, his brown eyes wide. "What sort of accident? Were there blood and guts?"

The memory of Bernard's bashed and bloody head made her stomach cramp again. Tiffany quickly brought her hand to her mouth and took a few calming breaths. "Unfortunately, yes, Captain. A former footman at the palace died."

"Which one?"

"Do you recall Mr. Coram? A very tall footman with pale hair?"

He shook his head. "No. But may I see the body?"

"No. Your mother would kill me if I let you."

Beau huffed. "But I am your captain!"

Tiffany shrugged her shoulders. "But your mother pays my wages, darling."

His little face looked positively mutinous. Tiffany had to suppress a smile. She'd been quite put out when the dowager Duchess of Beaufort had added teaching her son to Tiffany's duties as librarian. The duchess had assured her that the arrangement would only be temporary while she found a proper governess. Five months later, Tiffany was wondering if the duchess would ever find a suitable candidate; and part of her was hoping that she wouldn't. Tiffany had never had much to do with children and certainly not with a bossy six-year-old who was already a duke. But Beau had quite stolen her heart, and she loved him as if he were her own son. The little boy had filled a hole in her life.

"Would it please the captain if we started by reading *Gulliver's Travels*?" she asked. "And waited on spelling and sounds until after luncheon?"

Beau dropped the wooden sword and ran over to the table to pick up the heavy volume. He brought it over to her, and they snuggled together on a settee near the fire. Beau leaned his head against her arm, and Tiffany felt warm all the way through.

"Now, where were we?"

"Gulliver has returned to England, but he has set out again and was attacked by pirates near India. But then he was rescued by the flying island of Laputa that uses mathematics instead of weapons to fight."

Sort of.

Tiffany had to make math more exciting somehow; and what better than mathematical pirates that flew around the world on a floating island? She hoped the author, Jonathan Swift, didn't mind her adaptations.

The continent, as far as it is subject to the monarch of the flying island, passes under the general name of Balnibarbi; and the metropolis, as I said before, is called Lagado . . .

Tiffany read several pages, until she noticed her small partner stirring. It was clearly time for a battle.

She closed the book with a loud snap. "Captain, I see pirates ahead. They are five chairs and two tables away. How long until they get here?"

Beau jumped to his feet. "They'll be here in seven! Get your sword, First Mate Woodall."

Tiffany did not have to be asked twice. She rushed across the library and grabbed her own wooden sword. She returned to Beau's side and they slashed the air with their play swords at fierce pretend pirates.

"How many have you felled, Captain?"

"Eight!"

"Oh dear," she admitted. "I've only felled two. How many is that altogether?"

"Ten. But then I got another, so now it is eleven," he said. "But there are more coming. To the ship!"

She grinned. Sailing on the ladder was her favorite part of the game. She followed Beau over to the iron ladder that was over fifteen feet high. He nimbly climbed it as well as a sailor scaling the rigging. Tiffany took her perch on the first step and waited for her captain's nod before she pushed them with one foot, and the ladder sailed across the bookshelves to the other side of the room.

Tiffany put a foot down to stop them from colliding with another bookcase. "We are cornered, Captain. We must fight! There are four female pirates and five male pirates. How many are we facing?"

Beau dropped his wooden sword, and luckily it missed Tiffany by a few inches. He held up both of his hands, making the number nine with his fingers.

"Perfect, Captain, but please retrieve your sword."

"Aye, first mate," Beau agreed, climbing back down and picking up the wooden weapon. "We must plunder and pillage."

Tiffany nodded and continued to swing her own wooden sword against the invisible opponents.

"You don't need to fight anymore, First Mate Woodall," Beau informed her. "They are all dead now, and we must send them to the depths of the sea."

Obligingly, she put down her sword and carried invisible people to the side of the rug and tossed them in the air.

Beau gave her back her sword. "Now, we must practice our sword fighting with each other."

"Very good," Tiffany said, raising the weapon to her face. "En garde!"

Neither she nor Beau had any practical knowledge of fencing, so they mostly hit each other's weapons and tried to make the other person drop their sword.

Parry. Hit. Crack.

Tiffany retreated a few steps and readied herself for the second onslaught, but the door to the library opened, and the Duchess of Beaufort walked in, followed by her lady's maid, Miss Emily Jones. The duchess, like Tiffany, was in her early forties. But no one could have guessed that, with her impressive wigs and beautiful French gowns. She was like a walking work of art: powdered, painted perfection. Emily made a lovely contrast with her youthful face and figure, her glowing brown locks, and her simple beauty. She was Mary's elder sister.

The duchess smiled at her young son, and it transformed her otherwise rather cold face. "Oh dear, are you two being Lilliputians again?"

"The Lilliputians were two weeks ago, Mama," he said, running to kiss his mother's cheek. "Last week, we were giants, and this week we are pirates."

"Mathematical pirates," Tiffany interjected. "I assure you that a great deal of algebra and geometry is required to be a successful pillager."

"We are on the flying island of Laputa, and we throw rocks at people below us," Beau added.

She winced and wished that Beau wouldn't have mentioned that. Yesterday, they had thrown rocks into the lake on the estate, but when they arrived back at the palace, Beau threw a rock through a window near the kitchen. She carefully explained to him that all rock throwing had to be away from buildings and people. Tiffany half wondered if the duchess was coming to talk to her about the broken window. It was *partially* her fault.

"Have your mathematical pirates stolen any goods, Miss Woodall?" the Duchess of Beaufort asked, her tone cold.

Tiffany's face felt rather hot as she turned to look at Beau. "Captain Beaufort, you haven't been pillaging outside of the library, have you?"

"First Mate Tiffany that is insu-aboard-a-nation." Two bright red spots appeared in his little cheeks.

"*Insubordination*—very close, darling. I mean Captain. And please tell me the truth."

He shrugged one narrow shoulder. "Maybe."

Her stomach cramped tightly, and Tiffany felt miserable from the roots of her hair to her toenails.

The Duchess of Beaufort cleared her throat. "Jones, would you please take Master Beau out for a walk? A long walk."

Emily bobbed a curtsy. "Yes, Your Grace."

"May I bring my sword?" Beau asked.

"Very well," his mother said sternly, "but you must wear a coat and keep it buttoned up the entire time."

Emily held out her hand to the young duke, and Beau put his in hers.

Tiffany swallowed and tasted again the rotten bile. "Don't walk too close to my cottage. There has been an accident."

The lady's maid nodded, her face pale, and she led Beau out of the room. He looked over his shoulder and gave her a little wink. The sweetheart.

When the door closed behind the pair, Tiffany knew she was in deep trouble. The Duchess of Beaufort did not approve of her teaching methods.

The duchess moved to the settee, by the fire, that Tiffany and Beau had recently shared, and sat down. She gestured with one elegantly mitted hand for Tiffany to also take a seat in the chair beside her. Tiffany placed her hands in her lap and crossed her heels, keeping her eyes on the floor.

"It is that time of month?" the duchess asked, her tone softer than before. Less commanding.

Tiffany glanced up in surprise, unsure of what the duchess was referring to. "For *Gulliver's Travels*?"

The exquisitely dressed woman rolled her eyes. "Please, Miss Woodall, I see with my own eyes that you are pale. Is it the time of your monthly bleeding?"

She clutched her cramping stomach. "Yes, but finding Mr. Bernard Coram's corpse in front of my cottage this morning did nothing to help."

The duchess shook her head. "He was such a dreadful young man. I knew that he would come to a nasty end."

"I only wish it hadn't been in front of my house."

Her Grace nodded. "And so close to the palace. I can only be grateful that Thomas is away in London for another few days. Their dislike of each other was well known among the staff and village. I should have hated for suspicion to be cast on my son a second time."

She too felt relieved. Tiffany and Thomas had become fast friends in prison and had helped prove each other's innocence. The Duchess of Beaufort had been so grateful to Tiffany for exonerating her adopted son that she'd given her Bristle Cottage and the three acres surrounding it. For the first time in her life, Tiffany had a home of her own.

"Thomas will be returning with a proper governess, a Miss Drummond. She's the daughter of a vicar and has already been a governess for ten years."

Tiffany's face fell. She would miss spending time with Beau. Her librarian duties were hardly strenuous, and teaching the young duke had become the sunshine of her day. His smiles. His snuggles. His sweetness. She touched her flat stomach, wishing for a child of her own.

"I'll miss being a mathematical pirate."

The duchess barked a short laugh. "I will not miss your rock-throwing pirates. Yes, Mr. Ford informed me of the broken window. But Beau confessed to him and to me. He also told me that he'd pilfered items from around the palace as a part of pirating. I should like for you two to return them this week, before the new governess starts."

She nodded, praying that Beau remembered where he'd hidden the items (including her priceless diamond cluster pin— their first piece of treasure). "Of course, Your Grace."

The duchess stood up and walked to the door, waiting in front of it. Tiffany rushed to turn the handle and open it for her.

"Why don't you take off the rest of the day, Miss Woodall?" the duchess said. "I am sure Constable Lathrop will wish to discuss your finding of Mr. Coram's corpse, and perhaps you could urge him about another personal matter."

"What personal matter?"

Sighing, Lady Beaufort shook her head. "Marriage, Miss Woodall. If you want to have a child of your own, you and your bookseller ought to marry sooner rather than later. You are neither of you getting any younger."

Tiffany's mouth fell open, and her face went red. The duchess didn't see, however, for she walked through the door without another word or glance at Tiffany.

Was the Duchess of Beaufort matchmaking?

Tiffany giggled at the thought. But sobered when she remembered her purpose. She should set off for the village at once to talk to Samir about the body, and her own feelings. There was nothing like death to remind one how short life truly was.

Chapter 3

Happily, Mr. Bernard Coram's body was not in the road in front of her cottage as she passed by. Samir must have already collected it. Tiffany couldn't help but feel a bit relieved. She opened the door to her home to check on Mary. She called out her name, but there was no response. Walking through the rooms, she noticed that no fires were lit. The house was dark and cold and empty.

Wherever could Mary be?

Tiffany assumed she must still be in the village. She washed her hands and took out yesterday's bread and cut herself a slice. It was dry, but it helped calm her poor cramping stomach.

She put back on her calash bonnet and left the cottage. At least the rain and sleet had stopped. The ground was still more muddy than not, but Tiffany chose her steps carefully on the way to Mapledown so that only the edge of her dress and petticoat showed a bit of mud. Her heartbeat quickened when she saw Samir's bookshop. There was no smell she liked better than that of books and ink and Samir. Taking a fortifying breath, she strode purposely to the door and opened it.

Samir stood on the other side, with his tricorn hat and coat on as if he'd been about to leave. He stiffened as she entered, and his full lips tightened into a line. His handsome face looked more dismayed than delighted to see her. Hardly an auspicious start to the bearing of her heart. But perhaps he was concentrating on his duty, and his somberness had nothing to do with her.

"Were you on your way to see me?" she asked.

"Yes. No," he said, taking off his hat with one hand and running his fingers through his dark curls with the other. "I intended to come question you after I informed Farmer Coram of the death of his son."

Bernard's father. That would certainly be an unpleasant visit, and the prospect of that would make anyone feel dismayed.

"I could accompany you, if you'd like. I am sure you don't want to make such a visit alone."

Samir put on his hat, but he didn't agree with her. He merely opened the door again to let her out and locked it behind them. He started to walk toward the long road that led to her home (the shorter path was near the rectory). Tiffany had to jog a few steps to catch up to him. Samir's pace was uncharacteristically quick.

"Are you well acquainted with Farmer Coram?" she asked, for she did not know Bernard's family at all.

His nostrils flared. "I haven't been inside his cottage in ten years. He's a mean old bigot, and his second wife is scarcely better."

The apple didn't fall too far from the tree then. Bernard had also been a most unpleasant young man and highly distrustful of foreigners and anyone different from him. She'd heard him say the most terrible things about Samir and Monsieur Bonne.

Tiffany increased her speed as they passed the last house in town and continued down the muddy road. "I know that now

is not the best time . . . but there never seems to be a good time
these days. Or at least a time when we are on our own. The
thing is . . . I, um, well—"

Samir stopped and turned to face her. She wished he hadn't.
Confessing her feelings to his shoulder was far less intimidating
than to his face.

"What would you like to tell me, Tiffany?" he asked, his
tone soft and the look in his eyes even softer.

Despite her doubts, she was sure that Samir cared for her.
But then why had *he* not spoken again to her about his love?
Was it because the last time he'd tried to confess his heart,
she'd stopped him?

Swallowing heavily, Tiffany took a deep breath. "Samir, I-I
love you and I was h-hoping that you felt the same way about
me."

His eyes dropped to the muddy path beneath them. She
heard him inhale and exhale. Nature around them was even
quiet, waiting for his response. Not a bird tweeted or a fly
buzzed.

"I-I am so sorry. At this time, I am not able to give you
what you wish," he said, then walked away.

Tiffany felt as if she'd been slapped. His rejection stung
deep in her soul. She had terribly misjudged his feelings for
her. All these months of hoping, praying, and pining. She had
thought he loved her like she did him, but he must have only
felt friendship. Trying not to cry, she followed him down the
road like a beaten dog. Her ears were ringing and her limbs
were shaky. She wanted to go home, but decided it was best to
get both unpleasant interviews over with first.

By the time she caught up with Samir, the door to a small,
thatched cottage opened. The woman who answered it was not

much older than Tiffany, and her left eye was bruised purple. Her brown hair, however, was in a tidy bun, and her dress and apron clean.

The woman curtsied to them. "What can I help you with, Constable?"

Samir took off his hat. "Is your husband at home, Mrs. Coram?"

She shook her head. "He's in the fields with our sons, like a proper working man."

"Of course," Samir said, lowering his chin. "Unfortunately, we come bearing some sad tidings. Your stepson, Bernard Coram, was found dead on the road this morning . . . It appears that he was murdered."

Mrs. Coram shook her head again and clenched her teeth. Tiffany expected her to cry, but she didn't.

The woman wiped her already clean hands on her apron. "I knew he'd come to a bad end. Told m'husband more than once, but he'd hear nothing against his precious Bernard. So, what are you here for? Money for the funeral? Ye can tell the sapskull priest and spineless coffin maker that we're good for it."

Then she slammed the door in their faces, never once acknowledging Tiffany's presence as she stood next to Samir.

CHAPTER 4

"Shall I tell you how I found him?" Tiffany asked as they began walking back to Mapledown.

Samir didn't look at her as he said, "You might as well save your story until we reach Doctor Hudson's house. He's examining the body, and he will probably want to know all the details as well. Sir Walter Abney has requested that he take a more active role in this murder case."

Tiffany rubbed her lips and wondered why the justice of the peace would request the village doctor to help in the investigation, when Samir was the constable. She didn't dare ask, and so they walked next to each other in silence. At least his pace was slower now. But Samir seemed changed beyond reason. Had Bernard's death affected him this much? Or was he purposely being cold to Tiffany to emphasize that he was not interested in her romantically? Shivering, she would not have thought he would ever treat her thus. It was almost as if he were another person entirely.

She felt relieved when she saw Doctor Hudson's house. The front door was painted a bright blue, which made it easy to locate amid the brick and stone buildings on the main street. She didn't wait for Samir, but briskly knocked on the wood.

Doctor Hudson's housekeeper, Mrs. Balogh, opened it. She was a plump and pleasant lady with an abundance of brown hair, liberally streaked with gray, and somewhere in her late fifties. Her face was round, as was the end of her nose.

She smiled warmly at Tiffany and gave her a quick curtsy. "Miss Woodall, I didn't expect to see you here. Constable Lathrop, the doctor is waiting for you."

Tiffany bowed her head. "I wish I were here under more pleasant circumstances, Mrs. Balogh. I was the one who found the body outside of my cottage this morning."

Mrs. Balogh put a hand on her ample chest. "Lord, bless me. What a shock that must have been."

It had been a very great shock, but compared to the other shocks of the day, it had paled a little. Tiffany only nodded.

Mrs. Balogh gestured for her to come inside. "'Tis no wonder you're looking peaky. Let me get you a cup of tea before you see the doctor. He's with the body. Constable, it's just right through that door."

Tiffany watched Samir go the other direction, before following the housekeeper into the kitchen.

"What a conscientious man our constable is, and fine-looking too," Mrs. Balogh said with a wink.

She had thought so too, but her heart still stung from his rejection.

Mrs. Balogh handed her a hot cup of tea on a saucer. Tiffany took a small sip. The warm, spicy ginger liquid seemed to calm her cramping stomach.

"How 'bout a biscuit?" the housekeeper said, opening a tin of round sugar biscuits.

"Oh, I couldn't."

Mrs. Balogh smiled and held the tin closer to Tiffany. "It will be good for your monthlies."

Tiffany very nearly dropped her teacup. It clattered on the saucer, and she spilled hot tea on her gloves. "Excuse me?"

"Ginger tea will help with the cramping, as will dry foods like biscuits."

Tiffany set down the teacup with one shaking hand. It had already been a very trying day. "I-I don't know what to say."

The housekeeper shook her head. "I were a midwife for thirty years before I become the doctor's housekeeper and assistant. I know all there is about a woman's monthly bleeding."

Her hands still shaking, Tiffany reached out and took a biscuit. It was perfectly round and pale golden, sprinkled with sugar. She took a small nibble, and Mrs. Balogh had been right. The dry texture felt good on her tongue and even better going down. Tiffany was even able to drink the rest of the tea in her cup while finishing the biscuit.

"Thank you," Tiffany said.

Mrs. Balogh led her from the warm kitchen, down a hall, to the examination room. Doctor Hudson was in his mid-twenties with a pair of closely set eyes, a long pointy nose, and a spotted face. His light brown hair was pulled into a low ponytail at the back of his head. He bowed to Tiffany. She curtsied back, but her eyes were on Samir. She felt a surge of love at the very sight of him. He was so tall and strong and solid. Yet, he did not return her feelings. She forced her gaze away from him and back to the young doctor.

"Miss Woodall," Mr. Hudson began, "I am relieved that you have come with the good constable. I have some questions for you about your discovery of Mr. Bernard Coram's corpse."

Tiffany kept her straying eyes on the doctor. "That is why I am here."

"When you discovered the body, did you by chance try to offer any aid to him? Did you wipe up any blood on the back of his head? Or clean up the scene around him at all?"

She shook her head, her eyes falling to the inert form on the table. "I am afraid that I was late for my position at the palace when I quite literally stumbled over Bernard. Since I was already on my knees, I checked to see if he needed any help, but his skin was cold. I was able to turn him over and saw that his lips were blue. I noticed the blood on the back of his head and knew that he was dead. Then I returned to my cottage, to wash and change, and requested that my maid, Mary, go and get the constable."

The urge to look at Samir when she said his title was nearly overwhelming, but she kept her eyes on the corpse. She again noticed that there were scratches on his cheek that she'd initially thought were from an animal. But now they looked as if they had been inflicted by human fingernails. Bernard's torso was naked. Tiffany could see that he had been a muscular man. Who could possibly have inflicted such harm on him? And why?

"This is quite awkward, Miss Woodall," Doctor Hudson continued, "for the constable and myself walked through your house and found bloody rags in your room . . . Are you certain that you did not see what happened to Mr. Bernard Coram and that you did not clean up his wound?"

Heat rushed to Tiffany's face. The doctor and Samir must have seen her used rags from last night and this morning. She ought to have washed the blood out of them instead of waiting to do it after work.

Grasping her hot neck with one hand, Tiffany exhaled slowly. "The blood on the rags was not from Mr. Coram, Doctor. It is the time of my monthly bleeding. If you would like your housekeeper to examine me for the truth, I am willing."

"There is no need for that, Miss Woodall," Samir said, a little color in his own cheeks. "I already told the doctor at Bristle Cottage that a lady's monthly bleeding has a different smell and color than blood from a wound."

If anything, Tiffany's face felt hotter at his words. Samir was correct, but she couldn't help but wonder how he knew so much about a woman's menses. Her chin trembled and her toes curled up in her boots in embarrassment. He'd seen her soiled rags.

Doctor Hudson didn't appear to be embarrassed at all by their discussion. He picked up Bernard's right hand and showed it to Tiffany. "Do you see this bite mark on his thumb? Whoever bit him had perfectly straight teeth. A rare trait in a village."

Tiffany couldn't help but run her tongue over her own set of straight teeth. "Good heavens! You're not suggesting that I killed Mr. Bernard Coram?"

But of course, he was. That was why the doctor had mentioned the bloody rags. Tiffany blinked rapidly, and her limbs shook. Could this day get any worse?

Doctor Hudson cleared his throat, and she could see his Adam's apple bob up and down. "The thing is, Miss Woodall, when—er, you were dressed as your brother, you slapped Bernard's face and offered violence on his person."

Her eyes moved to Samir. Could he have betrayed her? The doctor had not been at Astwell Palace that day, but Samir had. She'd been defending *him* after Bernard had called Samir, a "bleedin' dark-skinned Indian." The memory still brought rage to her soul. Yet, Samir had done nothing. As if he was used to such terrible treatment.

"I heard about the incident from another member of the staff, not from the constable," Doctor Hudson continued, "and that you are also particularly close to Mr. Thomas Montague. Another gentleman who disliked the deceased."

Tiffany gritted her unfortunately straight teeth, trying to keep them from chattering. She took a few deep breaths through her nose before speaking. "I should be shocked if you found anyone who liked the deceased."

Samir barked out a laugh, and even the doctor gave a wry smile.

"Be that as it may, Miss Woodall, I was hoping to get an impression of your teeth to compare to the bite mark on the body."

"It would help clear some of the suspicion," Samir added; his countenance seemed to ask her to comply. "We met with Sir Walter Abney after retrieving the body, and he is of the belief that you are the most likely candidate based on the location of the corpse. He has tasked both Doctor Hudson and myself to investigate you most thoroughly. He feared that I may be biased because of our friendship."

Samir had known she was under suspicion for the murder when she entered his shop and accompanied him to the Coram farm. Could that be why he'd rebuffed her romantic advances? He hadn't said that he didn't love her. Only that he was sorry and that *"At this time, I am not able to give you what you wish."* Would he be able to return her regard in the future? When she wasn't the prime suspect in a murder investigation?

Blinking rapidly, Tiffany recalled that the justice of the peace, Sir Walter Abney, believed her to be a murderess. Her spinster state was the least of her current problems.

She took a deep breath; she could almost taste the metallic smell of blood in the air. "You are welcome to take an imprint of my teeth, sir. I have nothing to hide. I have not spoken a word to this man in nearly six months. Nor have I seen him in church."

Doctor Hudson turned and took a jar out of his sideboard. He opened the lid and took out a bit of gray clay, rubbing it together to make it more malleable. He formed it into a round biscuit-like shape. Reaching out, he offered it to Tiffany.

She could only be glad that Mrs. Balogh had helped relieve her stomach cramps, for otherwise, she would not have been able to put the clay in her mouth, nor to make a small bite with her teeth. Even still, Tiffany gagged as she handed it back to the doctor. He took out a knife and carved: "T. W." Then he brought the sampling next to Bernard's thumb. Tiffany didn't dare breathe as he compared the two bite marks.

"Miss Woodall's mouth is clearly larger than that of the person who bit the corpse," Doctor Hudson said, pointing out the shape to Samir. "Her jaw circumference is nearly a centimeter wider, and it appears that her teeth are larger too."

Tiffany snorted, trying to keep in a hysterical laugh of relief. But she couldn't. For the first time in her life, her large mouth had saved her from getting into trouble, instead of the reverse. Neither her strict father nor her joyless half brother would have ever believed it.

"Miss Woodall, are you quite well?" the doctor asked, grabbing a bottle of smelling salts from his sideboard and offering it to her.

She held up a hand. "I am sorry. It is only that my big mouth has landed me into a mess many times. It is ironic that today it has saved me. But surely Bernard was not murdered by a bite. I have seen the back of his head. That wound must have been what killed him."

Doctor Hudson set down the smelling salts on the table with the corpse and turned the head slightly so that Tiffany could see the wound. It had been washed clean, presumably by the good doctor and Samir, but it still looked menacing. At least a two-inch impression through the bone of the skull. Tiffany couldn't conceive anyone with enough force to give such a blow.

"A head injury like this one would have bled pretty freely," the doctor said. "But the constable and myself did not find any blood near the body or on the road in front of your cottage. If you did not clean up the wound, that leads me to believe—"

"He wasn't killed there," Tiffany said, completing the thought for him. "Only why would someone leave his body in front of my cottage for me to find? I cannot think of anyone with whom I have a quarrel. Except perhaps the rector. But refusing an offer of marriage nearly a half a year ago can hardly be a reasonable excuse to drop a corpse at my home. Besides, the rector has since remarried."

Samir stepped closer to the table. "Maybe the location had nothing to do with you or your cottage. Perhaps, it is because your home is halfway between Mapledown Village and Astwell Palace."

"Then was Bernard Coram killed closer to the village or the palace?" Tiffany asked.

Samir shook his head, shrugging his shoulders. "I have no idea."

Doctor Hudson sighed. "If we found any blood, it would help us tremendously to locate the murder weapon and the person who perpetrated it. But unless the death happened indoors, the rain and mud will have destroyed all the evidence."

"How would we know if the death happened inside?"

Samir cleared his throat. "Blood stains wood. It is easy to discover where a crime has been committed."

Tiffany thought of her own wooden floors and was glad that no blood stained them. And that her mouth was overly large. But it seemed since the body had been found by her cottage, that suspicion was cast on her. No matter how innocent she was. What a terrible time for her monthly flow!

Glancing down at the body again, she saw a strand of yellow thread in the nail of his index finger. The color was bright and did not match his current apparel of buckskin breeches and a black jacket. It had to belong to someone else's clothing. Possibly the killer's. Swallowing her distaste, she picked up Bernard's cold hand and pointed at the string. "Do either of you recognize this particular shade of yellow? Perhaps Bernard fought off his attacker, and this is a thread of their clothing?"

Doctor Hudson picked up a magnifying glass and took the corpse's hand from Tiffany. She was only too happy to relinquish it to him. She took a step back from the table and the body. The doctor examined the thread lodged in the fingernail before yanking it out and placing it on a silver tray on the table.

"Constable Lathrop, do you know anyone with this shade of cloth?"

Samir folded his arms across his broad chest. "Can't say that I do. It's a bright yellow. I doubt I know of any man in the village who wears a yellow coat or shirt."

The doctor rubbed his long pointy nose and then looked through the magnifying glass at the yellow thread again. "I would think such a color would be from a woman's dress."

Tiffany pinched her lips together. Surely the doctor wasn't trying to throw suspicion on her again? "Neither myself nor my maid own any gown of that shade. It would clash with our coloring. Were there any other clues on his person? In his clothing?"

Samir turned and picked up the coat that Bernard had been wearing. "He had three pennies in his purse. The murderer did not take the money, which means that the violence was not theft. Whoever killed this man, it was personal. And the only other thing in his pocket were some herbs in this small packet."

He presented Tiffany with the herbs, and she could see a few flecks of blood on the burlap bag. Untying the knot, she took a deep sniff of the dried plants. "It's Queen Anne's lace."

The doctor took the packet from her. "It is also known as wild carrot seed. I am surprised a lady like yourself would recognize it."

Tiffany felt her face go red. "I used to buy some from the apothecary for my late half brother. Mr. Canning said that it would help with his loose bowels, but not to take any myself, for it causes constipation."

"Yes, it can, Miss Woodall. But it's main use is to prevent an unwanted pregnancy. The seeds are best taken within a week of sexual congress. You can also make it into a tea."

Stealing a glance across the table, Tiffany realized that she was not the only person in the room blushing. Only Samir wasn't interested in her that way. At least not at this time. Whatever that meant.

She swallowed, and her mouth still tasted of clay. "Can a man take it for an unwanted pregnancy, or is it only for a woman?"

A bit of pink stole into the young doctor's cheeks. "Only a woman."

"Then if Bernard was carrying it, the Queen Anne's lace was not for him, but presumably for a woman of childbearing years. He was rather free with his sexual attentions at Astwell Palace. I saw him with the late Miss Sarah Doddridge. And sneaking about with Miss Chandler, an upper maid. Perhaps the mixture was for her."

"I shall speak to her," Samir said.

Tiffany touched the back of her burning neck again. "I did not mean to tell tales. I only saw them kissing. It may have been nothing more. I should not wish to damage Miss Chandler's reputation, nor her position in the palace."

She could hardly throw stones at another woman when she herself was so flawed. Nor did she want to cast suspicion on another innocent person.

Samir nodded curtly. "I shall be discreet and inquire privately with all the servants of the palace. I will not draw attention to her in any way. I am sure Doctor Hudson knows the value of discretion in his profession."

Her heart warmed. This was the honorable man she knew and loved.

"Of course, Mr. Lathrop," the doctor said. "I would not dream of spreading tales about my clients. But perhaps you will allow me to accompany you. I should like to get the teeth indentations of all the major suspects, to compare them with those on the corpse. The body is already starting to rot, so speed is of the essence."

"Wouldn't the cold preserve the body longer?" Tiffany asked.

The doctor sighed. "Yes, but I do not care to have a body decomposing on my examination table."

"Then why not take it to the prison? Surely it would be safe enough there. And cold, for since it is not occupied, there are no fires lit there."

Samir bit his lower lip. "I think Miss Woodall has given us a sound suggestion. Perhaps we can have the undertaker prepare the body and place it in the coffin, but not hammer on the lid. That will give us a few extra days to discover all that we can before Bernard's body is returned to his parents' home for the funeral procession."

"Better take the three pennies with you to the undertaker," Doctor Hudson said. "Mr. Anstey does nothing for free."

"Neither does the rector," Tiffany added.

Samir shrugged his shoulders. "Death is entirely too profitable. Miss Woodall, would you mind accompanying me to the undertaker's?"

It was a grim sort of proposal, but Tiffany didn't dare decline it. She needed to find the true murderer, and any additional information would only help her. "Of course, Constable. Good day, Doctor Hudson."

The young man bowed to her as Samir took her elbow. She felt the slight warmth of his touch emanate through her arm and then to her entire body. Her skin tingled with awareness of him. Samir lightly guided her out of the examination room, down the hall, and out of the house. Once they were on the road, he released his hold on her. If only her own heart could let go of him so easily.

Chapter 5

Unfortunately, Mr. Anstey's house was across the road from the rectory. No doubt it was a convenient location for coffins and funerals, but it was rather too close for her own liking. Tiffany had not stepped foot in Mr. Shirley's home dressed as herself since Sarah Doddridge's funeral. And even when she attended church on Sundays, her legs were restless as she sat in the pew. As if they wanted to run at the first opportunity. Happily, the rector never looked in her direction. The reprimand from his bishop must have done the trick.

Breathing in deeply, Tiffany knocked on the black door. She waited only a few moments before a woman about her own age answered it. Her hair was fiery red underneath her white cap, and her skin liberally graced with freckles. She was neither thin, nor fat, but comfortably in the middle. On her hip was a small child. Tiffany would guess the babe was around a year old. It wore a sweet little white dress and had strawberry-blond curls. It was impossible for Tiffany to tell if the child was a boy or a girl.

Mrs. Anstey bowed, still holding the baby. "Miss Woodall, I did not expect to see you today. And the constable."

Tiffany gave the woman a tight smile as she curtsied. "Alas, I wish our visit was for congenial purposes, but I am afraid there has been another death in the town."

The woman nodded, but she didn't seem surprised. News traveled fast in a small village like theirs. "'Tis sad, of course. But 'tis also good business. Would you like to come in and discuss the arrangements?"

"Thank you," Samir said, taking off his hat and bowing his head to her. "A seat and a warm fire would be most appreciated."

Mrs. Anstey opened the door wider, and they followed her inside. The parlor and kitchen were all one big room. There was a set of stairs that Tiffany assumed went up to the bedchambers. A young woman with matching fiery red hair was washing dishes at the sink. She was clearly Mrs. Anstey's daughter. The young woman had a petite, curvaceous figure that Tiffany, with her own tall beanpole body, could only envy.

"Caro, curtsy to Miss Woodall and Mr. Lathrop," her mother said. "They've come visiting with business and news."

Tiffany found herself making a wry smile. Mrs. Anstey wanted to know all of the gossip about the murder before her neighbors.

The young woman bobbed a quick curtsy, and one of her wild red curls fell across her face charmingly. Tiffany's own blond hair never behaved charmingly and resisted curling at every opportunity.

"Pleased to see you, Miss Woodall, Mr. Lathrop."

Tiffany returned the gesture. "As am I. Shall I call you Miss Anstey or Miss Caro?"

"Sit, Miss Woodall, Constable," Mrs. Anstey commanded with a wave of her hand. "You can just call me girl Caro. She's too young to be putting on any airs."

A bright flush suffused the poor young woman's cheeks. Tiffany felt for her. How awkward it was to be not a child, but not quite a grown woman either. Tiffany took a seat in a comfortable wingback chair, nearest to the fire. She held out her mitted hands toward the orange flame. The chill that had entered her bones since finding Bernard Coram that morning finally began to ebb away in the warmth. Samir was seated in the farthest chair away from her. She wondered if it was by design.

Tiffany raised her eyebrows at Mrs. Anstey, who sat down beside her, the babe in her lap. "Mrs. Anstey, I do believe you have forgotten to introduce us to this lovely young person."

The other woman kissed the strawberry-blond curls. "This is little Luke. Named after his father, he is."

The little boy smiled at Tiffany, and she could see at least two teeth. She couldn't help but grin back at him and wave. "I don't think I've ever seen a sweeter babe in all my life. How blessed you are, Mrs. Anstey."

She nodded. "Aye, my husband and I had given up on hoping for another child. We've only got the two: Caro and Luke."

A sixteen or seventeen year gap between the two children was certainly a large one. Not that Tiffany was by any means an expert on midwifery. She was a forty-year-old spinster after all.

"A fine family," Samir said, crossing his legs and resting his hat on his knee.

Tiffany clasped her hands together. "And a beautiful one, Mrs. Anstey. It is no wonder that you are proud."

Mrs. Anstey sighed with a sound like contentment. "I am. So, what's this we've all been hearing in the village about a body being found outside your cottage, Miss Woodall?"

"Actually, Bernard Coram's body was in the road in front of my cottage. Not on my property at all." Tiffany wasn't quite sure why she added that last part.

Caro set down a wet pot, with a clunk, and the sound made Tiffany jump. "How did he die, Constable?"

Tiffany clenched her perfectly straight teeth. She couldn't help but notice that Mrs. Anstey was missing three of her upper teeth and that Caro's two front teeth came out to meet you. Neither of them could have made the bite mark on the corpse's thumb. Not that she thought they had.

"There was a wound on the back of his head," Samir said quietly. "I believe there must have been a killing blow, although who could administer such a hit to a tall, strapping young man, I do not know."

Mrs. Anstey nodded, her whole body moving forward and back. "It must have required a great deal of force. I daresay only another man could have done it."

Or a tall woman, Tiffany thought, but being the tallest woman in the village, she decided not to give them more reasons to be suspicious of her.

"Possibly," Samir said with a bow of his head. "I would like to order a wooden coffin for Mr. Bernard Coram's body to be taken to Doctor Hudson's home. We are going to remove the body to the prison, to keep it from decomposing faster." He held out the coin purse to Mrs. Anstey, who didn't hesitate to take it. "There are only three pennies inside. They were found in Bernard's possessions. Your husband may expect the rest of the payment from Farmer Coram on receipt of the coffin and removal from the doctor's examination room."

Little Luke tried to take the coin purse, but Mrs. Anstey held it out of his reach. The baby started to cry and said, "Oh oh."

"Caro, take your brother upstairs for a nap," Mrs. Anstey said, lifting the child off her lap and into his sister's arms. The little baby burrowed his face into his sister's bosom as Caro carried him up the stairs.

Tiffany felt her cheeks grow warm. A woman's breasts were made to feed her babies. There was absolutely no reason for Tiffany to blush for the small child or herself. She got to her feet. "Thank you for inviting me inside your lovely home, Mrs. Anstey, and letting me warm myself by the fire. It has made me ready for the long walk to my own cottage."

Mrs. Anstey stood up, her face pensive. "'Tis an odd place to leave a body. Out there by your cottage on the road. T'weren't anything else interesting about it, were there?"

Tiffany shook her head. "I am afraid not. His skin was quite cold by the time I happened across Bernard. He must have passed away several hours before."

Samir cleared his throat and also got to his feet. "Dr. Hudson also noticed a bite mark on his right thumb, and there were scratch marks on his cheek."

"A bite mark or a scratch couldn't have killed a virile young man," Mrs. Anstey said quickly, opening the door for them. "They probably have nothing to do with his murder."

He nodded. "I agree, but there is a lack of other evidence. They are the only clues that Doctor Hudson and I have to go on besides a small yellow thread in the deceased's fingernail. Do you know anyone with a yellow gown?"

Shaking her head, Mrs. Anstey tutted. "No, sir. Yellow is a bit garish, innit? And murder 'tis bad business, no matter how many coins we earn."

Tiffany curtsied one last time. "Good day, Mrs. Anstey."

She left the house, turned around, and trudged home without another word to Samir, shivering the entire way from the cold and embarrassment. The walk to her cottage felt twice as long as usual. Her feet were like blocks of ice by the time she reached her door. It was unlocked, but perhaps it would be wise, for both Mary's safety and her own, to keep it locked even when they were home. She closed it behind her and took off her wet effects.

There was a chill in the air of the parlor, but Tiffany could hear sounds in the kitchen. She followed the noises to find a large fire in the hearth and Mary cooking a kettle of soup over it.

"Did you have a good day at work, Miss Woodall?"

Then Mary smiled at her—and her teeth were perfectly straight.

CHAPTER 6

"A terrible one," Tiffany said with a huff, hanging up her wet scarf. "It started badly and only got worse as the day went on. How about you, my dear? I noticed you were not here when I stopped at midday."

Mary lifted the pot from the fire, using a potholder. "We were running low on sugar, so I stopped by Mr. Nix's shop to purchase some with the coins in the housekeeping tin. Then I had a little pick me up at the Black Cauldron public house, but I didn't use yer coins. Miss Day gave me the cup for nothing when I told her all about finding Bernard's body by our cottage."

"How thoughtful of you to pick us up supplies," Tiffany said, unwrapping the last of the bread and slicing it into one-inch-thick pieces. "But we might need to be a bit more frugal in our usage of sugar in the future."

Her maid dished them both up a bowl of soup, and Tiffany set the slices of bread on the side of them. "Why is that, Miss Woodall?"

Tiffany took one of the bowls and brought it to the table that Mary had already set with spoons and two glasses of water. "We are spending my income as fast as I receive it. We need to be better at saving some coins for a rainy day. And perhaps it would be best at the present if you didn't talk in the village as much. Our position is a little precarious, with the body being found in front of our home. Suspicion has been cast on me."

Mary sat down across from her. "They think you done it?"

Sighing, Tiffany picked up her glass of water. "I did not like Bernard Coram."

"Whyever not? He were a handsome bloke, talked flash, and dressed all the crack."

Tiffany nodded; he had been an attractive young man. "You see, before you came to live with me, he accused my friends Monsieur Bonne and Mr. Montague of attempting to murder him."

Mary set down her spoon with a clatter. "The cheek! And if you're worried about money, ye don't have to pay me wages no more, Miss Woodall. That'll save ye a few coins."

"I will not rob you. Women are paid too little in this world already."

"But ye don't charge me for my reading lessons neither," Mary said.

It was less about the money and more about Mary holding her tongue in the village, but Tiffany didn't wish to offend the young girl's sensibilities. "I enjoy the lessons. Let us speak no more about it."

After the evening meal, Tiffany and Mary washed up the dishes together. Tiffany would need to bake some bread in the morning while Mary fetched the eggs and fed the chickens. The chickens were the only animals in the small barn. She was sure that it could fit a larger animal, perhaps a cow that could provide them milk. One less item to go into the village and pay for.

Setting down the newly dried pot, Tiffany asked, "Do you happen to know how to milk a cow?"

"Yes, miss, I do."

"How would you feel if I were to purchase a dairy cow? You would have to teach me how to milk it. But at least we'd have fresh milk and eggs. We could even make our own butter. Then we could also eat the vegetables from our summer garden. I daresay we wouldn't have to go to the village for supplies more than once a month."

Mary placed a hand on Tiffany's arm. "I would love a cow. Might I find one for us? Anyone in the village will charge ye more because you're a lady."

"I should be most grateful to you," Tiffany said, folding her arms. "And now, for your lessons."

They sat next to each other at the table, and Tiffany watched as Mary wrote her alphabet on the slate with chalk. Mary still mixed up her *b*'s and *d*'s, but otherwise she was picking up the letters and sounds very quickly. Tiffany wiped off the slate and wrote a few short words: *to, do, so, low.* Mary sounded them out and then copied them in her own hand. Her handwriting did not have the surety of Tiffany's copperplate, but it was greatly improving in tidiness each day.

Mary put away their school supplies and brought out a book, *The Castle of Otranto.* "Please say you'll read me a few chapters, Miss Woodall? I must find out what will happen to Isabella."

Tiffany smiled and took the book from her. "Only a few chapters, for I am quite done in today."

Mary sat next to her and leaned over her shoulder to see every word, even though she didn't know what they all meant yet.

Tiffany read four chapters before her throat felt dry and she yawned. "We can read more tomorrow."

Her maid leaned her chin on her hand. "I like the story. But it's not really accurate is it, Miss Woodall? I mean how does a helmet fall from the sky without someone dropping it? It's not a proper murder at all."

Tiffany got slowly to her feet. "I don't think there is such a thing as a proper murder."

"I mean Bernard Coram had a big gash in the back of his head, but no one went looking for a falling helmet. Mrs. Day at the Black Cauldron said that Bernard gots into a fight the night before with Mr. Hadfield."

A proper lady did not gossip. Nor would she press her maid for more information acquired in a public house that was clearly not genteel. But then again, Tiffany was no longer a proper lady in any sense. "Did Mrs. Day happen to mention what the fight was about?"

Mary got to her feet and moved closer to Tiffany, as if sharing a secret. "'Twere over Caro Anstey. Both blokes fancy her, and who could blame 'em? She's the prettiest lass in town. But Bernard must have got a bit rough with her, for Mrs. Day said that Caro scratched his cheek. Mr. Hadfield punched Bernard in the eye, but he's half his size, ain't he? Bernard sent the fellow sprawling to the ground with an uppercut. Then Mr. Day tossed 'em both out of the public house, and that were the last time they saw him alives."

Mrs. Anstey must have known about the scratches on his face, for she'd made a point of telling Tiffany that they had nothing to do with his death. And that a *man* must have killed him. Did Caro have a yellow dress?

Last night, Bernard Coram had been at the Black Cauldron in Mapledown Village. When had he left it, where had he gone to? "Mrs. Day didn't happen to mention the time of the fight?"

Mary nodded solemnly. "She told me it were about half past nine. Most folks leave by half past ten at night, for they have to work the next morning."

"So, there would have been many people in the taproom to witness the fight?"

"At least half the adults in town."

Tiffany banked the fire in the kitchen and handed Mary her own candle as they went up the stairs to their individual rooms. Tiffany quickly undressed and put on her nightgown before jumping underneath her covers. She shivered as her body temperature began to heat up the linens of her bed. The sooner she or Samir found the true murder, the sooner suspicion would be away from herself.

Samir.

She loved him and he didn't want her. The tears in her eyes that had threatened to fall all day now trailed freely down her cheeks.

CHAPTER 7

Cleaning bloodstains out of her sheets was not how she wished to start her morning, but she couldn't allow them to stay. The stains would set in the cloth, and the villagers might think it was Bernard's blood and not her menstrual discharge. She started the fire in the kitchen hearth and fetched fresh water from the well in the back garden to boil the wash along with the soiled rags. At least it wasn't raining today. She hung them up on her line and returned to her kitchen.

"You're up early, Miss Woodall," Mary said.

Turning, Tiffany saw that her young maid was looking bright-eyed and chipper. "I wanted to have enough time for the bread to rise."

Mary smiled and set the breakfast table with plates, glasses, and cutlery. "I'll go fetch the eggs. I can hardly wait until we have our own cow and fresh milk each morning and evening. And I can teach ye how to make butter."

Tiffany's own stomach was churning enough to make butter inside of it. "I should like that very much indeed. And while you're out looking for a cow in the village, perhaps you could purchase some ginger for tea? I've had a bit of a craving for it."

"Aye," Mary said with a wink. "Oh, and you gots another letter from the Duchess of Surrey yesterday. I forgot to tell you. I lefts it on the mantle."

"Thank you, Mary," Tiffany said, but she had no intention of reading the letter immediately. Tess, the Duchess of Surrey, had proved to be a great letter writer and was always thoughtful enough to have her son frank the envelope so that Tiffany did not have to pay to receive it. Tiffany enjoyed their correspondence, but Tess always complained about being ostracized by the beau monde for her unfortunate (and unwitting) part in the murders. Tiffany would always sympathize with her old friend, but at the moment, her own problems loomed rather too large.

She put the loaves in the oven before leaving the warm kitchen to go dress for the day. And if Tiffany selected her best green silk taffeta dress and took extra time with her coiffure, it had everything to do with her lofty position as librarian and nothing to do with the fact that Samir would be questioning the servants of the palace today. She even tied a ribbon around her neck for a little extra something. Her diamond cluster pin would look well on the lapel of her gown, but she would have to follow their pirate's map to find it first.

Tiffany's appetite returned a little when Mary told her at breakfast, "Why ye're lookin' fine as five-pence, Miss Woodall."

Blushing, she touched her hot cheek. "Thank you, Mary. You are like living with my own personal sunshine."

Her maid shooed her away. "Oh, go on. I'll get the bread out. I won't forget again."

Tiffany returned the wave and headed to the door to put on her cloak, bonnet, and pattens. It was not currently raining, but the road was still more mud than anything else. She opened the door and found Samir standing on the step.

He took off his tricorn hat. "Tiffany, I was hoping to walk you to Astwell Palace this morning. If you are agreeable."

She was always agreeable, but he did not return her affections. "Of course, Mr. Lathrop, I should be glad for your company."

Samir put on his hat and offered her his arm. Tiffany took a sharp breath before she lightly set her three middle fingers on the crook of it.

They walked away from the cottage and down the road before Samir spoke. "I am Mr. Lathrop this morning, I see. I am sorry that I was terse with you yesterday—it had everything to do with the circumstances and nothing to do with you."

His words mollified her pride, but not the pain in her heart.

Tiffany took a few steps forward. "I suppose you too learned where the late Bernard received those scratches on his face."

"I did not," he said, placing his hand over her fingers on his arm. "The townsfolk are less likely to confide in me because of the color of my skin and my uncertain station. They cannot decide if I am a commoner or gentleman. I am educated, but I am also partly foreign. I am both above and below them; hence I have no place among them."

He spoke these words as if they were fact, without any remorse or anger. Tiffany too had experienced having a nebulous place in society. She was born a lady, but she worked. She did not fit anywhere in the puzzle of social classes.

"Mary stopped in the public house yesterday and learned that Bernard Coram and Mr. Hadfield had a scuffle, but it was Miss Anstey who scratched the late footman's face."

"Did she bite him as well?"

Tiffany absentmindedly stroked her thumb over Samir's forearm. "I don't think so. When we went to the Anstey's home yesterday, to order the coffin, I saw that her smile was not straight. She is a lovely young woman, but she has buck teeth. I also noticed that her mother, Mrs. Anstey, was missing several teeth. The bite mark on Bernard's thumb could not have come from either of them."

"It would not hurt for me to go and speak to Mr. Hadfield and hear his side of the story."

"Where does Mr. Hadfield live?"

"He's a freehold farmer. His place is a couple of miles away from town. He has close to fifteen acres. Mr. Hadfield is an affable young man in his twenties. I've only spoken to him a few times, but he is well thought of in the village."

Tiffany shook her head slightly. "I do not recall seeing him in church."

Samir gave a short mirthless laugh. "One can hardly blame him for missing Mr. Shirley's sermons. If you've heard one, you've heard them all."

"Yes. We are all terrible sinners on our way to hell."

"But you've put it too succinctly. Our rector takes at least an hour or more each week to pontificate about the hot fires of the devil."

"Is Bernard Coram's father also a freeholder?"

"No," he said. "He is a tenant farmer of the Duke of Beaufort."

She had noticed the Coram cottage, but she'd never bothered to learn who lived there, before visiting it yesterday with Samir. "So, if someone had been returning the late Bernard Coram's body to his home, it is reasonable to think that they might have been on their way there when they left it here. But then why would they leave it outside of my house?"

Samir shrugged his broad shoulders. "I do not think that it was a sinister joke. Or that you have any enemies that would wish you harm."

"The only people in the village who disliked me, that I am aware of, were Bernard and Mr. Shirley," Tiffany admitted. "But there was one other odd thing. Yesterday morning when I told Mr. Ford there had been an accident, he immediately assumed it was murder. I would not have jumped to the same conclusion."

His lips quirked up into a small smile. "I can ask Mr. Ford, but the butler could put a king out of countenance with his stare. I've known him my whole life, and I don't think I will get much out of him."

"He's not intimidated by your lofty position of constable?" she teased.

"No indeed. I fear if I try to examine him, he will bring up the time that I drank the sacramental wine."

Tiffany touched her chest dramatically and sighed. "Samir Lathrop, I am shocked to my very soul."

"I was eleven."

"And here I was thinking that it was only last year."

He grinned widely at her poor jest, causing her heart to tighten in her chest. But he only wanted friendship.

Tiffany opened her mouth, but before she could speak the words, the sound of a buggy behind them caused them both to turn.

It was Doctor Hudson, and he was driving a two-wheeled gig with a brown mare pulling it. He tugged the reins to a halt.

"May I offer you both a lift to the palace? I daresay we can all three fit across the seat if we squeeze together a bit."

Still tender from yesterday's spurning, Tiffany quickly agreed to it. Samir helped her up into the buggy, and she sat between the two men. It was a good thing that all of them were slim, for it was a rather tight fit. Tiffany could feel the pressure and warmth of Samir's leg against hers. His torso was slightly turned, so Tiffany's back was resting against his shoulder and chest. It felt hard and strong and positively wonderful. Her knee was against Doctor Hudson's, but it was as cold as touching a stone. She had no feelings for any man but Samir. No wish to be touched or held by anyone else.

But he didn't want her for a wife.

CHAPTER 8

Doctor Hudson and Samir walked with Tiffany through the servant's entrance into Astwell Palace. Not even physicians and constables were worthy of the front door. Tiffany took off her muddy pattens and carefully removed her calash bonnet. She'd worked too hard on her hair this morning to have it ruined by her own negligence. Giving her paper curls a pat, she took a deep breath.

Mr. Ford came into the mudroom, and Tiffany had to admit that the old butler did have quite a presence; and a noticeable limp. She doubted he had moved any corpse through the mud at night. Her suspicions now seemed as ludicrous as Samir's youthful sacramental wine drinking.

He bowed to her first. "Miss Woodall, the Duke of Beaufort would like me to inform you that he is currently extracting sunbeams from cucumbers and should appreciate your immediate assistance."

"Excuse me?" Doctor Hudson said, a curious look on his face.

Tiffany swallowed. "We are reading *Gulliver's Travels*, by Jonathan Swift, and are currently visiting the capital city of Lagado, which is Balnibarbi; the home of a rather foolish academy that suggests impractical projects to the people. It is meant to be a satirical farce."

"Hence extracting sunbeams from cucumbers," Samir said with a slight smile.

"Precisely," Tiffany said, and then glanced at the butler in realization. "You didn't give Beau real cucumbers, did you? Surely, they are out of season."

"*I* did not," Mr. Ford said loftily. "However, Monsieur Bonne gave him some from the hothouse."

She brought her hands to her face and shook her head. Beau could have plastered half the library with cucumbers by now. She'd best hurry. "I shall bid you all adieu. Thank you for the lift, Doctor Hudson."

Tiffany had tried to keep her eyes on the butler or the doctor, but inevitably they had fallen on Samir and his beautifully proportioned lips. She forced herself to turn and walk away from him. Again. Each time it proved harder to do.

Her feet retraced her now well-known path to the library, and she opened the door to see what sort of shenanigans the young duke had gotten into before her arrival. Beau was carrying her wooden sword and had a sash tied around his head (very pirate-ish). Lifting the wooden sword over his head, he brought it down hard over the poor green vegetable. It splattered and broke in half.

She rushed forward as he set another cucumber on the table. "Beau! You must stop at once. There are no sunbeams in cucumbers. It's just a silly story."

He looked at her, his brown eyes wide in his small face. "Are there no mathematical pirates or floating islands either?"

Tiffany picked up the crushed and juicy cucumber. "There are indeed pirates, and I am sure that they need to understand addition and subtraction for their work."

"Of pillaging."

"Precisely," she agreed. "The floating islands, on the other hand, I do think are only in Mr. Swift's imagination. I mean, you saw what happened when we threw the rocks. They all fell to the ground because of Sir Isaac Newton's laws of gravity. I would assume that an island would suffer the same fate."

"What of little people and giants?"

Tiffany did not wish to crush his imagination, nor did she want to lie to him. "Most giants are only as tall as your brother Thomas. Around or slightly over six feet. And I have seen little people before in the village I used to live in, but they are a great deal larger than the six inches of the Lilliputians. I would say they are about three feet tall."

"About the size I am now?" Beau asked.

"Yes," she agreed. "But now it is time for all the pirates of the library to swab the deck. Do you know what that means?"

"Clean up the cucumbers?"

Tiffany passed Beau her handkerchief. "Yes."

He took it and glanced at her uncertainly. "But dukes don't help clean up."

"Pirate captains must know how to do every task that they assign their sailors. So we must wash up our 'deck' and be prepared for an imminent attack."

Beau giggled. "Who is going to attack us?"

"The HMS *Duchess*, if we don't clean up and get to our studies this morning," Tiffany replied.

Together they gathered the cucumbers, both the decapitated and whole ones, to bring back to the kitchen. A maid would no doubt have to scrub up the table and the floor, but the library was a great deal cleaner after their efforts. Beau turned the unharmed cucumbers over to Monsieur Bonne, the

French chef, and Tiffany took the bits to the compost pile outside the kitchen door.

Returning to the kitchen, she found Beau sitting on a stool, eating a biscuit. He waved merrily when he saw Tiffany.

"Pirates get hungry," he explained, and offered her a biscuit from the three-tiered tray in front of him. Monsieur Bonne was spoiling Beau even more than she did.

Tiffany took one and bit into it. "Even first mates."

After they finished their biscuits and thanked the chef, Tiffany led Beau back to the library, where they worked on spelling and writing his letters, read a little from *Gulliver's Travels*, and then drew a treasure map.

"Now it is important that *X* marks the spot where we hid the treasure, so that when we come back, we can find it."

"First Mate Woodall?"

"Yes, Captain."

"I should have done that before I hid the treasure."

"Alas, we are still apprentice pirates and are learning as we go," Tiffany said. "Do you have any idea where we should start looking for the jewels?"

Beau shook his head, his guinea-colored curls gleaming in the light.

"Let's start with a map of the library, and we will mark everywhere the treasure is not."

She watched Beau make a large rectangle on the paper and add the physical locations of their reading sofa, her desk, and the fireplaces. They subsequently checked those three places, but discovered no treasure there. Next, they took turns climbing the library ladder to see if the jewels had been placed on a high shelf. Or on the south side, the second-story mezzanine, which consisted of only Latin books. After nearly an hour of searching, Tiffany came to the conclusion that the treasure was not located in the library.

"I must have taken the treasure somewhere else," Beau said. "Where should we look next?"

"The nursery."

She gestured toward the hallway. "Lead on, Captain."

With a sweet giggle, Beau ran from the room, and Tiffany walked more slowly behind him. The nursery was large and located on the first floor near the family rooms; Beau's bed-chamber and one for a nurse were attached to it. A few months before, Tiffany had learned that there was a secret passageway from the duchess's rooms to the nursery. All one had to do was push the pig's snout on the fireplace to access it. Thomas Montague, the duchess's adopted son, had told her about it. She wished Thomas were here now. He was a dear friend with whom she could confide her darkest of secrets, knowing that he would not judge her too harshly.

Wooden blocks were scattered all over the black and white checkerboard marble floor of the nursery, and there was a wooden rocking horse beneath the far window. Beau had clearly already visited the room that day. Her delightful little duke seemed to create mayhem and messes wherever he went. He opened the doors to a wardrobe, and Tiffany saw that there were even more toys inside. In her entire childhood, she'd owned only two dolls. But Beau possessed at least a dozen dolls, with a furnished house; two different toy armies (with little lead cannons); two dozen tops of different colors; and a bilbo-quet (cup-and-ball toy). There were also several games: lawn bowling, sheep's knuckles, quoits, draughts, and chess pieces.

Her half brother, Uriah, had owned a bilboquet, and he'd never once let Tiffany try it. Impulsively, she reached into the cupboard and took out the cup and ball, tied together with a string. Something fell out of the cup and bounced on the floor. She bent down to see that it was her diamond cluster pin. How foolish she'd been to leave it about. It was the only item of value that she owned, and she felt a familial connection to it, for it had once belonged to her father. He would have been ashamed of how carelessly she'd lost it.

Holding the pin between her thumb and pointer finger, she showed it to Beau. "Is this a part of the treasure we are looking for?"

Beau grinned, nodding. "You left it on your desk, and I pilfered it."

Oh dear.

Tiffany cleared her throat. "I do not mind that you pilfered my pin, but we are not real pirates. Therefore, we should never take something that isn't ours."

His little shoulders slumped, and he stuck out his lower lip. Even angry and disappointed, he was adorable. "And pretend pirates can't throw rocks at windows either."

She had to bite her lower lip to hold back a smile as she pinned the diamond onto the lace of her gown. Once she was able to control her emotions, she nodded gravely. "It is important to remember when playing that we must still be responsible. Now, your mother mentioned that other items had been *pilfered*. Should we look in the wardrobe? And do you remember what you took?"

Beau shook his head.

Heaven help her. She took a deep breath and then attempted to catch the ball into the wooden cup. It took her four tries before she managed to swing the ball on the end of the string into the wooden bowl. Bilboquet was surprisingly enjoyable.

She was trying to catch the ball a second time when the secret passageway groaned open, and the Duchess of Beaufort walked through it.

Tiffany had literally been caught playing, by the duchess. She felt heat rush to her face as she quickly curtsied, causing the ball to fall out of the cup again.

"Look, Mama, we found one of the treasures," Beau said, pointing to Tiffany's diamond cluster pin.

The duchess smiled warmly at her young son. "How clever of you! Now, all you need to find are my pair of ruby earrings, six gold bangles, and an amethyst brooch."

Tiffany couldn't help but sigh, hoping that those were the end of the stolen treasures. "We didn't find any pirate's booty in the library, so we decided to search the nursery. We'll keep looking and see if we can locate your missing jewelry, Your Grace."

Beau stepped forward and began to pull out small wooden boxes and crates, dumping them on the floor. A small battalion of red-coated soldiers attacked the duchess's pretty pink embroidered heels.

The duchess stepped back. "I shall leave you to your search, Captain Beaufort and First Mate Woodall." She walked back to the fireplace and pushed the pig's snout, and again the secret door to the passageway groaned. The duchess glanced over her shoulder. "Am I to congratulate you yet, Miss Woodall?"

She blinked and realized that the duchess was referring to Tiffany telling Samir how she felt about him. Tiffany wasn't ready to admit to a practical stranger that she had offered her heart fully and it had been trampled on.

Instead, Tiffany forced her lips to curl up into a half smile. "There has not been time yet to discuss it with Mr. Lathrop, with the unfortunate death of Bernard Coram."

The duchess sighed. "Don't take too long," she said, and then pointed to Tiffany's pin. "You should turn your diamond cluster into a wedding ring."

Tiffany's hand moved to the pin, and she poked her finger on the end of it, drawing blood. Before she could move her finger to her mouth, a small droplet of blood fell onto the white marble tile. Tiffany sucked on her finger and glanced at the red spot. Wherever Bernard had died there would have been a great deal of blood. But where?

CHAPTER 9

Despite being a mathematical pirate, Tiffany could only boast that she had searched twenty-three of the sixty-seven rooms in Astwell Palace. Roughly one-third. Perhaps playing pirates had not been a very wise idea. No other lost items had been retrieved besides her diamond cluster pin.

She sighed.

"A long day for you as well?" Samir asked from behind her.

Tiffany turned to the servant's door and saw him walking out of it. She couldn't stop her mouth from smiling at him, but she forced her hands to stay at her sides. Which was punishment enough, for she longed to be held by him. To sob out her worries on his shoulder. But all she could do was give him a smile.

"I'm afraid that pirates and studies do not go as well together as I'd previously thought," she admitted. "Beau has pilfered and lost several of the duchess's jewels. We spent the entire day searching room after room. I had no idea he'd wandered in and out of so many of them."

Samir grinned, nodding. "The lad does need a governess to keep a closer eye on him. Not that you're not doing a wonderful job teaching him to read and do math during the day, but a young boy like Beau needs supervision in the mornings and evenings as well. And friends his own age."

"He's certainly a handful. How did the doctor's bite marks go? Any matches?"

Samir stepped closer, and Tiffany caught a hint of musk and leather. She wanted to breathe him in like incense.

He shook his head. "Alas, Doctor Hudson and I spoke to all of the servants individually and took clay bite marks of all the women, including Miss Chandler, whom you mentioned had a romantic entanglement with Bernard Coram. She is missing one of her canine teeth, and another maid, Emily, vouched that the tooth has been gone for more than a year. None of their jaws were straight enough to belong to the biter of Bernard. And Mr. Ford assured us that all of the doors had been locked, and there was no other way for the former footman to have entered the palace."

She began to walk. "Are there any other leads?"

He sighed. "Doctor Hudson intended to check your maid Mary's teeth as well, on his way home."

Tiffany stiffened. "Mary had nothing to do with Bernard's death."

"Sir Walter Abney believes you are the only person with the means, motive, and opportunity to kill Bernard Coram. He also found it very suspicious that you sent Mary to tell me, instead of coming yourself. It is best for you if the doctor and I examine every other possibility."

Biting down on her lower lip, Tiffany's eyes watered, and she would have cried if she'd been alone. Yet, he was trying to save her. Samir might not love her like she did him, but he believed in her.

Samir kept pace with her as they reached the edge of the lake. "I need to go and speak to Mr. Hadfield. He is obviously a suspect because he had a fight with Bernard the night of the murder. He is a smaller man, and a blow from behind would have been his best option to take down Bernard. You said that they were thrown out of the public house at the same time."

Tiffany stole a glance at Samir's profile: his dark brows, strong nose, and soft lips. A warmth radiated from her heart to her arms and legs.

"I wonder if they continued their fight once they left the taproom?" she asked.

Frowning, Samir grimaced. "I don't know, and I am not sure if anyone will tell me. What I do know is that their homes were in opposite directions. Mr. Hadfield's freeholding is nearer Sir Walter Abney's estate; which is north of town, and Bernard Coram's father's farm is to the southwest."

"Are you heading to Mr. Hadfield's holdings next?"

"Aye. If you'd care to accompany me, I could borrow a horse and gig in the village."

Tiffany should go home and check on Mary, who was now also a suspect. More time spent in Samir's company would only further pain her. She opened her mouth to tell him no, but found herself saying, "I should be pleased to accompany you."

They passed Bristle Cottage, and Samir led her the long way to the village, and then they passed the Corams' cottage. Despite not wanting to like anything about the former footman, Tiffany couldn't help but notice that the house was well kept, and the fields around it were tidy. She had rarely seen a farm property in better condition. She remembered that Samir had told her that Farmer Coram was one of Beau's tenants.

Tiffany turned around in a circle. "Then all of this land belongs to Beau?"

He nodded. "Every bit of land between Mapledown and Bardsley belongs to the Duke of Beaufort, except for three acres and a cottage."

Her property.

She smiled widely. "The best three acres."

"Of course," he agreed with a nod. "Sir Walter Abney owns most of the land east of Mapledown. That is where his estate Maplehurst Park is. But directly north of the village are the two freeholdings."

When they arrived in Mapledown, Samir ducked into the Black Cauldron to ask to borrow Mr. Day's horse and wagon. The answer must have been yes, for a large man with arms the size of pint barrels followed him outside and hooked the gig to the horse. Samir tipped his hat to Mr. Day and helped Tiffany inside the two-wheeled carriage. Once seated, she gave a thankful smile to Mr. Day. He glared back at her. His black beard was long and scraggly over a wide neck. There was a long white scar that cut through his left eye and down his cheek. Tiffany had no trouble believing that he had tossed both Bernard and Mr. Hadfield out of his pub. His short, compact body seemed to be made purely of muscle.

Mr. Day touched his pointer finger to his hat, and Samir urged the horse forward.

Once they were a safe distance away from the public house, Tiffany commented, "Not the friendliest tapster I have ever met."

Samir chuckled. "No, but a good man. Mrs. Day is friendly enough for the pair of them. And luckily enough, their three daughters take after her."

Tiffany tried to picture a feminine version of Mr. Day's squat, muscular, and scarred body. She failed with a giggle. "I am glad for their sakes."

He was silent for several minutes, and she watched him effortlessly drive the wagon. His grip was strong and sure on the reins. Another part of him that she admired. He urged the horse out of town and down a country road that Tiffany had never before gone on. It occurred to her how very small her life still was. The entirety of her days were spent at either Astwell Palace or her own cottage. She had never gone as far as Bardsley. Nor had she laid eyes on Sir Walter Abney's estate before. She could see it now, a red brick mansion with six prominent white colonnades in front. There was a large pond on the left side of the building, with a spraying fountain in the center.

They passed several fields separated by stone fences before Tiffany saw a gray stone cottage with a thatched roof.

Samir pulled up. "Whoa."

He transferred the reins to her and easily hopped out of the vehicle to the ground. Then he took back the ribbons and tied them to the fence. Samir came to the side of the gig and held out his hand to her. She felt the spark of warmth move from his hand to hers and up her arm. She could barely feel her body as she stepped onto the gravel road and away from the wagon. He did not let go of her gloved hand, and she could not pull it away from him.

The cottage door was painted red. Samir knocked sharply on it. Only a few moments later, an older woman answered it. She was a very small person, her head barely reaching above Tiffany's waist. Her brown and gray hair was mostly hidden beneath a lacy white cap. Her brown eyes were deeply wrinkled, and her thin lips were set in a tight line.

"How can I 'elp you, Constable," she asked, her eyes darting from him to Tiffany, her tone suspicious.

Samir took off his tricorn hat, and Tiffany saw that his hair was a mess of curls. How she longed to have the right to smooth them into place!

"Mrs. Hadfield, good day to thee," he said. "I was hoping to have some words with your son."

"Lawrence is still out in the fields, he is. Unlike some folks, he can't be lollygagging around all day."

Mrs. Hadfield's eyes fell on Tiffany as she made this comment, which felt unfair, for Tiffany had worked very hard all day long, searching for the lost pirate's treasure.

"Which area, Mrs. Hadfield?" Samir asked. "We'll go out and meet him."

She harrumphed but pointed to the field left of the cottage. "Mind you don't step where he's already sowed the seeds."

Samir put back on his hat. "We will keep to the fence. Thank you, ma'am."

Mrs. Hadfield gave them one final harrumph before she closed the red door in their faces. Tiffany couldn't help but wonder if the older woman treated them suspiciously because Samir represented the law or because of the color of his skin. Either way, she had certainly not been polite or pleasant with them.

Samir took Tiffany's elbow as he helped her over a stile and into the field. Remembering Mrs. Hadfield's warning, they kept to the side of the stone fence and walked until they saw a man wearing a smock and a large straw hat.

"Mr. Hadfield!" Samir called out, cupping his mouth with both hands.

The man dropped the rake he was holding and came toward them. He took off his hat and bowed to Samir and Tiffany.

Unlike his mother, he smiled at them in greeting. She saw that one of his front teeth was a snaggletooth. It came forward and crookedly covered part of the other. His hair was the color of straw, and his eyes were a dark brown. Tiffany could see a blue and yellow discoloration on his right cheek and jaw. Presumably from the bar brawl.

"Constable, it's good to see you." Mr. Hadfield held out his hand and Samir shook it.

"I wish it were under better circumstances, Mr. Hadfield," Samir said, dropping his own arm.

Mr. Hadfield nodded, his face suddenly grave. The farmer was at least a head shorter than both Samir and herself. "I can't say that I am sad that he's dead. The fellow was a rotten seed. He reaped what he sowed. But I am sorry for the way of it and for the shock it must have given ye, Miss Woodall."

Tiffany blinked. She did not know that Mr. Hadfield knew who she was; but then she was rather infamous in Mapledown, for she had buried her half brother in the back garden and masqueraded in his place to keep his cottage and position as librarian.

"Thank you, Mr. Hadfield," she said, nodding her head. "It was a most alarming morning, to be sure."

Samir cleared his throat. "You mentioned that Bernard was a bad seed. Could you tell me more?"

Mr. Hadfield tugged at his smock, and his eyes fell to the freshly tilled earth. "My pa said that the measure of a man was how he treated womenfolk, and Bernard was not a good man. He thought because he was tall and fine-lookin' that he could kiss and fondle any lass that he wanted."

"I have heard that the fight in the taproom had to do with Miss Anstey. Did Bernard Coram try to kiss her?"

Tiffany saw Mr. Hadfield's hands clench into tight fists.

"The blasted fellow couldn't keep his mitts off her despite Caro asking him several times to keep his hands to hisself. She finally scratched his face."

A shiver of discomfort ran down her spine. She hated when men touched her without permission. Even a tap on the shoulder or a brush of her hair. A woman's body was her own, and she should be able to choose who touched it and how. Tiffany felt sympathetic toward both Mr. Hadfield and Miss Caro Anstey. Her opinion of the farmer rose with each of his words.

Mr. Hadfield clenched his teeth. "I told Coram to lay off touching her, and then he called her a straw damsel."

Samir gasped.

Tiffany didn't know precisely what *straw damsel* meant, but from the context she could tell that it was very offensive and had sexual undertones.

The farmer rubbed his left fist against his right hand as if he were still itching to hit someone or something. "I couldn't allow his words to go unpunished."

Nodding, Samir exhaled. "So you punched him?"

Mr. Hadfield hit his left fist into his right hand. The sound made Tiffany jump. But Mr. Hadfield didn't seem to notice. "The fella was practically a giant. I barely grazed his eye and got a couple good uppercuts to his gut before Mr. Day hauled us both out by the scruffs of our necks."

"What did you do after you were thrown out of the public house?" Samir asked.

He pointed to his bruised right cheek and jaw. "Coram's fist found my jaw, and it hurt something fierce. I hightailed it back to the farm and had my mum put a slab of steak on it. Took out most of the sting, it did."

Rubbing his own chin, Samir nodded again, as if he understood the pain. "Then you did not renew your brawl with Bernard?"

Mr. Hadfield shook his head. "I'm honorable, but I ain't dumb. The fella had three stone on me and at least a dozen inches. 'Twouldn't have been a fair fight."

"Did you happen to see what direction Bernard went after you left the Black Cauldron?"

The farmer raked his hands through his hair. "It were dark by then. But it looked to me like he was heading toward his pa's farm, on the pike road that leads to the palace. There's not much else to do in Mapledown after nine o'clock."

"Isn't that the truth," Samir said with a small smile. He held out his hand to the farmer, who shook it firmly. "Thank you for your time, Mr. Hadfield. I appreciate it."

"Did Miss Caro happen to wear a yellow dress that night?" Tiffany blurted out.

Mr. Hadfield tipped his head to one side and eyed her curiously. "No, miss. I dunna think Caro owns a yellow dress. It'd clash right dreadful with her hair, it would."

Tiffany couldn't help but agree that a redheaded woman would not look her best in a bright yellow.

The farmer turned to Samir. "And thank you, Mr. Lathrop. You're a good constable, no matter what folks say about your foreign blood."

Tiffany saw a slight flush in Samir's cheeks. She bobbed a curtsy. "It was good to make your acquaintance, sir. Good day to you."

Samir placed her hand on his arm, and she didn't have the heart to pull it away. It seemed to Tiffany that he needed the comfort of her touch. It was a balm she was only too willing to give. How difficult it must be for Samir to be judged based solely on his skin color and parentage; not on his merits or intelligence! To be treated with less than civility by women like the elderly Mrs. Hadfield, who was not *his* equal in education or position.

He helped her up into the wagon and then climbed in beside her. The drive back to Mapledown was mostly silent. The only thing Tiffany could say for certain was that she believed Mr. Hadfield had no part in Bernard Coram's death.

But then who had?

CHAPTER 10

They returned the wagon and horse to Mr. Day. Tiffany peeked through the windows of the Black Cauldron. She had never been inside of it. Public houses were for men and for ladies of the lower classes. She could see several tables and chairs, but not much else, for the light was dim inside the building.

"I'll see you home," Samir said. "Do you mind if I drop off my satchel at the bookstore first?"

Tiffany gave him a small smile. "Of course not."

They walked down the road to his bookshop, and Tiffany was surprised to see that there was a lantern lit inside. Not in the main shop, but the light came from the back of the building. A place that Tiffany had never visited. Had someone broken into the bookshop?

Samir touched her arm. "Wait here one moment."

"Did you leave the door unlocked?"

He shook his head and pressed a finger to the middle of his lips. Releasing her arm, Samir turned the handle of the door and entered. His fists were clenched at his sides, and Tiffany was not about to let him face intruders on his own. She followed behind him as he crept past the bookcases and down the hall to the source of the light. The lantern sat on a large desk. The back room must be his office.

The person sitting at the desk was not a ruffian, but a woman. Her age was hard to guess. Tiffany would have supposed her to be in her early thirties. Her hair was blond, but dirty. There was a layer of grime on her skin, and it highlighted the wrinkles near her eyes and mouth. She was tall and her clothing dark, but it did not conceal the obvious bump of her middle. This woman was expecting a child, and soon.

"What are you doing here, Evie?" Samir asked.

Tiffany wrapped her arms around herself in relief and surprise. Samir knew this woman's name.

The woman pointed a thumb at her chest. "I 'ave every right to be here, I do. I is yer wife."

"Ex-excuse me?" Tiffany said, blinking and sure that she had not heard this woman correctly. "You're his *what?*"

The younger woman stood up and placed her hands on her round belly. "His *wife*. Mrs. Evie Lathrop."

Tiffany's knees wobbled underneath her skirt, and her stomach cramped tightly. "Samir, you have a wife? Since when?"

And a child.

But Tiffany's lips could not seem to form those words. A feeling of cold rushed over her entire body, and her stomach hardened. It was no wonder that Samir couldn't return her affections. He was already married.

Samir turned his gaze from Evie to Tiffany. There was a flush in his cheeks and guilt in the lines around his eyes. "I tried to tell you, Tiffany . . . so many times."

The woman passed Samir and came toward Tiffany in a menacing manner. Tiffany was surprised that the woman was the same height as her. It was rare to find a man or a woman that tall. Evie Lathrop walked so close to Tiffany that her rounded middle bumped into her. Tiffany took a step back from her.

"I married Samir Lathrop in the year of our Lord 1774. And I's his legal wife," she said, pushing Tiffany's shoulders with both hands. The woman was surprisingly strong. "Don't think I 'aven't heard about you, *Miss* Woodall. My brother came and visited me in Bardsley and told me all about the ugly, old spinster my husband was making up to. Well, I've come to put a stop to it, I 'ave. I've come back to stay, so you'd best keep your distance."

Tiffany was forced to take a staggering step back from the push. Her whole body shuddered. "Who, pray, is your brother?"

"Mr. Bernard Coram," Evie spat. "And yous cost him his place at the palace and possibly his life. You and that slave."

Her words made Tiffany feel even sicker. Her jaw ached and her chest felt tight. Thomas was not a slave, even though his skin was black. He was the adopted son of the Duchess of Beaufort. A kind, intelligent young man who deserved respect—not harsh words from an uneducated shrew.

Samir stepped between Evie and Tiffany. "I don't know why you are here, Evie, but you will not touch Miss Woodall again."

Mrs. Evie Lathrop's mouth twitched into a sneer. "And neither will ye, husband."

"Why are you here?" Samir asked. "Do you want money?"

"I want to talk to m'husband alone."

Tiffany's hand stole to her throat, and she could feel her pulse thundering against it. "I will go."

Samir pivoted to face her, guilt shadowing his facial features. "Wait, Tiffany. I'll walk you home."

Wrapping her arms around herself, Tiffany shook her head. "You are too kind, Samir, but I need to stop at the apothecary first. I am sure that we will see each other again very soon."

She did not wait for him to reply before leaving the book-store and heading down the cobblestone street to the last shop. Her eyesight was blurry with tears, and she felt as if her heart were breaking. Samir had never been trying to tell her he loved her. He'd been trying to tell Tiffany that he already had a wife. A wife that was about to have a child. From the look of surprise on Samir's face, Tiffany believed that the baby was not his. Or maybe the child was his and he had not seen his wife in nearly nine months. Her friendship with Samir was barely six months old. She'd known him for less than a year, but that didn't change her feelings in the slightest.

Tiffany loved him.

Loved him as deeply as she'd loved Nathaniel Occom, whom she had known all of her life. But like Nathaniel, it was not meant to be. Nat had died at sea, and Samir was already married to another woman. One who was much younger than Tiffany and possibly prettier too, if she washed her face.

Sniffing, Tiffany opened the door to Mr. Canning's apoth-ecary, and immediately her senses were met with a dozen dif-ferent scents. Drying herbs and plants hung from the ceiling, and per usual there was a cauldron on the fire, bubbling with some sort of noxious concoction.

The many feelings in her stomach were also boiling together like the apothecary's brew: betrayal, love, pain, hurt, humilia-tion, doubt, unworthiness, lust, embarrassment, and jealousy.

Mr. Canning was an old man with a long white beard, a bulbous nose, and several missing teeth. He smiled at Tiffany. "Good evening, Miss Woodall. What can I get for ye? More tooth powder?"

Involuntarily, her tongue ran over her straight and even teeth. "Uh, no thank you, sir. I was hoping for some ginger, to make tea."

"Dry or fresh?"

She shrugged her shoulders. She should have asked Mrs. Balogh that very question, but she dared not confide about her monthlies to the apothecarist. "I am not sure. What would you suggest, Mr. Canning?"

He touched a crooked finger against his nose. "Powder stays fresh longer. I'll fetch you a packet."

Tiffany watched as he pulled out a small burlap sack and filled it with a yellowish powder.

Mr. Canning wrapped a piece of twine around the top, tied it, and then gave it to her. "Would you like to pay for it now or put it on your tab?"

She reached into her coat pocket, pulled out two coins, and set them on his counter. "And one more thing: Did you, by chance, sell Bernard Coram a packet of Queen Anne's lace?"

The wizened older man grunted. "No. 'Twouldn't give Bernard Coram nothin'. He already owes me nearly a pound. I tolds him not to come back without payment. Besides, Queen Anne's lace ain't as good as pennyroyal to prevent pregnancies. 'Twould you be needing some pennyroyal as well?"

Blushing, Tiffany demurred, "No, thank you, and good day."

Confirmed spinsters who were in love with married men did not need to learn the precautionary arts. She barely reached her cottage before it was completely dark, and managed to eat supper with Mary. She waited until she was alone in her room to bury her head in the pillow, and sobbed for the second night in a row.

CHAPTER 11

The following morning Tiffany woke up with swollen eyes and a cramping stomach, but with the help of the ginger tea, she was able to eat a boiled egg and a slice of bread for breakfast.

"Ye're lookin' more like yerself, Miss Woodall," Mary said, her mouth full of her own boiled egg.

Tiffany almost told her not to speak with her mouth full, but one should never correct kindness, even if her maid's table manners were sadly lacking. "Thank you, Mary. I am feeling more like myself."

Mary swallowed, a furrow between her brows. "Did you know that Doctor Hudson took an imprint of my teeth? Should I be frettin' about it?"

"Have you ever bitten Mr. Bernard Coram?"

The young woman shook her head. Tiffany couldn't help but feel relieved. Mary might be under suspicion, but she wasn't guilty.

Tiffany's own lips twitched upward. "Then I am afraid not. Doctor Hudson is looking for the teeth that match a bite on Bernard's hand."

Mary crossed herself. "Ye shouldn't speak so freely of the dead. 'Specially since he ain't buried yet. We dunna want him hauntin' the cottage."

"I am sure once he has had a proper burial, we will not have to worry about him again."

The maid crossed herself a second time for good measure and began to clear the breakfast dishes. Tiffany would have helped, but she needed to get to the palace and continue her search for treasure with Beau.

If only the dear boy remembered where he'd stashed the jewels!

Opening the front door, Tiffany was met by driving rain. She pulled out her umbrella and lifted her skirts, trying to keep the mud and wet off both her clothes and person. She was wildly unsuccessful at both.

She had only taken a few muddy steps when she saw him. Samir was standing in the road outside of her cottage. His hat and coat were sopping wet. The tip of his nose was a bit red, and it looked as if he'd stood outside her cottage for some time.

He held out his hands to her. "Dearest Tiffany, I am so sorry that you had to experience that last night."

Holding her umbrella, Tiffany returned the squeeze with one wet hand but then pulled it away. Again, she saw the hurt in his eyes. It echoed in her own heart. "Why did you not tell me about your wife? About Evie?"

Samir stepped back from her, back into the rain. He shook his head and took a deep breath. "I *was* married to Evie Coram nearly eleven years ago. But she left me shortly after and moved in with the blacksmith in Bardsley."

Tiffany's head and stomach were spinning. If this were the case, Evie's baby was definitely the blacksmith's and not Samir's. Her knees nearly buckled underneath her. "And you haven't seen or spoken to her since?"

Samir turned his head away from her. "No. I haven't seen or spoken to my wife since the day of our son William's funeral. He was premature and never breathed in this world. Evie wanted nothing to do with a brown-skinned baby. Mr. Shirley refused to baptize a dead child. He said that my son was going to hell. So I buried my child in a small wooden box at the top of my father's grave and named my son after him. Even in death, I could not bear the thought of my baby being alone. And when I came home, she was gone."

She reached out to touch him but dropped her arm. Instead, she wiped the tears that ran down her cheeks as the rain fell on his. "Oh Samir, I cannot even imagine your sorrow. I am so sorry. My dearest friend."

He stepped toward her, and she longed to comfort him. But she held him off. He was a married man. "Then the babe in her womb is not yours."

Samir raked his hands through his hair, knocking his tricorn hat to the ground. "I swear to you, Tiffany, on my father's soul, that her child is not mine. I promise that I have had no contact with her in a decade. After she left, I only followed her to make sure that she was safe and provided for. Evie was already living with the blacksmith. She didn't even come to the door when I knocked. After a year, I assumed that everything was final between us. And then another nine went by. We are still married in name, but in no other way."

"Why did you not tell me?" Tiffany asked in a small voice. The rain trailed down her cheeks like tears as she stepped forward to shield him with her umbrella.

He covered his wet face with his hands. "I never planned on meeting you. Or loving you. And once I did, I was too selfish to let you go, even though I knew that I could never marry you. I was trapped in a legal bargain that I made as a foolish young man, when I was naive enough to think that the world did not care about the color of my skin, but my character. But I was wrong. Evie never loved me, but rather the money I had inherited from my father. Our life together was a misery, and I felt only relief when she left."

Samir loved Tiffany.

It was all she had ever hoped for.

But it wasn't enough. He was legally the husband of another woman.

"Say something, Tiffany. For the love of all that is holy, please speak. Reprimand me if you must, but do not remain silent."

She cupped his wet cheek with her free hand. She longed to tell him of her own feelings—how she admired his goodness, intelligence, and warm heart. But Samir was already in enough pain. She would not add to it.

"Being your friend has been the most important relationship in my life," Tiffany said, her voice so full of emotion that she could only speak in a tone barely above a whisper. "I would not have missed it for any book or library in this world . . . But you have a wife, and she has returned to you."

He covered her hand with his larger one. "Evie had nowhere else to go. I could not turn her out, even if she had never been my wife."

Tiffany gazed into Samir's eyes. They were brown and deep, and she could easily have gotten lost in the warmth of their depths. "I am not angry with you, but that fact doesn't change that you have a wife, and such intimacies between us must be at an end."

A little color stole into his brown cheeks. "Evie hasn't been my wife in anything but name in over a decade. She slept in my spare room last night."

She dropped her hand and immediately missed the feel of his skin. Such an intimate gesture could not be repeated. According to the Church and the law of the land, he belonged to another woman.

"But she is your legal wife."

"I would divorce her if I could. Heaven knows that she has not been faithful. But there is nothing that I can do. I cannot put a bill through Parliament to end my marriage—I am not a member of the upper class. Nor do I have high connections in the Church of England for a religious divorce. There is no recourse for common people like us to end bad marriages. Or to find new happiness elsewhere."

Tiffany could only nod her head. Samir hadn't told her anything that she didn't already know. Divorces were rare and for the rich. "What do you intend to do with her?"

With us?

Samir cleared his throat. "I agreed to let her stay above the bookstore until she gave birth. Evie says that it will be any day now."

"And then what?"

He shook his head, exhaling. "I do not know. I cannot live with her. What little feeling I once felt for her died with our son. I will not be her husband again. I suppose I will have to pay for her and the child to live somewhere else, for she is not allowed to stay in her father's home."

"What about the baby's father?" Tiffany asked, touching her own flat stomach. "The blacksmith from Bardsley. Has he no interest in the child?"

"Evie refuses to speak of him."

Sympathy rose in Tiffany's chest for Evie. "Did she say why her own father refuses to let her come home? Bernard lived with him after being dismissed from his position."

Samir sighed. "It's not her father, but her stepmother who won't let her stay. I guess there is no love lost between them. The current Mrs. Coram is the mother of ten children of her own and has no need of another woman in the house, or another babe."

"She seems to be a most unpleasant woman. She did not even invite us into her cottage when you came to tell her husband the sad tidings of Bernard's death."

"I was never welcome in their home, even though I married their daughter," he said, wiping the rain from his face. "Sometimes I think the only reason Evie even married me was to escape her stepmother. They did not get on together . . . Last night, she said that she would rather die than take a scrap from her stepmother's table."

Tiffany lowered her own eyes, but they fell to his lips. How she longed to kiss him! Instead, she forced her gaze lower, to his neck. "Were you ever on better terms with Bernard?"

Samir swallowed, and his Adam's apple bobbed as rain continued to hit her umbrella. "At first, but things between us soured after Evie left. Before then, I taught him how to read and write. I even introduced him to Mr. Ford and helped him secure a position at Astwell Palace. He was untrained, but height is sought after in a footman. The taller, the better. So, Mr. Ford took on the arduous and thankless task of turning the lad into an obedient servant."

"What about his father's farm?" Tiffany asked. "As the eldest son, wouldn't he have inherited it?"

"That's typically the way of things, but according to Evie, her father hated his first wife and treated his children by her with disdain. Bernard came and lived with us after the wedding."

"Was Bernard always unpleasant?"

Samir gave a breathy laugh. "Only when he didn't get his way. Bernard seemed to think that his looks and his strength meant that he deserved special treatment. And I have to admit that both Evie and I doted on him. He was the friend I'd always hoped for. And Evie would have given him the shirt off her back. She was more mother to him than sister."

She didn't wish to feel sorry for Samir's wife, but she did. Tiffany knew how difficult it was to live with a father who didn't love you. Evie had given her love and affection to her younger brother instead. And now he was dead.

"His death must have been doubly hard for her."

"She's always blamed her brother's bad behaviors on their father. Bernard moved back in with him after he was dismissed," Samir said. "But I know that he was visiting Evie regularly—he told me himself. Bernard's only income came from borrowing coins from her and selling tokens he'd received from fine ladies who had visited the palace."

Tiffany tilted her head to the side. This did not surprise her in the least. Bernard had been altogether too free with his sexual favors among the staff. "Yet there were only three pennies in his purse. He must have run out of things to sell."

"Evie said that he asked her for money a couple of days before his death, but she didn't have any to give to him. She told me that her partner, Mr. Tate, the blacksmith, had already given him a pound not two months before. But he must have wasted it on drink and dice. Bernard could never keep two coins to rub together."

She closed her lips, but she couldn't keep herself from speaking the words in her head. "Mr. Tate will give money to her brother, but not pay for his own baby? Instead, he casts the woman bearing his child out of his house."

Samir sighed again. "I do not know the entire story. Evie refused to talk about the baby or Mr. Tate, beyond saying that he was a good man who had helped her brother."

Her arms akimbo, Tiffany huffed in exasperation. *Good men take care of their children.*

"You are a good man, Samir," she whispered. "And it breaks my heart that you will never be mine."

Wordlessly, still clutching her umbrella, she walked away from him, leaving him alone in the rain. Her heart crumbled further with every muddy step.

When she arrived at Astwell Palace, her face and hair were wet and dripping. She couldn't help but think that it was a good thing she didn't wear white face powder like her half brother had, for her entire skirt was soaked through and the bottom eight inches were liberally covered in mud. Her pattens were unspeakably dirty.

Tiffany attempted to remove her boots without soiling her gloves—a hopeless task. She was a muddy mess.

"Miss Woodall."

She turned to see Mr. Ford looking down at her over his beaklike nose. He bowed to her. Everything about his appearance was impeccable. Not a wrinkle could be found in his coat. Nor one of his gray hairs out of place on his head.

Brushing off her dress (little good it did her), Tiffany got to her feet and gave him a small curtsy. "Sir."

He cleared his throat and his silence spoke volumes. "Mr. Montague and the new governess arrived late last evening. Her Grace would like you to wait on them in the crimson drawing room."

Tiffany couldn't hold back a sigh. Today of all days she would have to appear before the duchess a right mess. "Very good, Mr. Ford."

The butler gave her a curt nod before limping away. She wondered, and not for the first time, what had caused the limp in his left leg. Picking up the rag, she gave one more attempt to remove the mud from her hemline before giving up. She let her skirts cover her soaked stockings; her boots were simply too muddy to even consider wearing in the pristine palace.

She made her way to the crimson drawing room, patting her wet hair and brushing at the mud on her dress. Her attempts made not the smallest difference in her appearance. By the time she reached the room, her hands were shaking as she touched the doorknob. She took one calming breath before entering the dark red room, with crimson furniture and no less than four fireplaces, all of which were currently alight.

The Duchess of Beaufort looked as if she were ready for a court assembly, not a discussion with a governess. Her yellow mantua was made from fine damask and elegantly embroidered with peacocks and leaves. It reminded Tiffany of the yellow thread that she had found in Bernard's fingernail. But Tiffany couldn't see any tear or snag on the beautiful gown. Nor on the matching yellow heels peeking out from underneath the duchess's skirt. The duchess was also wearing an enormous curly white wig that included a stuffed miniature peacock. Her face was painted white, with bright pink cheeks, red lips, and blue eye powder.

Lady Beaufort rapped her wig stick against the side table, causing Tiffany to jump, before the duchess used it to poke at the bugs in her artificial coiffure. "Fie! Are you always late, Miss Woodall?"

Tiffany curtsied and held up the sides of her skirt, displaying the mud. "Only when it rains."

"And when you find dead bodies, eh?"

She colored and nodded.

"I knew Mr. Bernard Coram would come to a bad end," Lady Beaufort said, picking up a bell and ringing it. "But I shall say no more on the matter, since he was no friend to my son."

A door on the opposite side of the room opened, and both of the duchess's sons walked in together, holding hands. Thomas Montague was a tall, strapping young man of African descent, with a handsome face. His large hand quite dwarfed his smaller brother's as Beau looked up at him with adoration. Tiffany couldn't help but put a hand to her own heart, the picture they made was so sweet. Beau's eyes widened when he saw her. He ran toward her and hugged her round her wet middle. She happily embraced him back.

"Did you fall into the drink, First Mate Woodall?"

Blushing, Tiffany answered, "No, Captain. I'm afraid that I am only wet from the rain."

Beau tugged on her slightly damp sleeve. "Mama says that you're not going to be my teacher anymore. That Miss Drummond is my new governess."

Tiffany felt another pang in her chest, but this one was not pleasant. "I am sure she is a lovely woman."

"She has a face like a ferret."

"Beau!" the duchess chided. "You mustn't say such things. It is not polite."

"I picked her myself, Beau," Thomas said, kneeling by his little brother, to look him eye to eye. "She is wise and a good teacher. You must give her a chance. She has prepared a family of five boys for school."

Beau's clasped Tiffany about the waist. "You won't leave me, will you?"

Tiffany knew her time with the young boy was coming to an end, and she would have no children of her own. "Never. But I am a librarian and not a governess."

Beau squeezed her more tightly, and Tiffany sniffed to hold back her tears. She had loved spending time with the little boy, reading to him, playing with him.

"I shall go and fetch Miss Drummond," Thomas said. "She was organizing the schoolroom and tidying the nursery this morning."

Chagrined, Tiffany blushed. Tiffany and Beau had made quite a mess of the nursery the day before.

"Are we to look for treasure today, First Mate?" Beau asked.

Tiffany sighed, biting her lower lip. "I think we must do whatever Miss Drummond wants us to."

He held her even tighter. "Is she the captain now?"

Thomas opened the door for a young woman with slicked back black hair in a severe bun and a plain gray dress. Tiffany had to admit to herself that Beau was right: Miss Euphemia Drummond did have a face like a ferret. She had dark eyes, a sharp nose that was rather pink at the end, a bit of light hair underneath her nose like whiskers, and thin lips. Tiffany would guess the woman was in her late twenties, but her severe apparel made her look older.

Thomas smiled. "Miss Drummond, may I present our librarian, Miss Woodall?"

She gave Tiffany a sharp bow. Her face was unsmiling. She was sterner than a captain in the Navy and appeared to be twice as formidable.

Tiffany returned the gesture with an awkward curtsy, still holding Beau's hand. "I am delighted to meet you, Miss Drummond. Beau is such a clever young boy and a delight to be around."

Miss Drummond sniffed. "I shall determine myself where he is academically."

Trying not to be affronted, Tiffany attempted to smile. "I am sure you are a very capable teacher."

"I would not be here if I weren't," she said and then reached for him. "Come, Master Peregrine. I should like to quiz you on your letters."

But Beau didn't move.

Tiffany tried to nudge him toward the governess. "He prefers to be called Captain Beau."

"I do not believe in nicknames or any such silliness. His name is Master Peregrine, and that is what I will call him."

Beau grabbed a handful of Tiffany's skirt. "My title is the Duke of Beaufort. If you won't call me Captain Beau, you may say Your Grace."

A giggle bubbled up in Tiffany's throat, but she ruthlessly kept her lips shut. Miss Drummond may have met her match with her stubborn young charge.

The governess sniffed again. "Very well, Your Grace, please accompany me to the school room. At once."

Beau turned to look at Tiffany. She smiled as she released her dress from his clutches and shooed him toward the strict young woman. "I promise we will finish *Gulliver's Travels* later, and then we will start a new story about a Big Bad Wolf." Tiffany raised her hand to her forehead and saluted him. "Captain Beau."

"If we have time after our studies," Miss Drummond interjected.

The little boy grinned back at Tiffany. "At ease, First Mate Woodall."

Miss Drummond marched out, with Beau trailing behind her. Thomas closed the door after them, and all three who remained in the room let out a collective sigh.

Thomas laughed, a deep, rich sound. "I wasn't sure who was going to win that battle of wills."

"She will be good for him," Lady Beaufort said, poking her wig again to scratch the side of her head. "You are too soft on my son, Tiffany. Not that I didn't appreciate your filling in until a proper governess could be found."

"I don't think we have to worry about Miss Drummond being too soft," Thomas said, with a smirk directed at Tiffany.

She smiled back at him. How she had missed her friend! And how much she needed his comfort now.

Turning to the duchess, Tiffany curtsied once more. "I shall return to the library and get to work. We are sadly lacking in children's literature for Beau. I shall do my best to order the best there is."

"No doubt your Mr. Lathrop will be pleased," Lady Beaufort said, her eyebrows raised.

Tiffany felt her face go red as she left the room. She didn't even notice that Thomas had followed her until she was several steps down the marble hall.

"My mother is truly grateful to you, Tiffany," Thomas said, hurrying to catch up to her. "She doesn't always know how to express it. The last few months have been very difficult for her. So many of her former friends and acquaintances have cut her after the scandalous death of her husband. She should be preparing to go to London for the season, but Mother fears that she won't receive any invitations. Even her own brother hasn't returned her letters."

Tiffany took his arm. "Oh, Thomas, I am not worried about what the duchess said. I am in the most terrible pickle."

His brown eyes watched a maid walk by carrying a basket of linens. "Let us go to the library, and you can tell me all about it."

Silently, they made their way to the library, Tiffany's favorite place in the world. Her refuge. She took her usual seat on the sofa, and Thomas sat beside her.

"What has happened?" he asked. "I have only been gone for a fortnight."

The blood rushed to her face again. She touched her cheek and reminded herself that Thomas was trustworthy. "I found Bernard Coram's dead body in front of my house, and everyone seems to know that I did not like him."

Her friend let out a low whistle. "Surely Samir doesn't suspect you?"

Tiffany bit her lower lip and shook her head. "No, but Doctor Hudson and Sir Walter Abney do. They've been asking my maid, Mary, questions, as if they believe she might have been involved with the murder too."

"I can't say that I am sorry he is dead, but I am sorry that you found him."

"But that is not the worst thing that has happened," she said. "I learned last night that Samir is already married to someone else. Mr. Bernard Coram's elder sister, of all people."

He shook his head incredulously. "I can't believe it. He has been alone for as long as I've known him."

Taking a deep breath, she continued, "He married Evie Coram eleven years ago, and they separated less than a year later; but the fact still remains that he cannot marry me when he is already legally married to her. Not that he asked me to."

"Where has she been for the last ten years?"

Tiffany shrugged her shoulders. "Bardsley, of all places. Living with the blacksmith there. And Thomas, as they say in the Bible, she is great with child and will deliver any day now."

Thomas's hands clenched on his knees. "Someone should bring that blacksmith up to scratch. If he's the father, he should provide for the child."

She touched the back of her neck. "I don't think Samir will take the blacksmith to task. How can he, when legally Evie is his wife and his financial responsibility?"

He got to his feet. "Then I will."

Leaning forward, Tiffany stood up. "And I shall come with you."

CHAPTER 12

By the time Thomas had called for a carriage, the rain had stopped, leaving only muddy puddles for what had once been the pike road. Again, Tiffany was embarrassed to admit that she had never gone down this particular road. Her world was very small indeed.

She saw several buildings clustered together. There were scarcely more than nine structures and none of them two stories high.

"Is Bardsley truly this small?"

Thomas shook his head. "This isn't Bardsley. It's the hamlet of Dee. It's made up mostly of the servants and gardeners who work at the palace."

Glancing out the window, Tiffany saw that the door to one of the cottages was open. A woman about ten years her senior with white-blond hair stepped out. The green cloth of her dress was sturdy rather than beautiful, but everything about her appearance was as neat as a pin. Her shawl was draped evenly over both shoulders. Her white lace cap covered the back of her hair. And Tiffany could not see a speck of mud on her polished boots. The woman also carried herself well and had a great deal of countenance. More than Tiffany, for certain. And more than the typical member of the working class.

Thomas tapped on the side of the carriage, and the driver came to a stop. Before Tiffany could ask him what he was doing, he bounded out of the carriage and to the woman. He swept her up into a warm hug. Tiffany saw only one of the woman's arms go around Thomas to return the embrace. She cautiously stepped out of the carriage. It would be too much for her to expect one of the scullery maids to clean the mud off her boots a second time in one day.

The woman's grave gray eyes turned to Tiffany, and her expression darkened. Tiffany admitted to herself that her appearance was rather slovenly after this morning, when she had talked with Samir in the rain, but it surprised her that the woman seemed disposed to dislike her on first glance. Her second shock came when she saw that the woman had a large bruise underneath her chin, all the way to her jaw. It was greenish and purple. What had happened to her? Or who?

"Miss Woodall," Thomas said, smiling and oblivious to the negative undercurrent between the two women. "May I present Mrs. Ford. I have known her since I was in leading strings. She has indulged me greatly since then."

Self-conscious about her appearance, Tiffany slowly curtsied, so as to not wobble. Then she raised her eyes to the woman. "It is always an honor to meet one of Mr. Montague's friends."

A bit of color stole into the woman's pale cheeks. She bowed her head. "You flatter me, Miss Woodall. But I am only the wife of a butler. The honor of our meeting is all mine."

This woman was Mr. Ford's wife? Tiffany hadn't known he was married. Not that she had ever thought to ask. It was only that most servants were not married. Or if they were, it was to another servant in the house of equal rank and status. This woman seemed a great deal too handsome for Mr. Ford, but she had the same precision of dress and neatness of person.

Tiffany smiled. "Then we shall both be honored."

Mrs. Ford returned a rather thin-lipped smile. "Mr. Montague, how was your trip to London? Were you able to find a suitable candidate for Master Peregrine's governess?"

Thomas nodded. "Miss Drummond is as strict as her name suggests. She will drum his studies into him, but she is not without humor, and I think she will be good for my brother."

The older woman gave a true smile. Her teeth were as straight and neat as the rest of her appearance. "She'll probably be the only person at the palace who does not indulge his every whim."

Tiffany felt her own cheeks grow hot. She could not think of one instance where she had told the little duke *no*. Not that he was a naughty or a mean child; but Tiffany could see that perhaps a little discipline would be beneficial in his rearing.

"I am afraid that I am guilty of indulging him," Tiffany admitted, folding her arms across her chest. "I have no children of my own, and it has been such a joy to spend time with him."

Mrs. Ford shook her head. "My husband is the worst. I do not think there is anything that he wouldn't do for the boy. He was the same with Thomas here when he was little."

Thomas grinned down at her, and Tiffany could see the affection between them.

"Do you have children of your own?"

The color that had entered Mrs. Ford's cheeks receded until her face was as pale as milk. "Mr. Ford and I were unable to have children."

Tiffany could have bitten her own tongue for asking such a question. She could see how much it distressed Mrs. Ford. "I am so sorry. I didn't mean to bring up a painful subject."

The older woman lifted her left hand and cupped Thomas's cheek. "We have been blessed by the duchess's children."

Thomas took her hand and kissed the top of it. "We are headed to Bardsley. Is there any errand that I may perform for you?"

"I am content, but it is so thoughtful of you to ask," Mrs. Ford said, giving him another warm smile.

Tiffany felt relieved to make her own escape. "Good day to you, Mrs. Ford."

She stepped over a puddle to reach the carriage door, where Thomas had rushed over to help her inside. He was such a kind friend. They sat side by side, facing forward, a position in the carriage that Tiffany had rarely experienced. Dependents and spinsters always sat with their backs to the front.

She touched her own neck. "You don't think that Mr. Ford is hitting his wife, do you? That was a terrible bruise on her neck."

Thomas sat up in his seat. "No. Mr. Ford would never hurt a fly . . . I don't know if you noticed, but Mrs. Ford's right arm doesn't work properly. It hangs limply to her side. She probably fell."

"Then she usually does not have bruises?"

"No. I have never seen one on her person before."

Tiffany exhaled with relief. She was glad that Mr. Ford was not an abusive husband. He'd once stood up and protected her from the violent Mr. Shirley. It would have lowered her opinion of him irrevocably if it were true.

Thomas folded his hands in his lap. "Mr. Ford dotes on his wife. When my mother went to the London season, I would often go and stay several days with them. And I have never met a more loving couple. They are completely devoted to each other."

"I am only sorry that they were unable to have children, but grateful that they treated you so well."

He looked at her pensively. "What are you going to do about Samir?

Tiffany shrugged. "Nothing. Because that is all I can do . . . I never thought I would love again after my fiancé, Nathaniel, died when I was seventeen; and to have met Samir, to have reveled in his intelligence and delightful company, is a gift that is worth the great price of loneliness."

Thomas placed his hand on hers, and the gentle touch filled her heart with warmth. She was thankful for his friendship.

CHAPTER 13

Tiffany's stomach began to roil with fear or cramping when they reached the real city of Bardsley. It was ten times the size of the hamlet of Dee. Tiffany could see a large stone church with stained-glass windows. She touched her diamond cluster pin as they passed a dozen shops and rowhouses. The carriage continued through almost the entire village, stopping at a low-pitched building on the edge of town. The exterior was made entirely of stone, and the structure had a thatched roof.

Thomas helped her out of the carriage, then offered his arm. A green door and a couple of windows marked the front of the cottage, but Thomas led her around to the back, where two large wooden double doors stood open. Tiffany felt heat suffuse her skin the moment they walked into the blacksmith's forge. Then she saw the blacksmith. He was not wearing a shirt, but she couldn't blame him in the heat of the room. Blushing, she noticed that his torso was both extremely muscular and dirty. His skin reminded her of the grime she'd seen on Evie Lathrop's hands and face. The blacksmith was bald but had a prodigious black beard.

He looked like a real pirate. She would have to tell Tess about him in her next letter. Tiffany had finally met a pirate. Alas, she would have greatly preferred to meet a mermaid.

The blacksmith must not have noticed their entrance, for he continued to pound his hammer against the molten steel, causing sparks to fly. The metal was almost orange from the heat, and Tiffany watched in fascination as the man bent it to his will. The strength he must possess!

"Mr. Tate, we are here to speak to you," Thomas said in a loud voice. "I am Mr. Montague, and my companion is Miss Woodall."

The blacksmith glanced up at them and grunted in response, not stopping his hammering for so much as a moment. Tiffany wondered if pausing would be to the harm of whatever item Mr. Tate was currently forging.

Thomas stepped forward, and Tiffany dropped her hand from his arm. "Mr. Tate, we are here to speak to you about Evie and her baby."

The man looked up from his work. "Did she have the bairn?"

Tiffany took a deep breath before coming forward. "She has not, but I believe she will give birth to your child at any moment."

Thomas cleared his throat. "You should take responsibility for your child and for the woman who has lived as your wife for nearly a decade."

Mr. Tate laughed.

It was the last thing Tiffany expected him to do.

He raised his hammer and slammed the burning metal. "Did the minx tell you that the child was mine?"

Thomas looked confusedly at Tiffany and then back to Mr. Tate. "Who else could the father be? Surely you aren't suggesting that Mr. Lathrop has fathered the child."

The blacksmith chuckled again, a great booming sound. "Nah. Evie wouldn't have him. I daresay the father is a bloke from Bardsley or a fella passing through. Evie is none too particular with her favors."

The forge was certainly hot, but Tiffany thought that her cheeks were hotter. It had never occurred to her that Evie might have had several lovers.

"How can you be certain that the child isn't yours?" Thomas pressed.

Mr. Tate set down his hammer, and Tiffany could see that he had created a horseshoe. "Got kicked in the family jewels when I's fourteen, by a donkey. Evie ain't the first lass I've shacked up with. None of them have got a child off me afore."

Tiffany swallowed, tasting the soot in the air. She glanced at Thomas and saw that his righteous indignation had cooled. They could hardly expect the blacksmith to take care of another man's child, any more than Samir should.

Thomas gave the man a sharp bow. "Forgive me, sir. I was misinformed."

Mr. Tate folded his arms across his barrel-like chest. "In more ways than one. I never sent Evie away. I don't mind that she's got the morals of a tomcat; the lass is the best ironworker in the county. And she don't put up a fuss if I don't come home at night. She's a good 'un 'cept fer that rotten seed of a brother of hers. Always begging for money."

All of Tiffany's body felt very hot. She'd never known that there could be such *open* relationships. Her father and her half brother would have been positively horrified. She brought her hand to her neck and felt the scrape of her diamond cluster pin. Glancing down, she unpinned it from her lapel and held it out to the blacksmith.

"Would you be able to turn this into a ring?"

His fingers and fingernails were liberally caked with black soot as he took it from her and brought it to his face. "Aye. It'll cost you five pence. Upfront."

"I am afraid that I didn't bring my coin purse," Tiffany began.

But Thomas interrupted: "I'll pay for it."

He took out the coins and placed them on the anvil, next to the cooling horseshoe. "When will Miss Woodall be able to pick up the ring?"

Mr. Tate turned the pin around; it looked particularly delicate in his large hands. "A couple of days to a week. 'Tis fine work and takes a bit longer than a nail or shoe."

"I'll return in a week," Tiffany said, walking to the double doors of the shop and feeling cool air on her face. She should have stopped and waited for Thomas, but her feet continued walking until she was in front of the cottage. Taking in a deep breath, she thought about their exchange. Why had Evie left Mr. Tate? Although they were an unlikely pairing, as was the nature of their relationship, it seemed to have worked for them. Why had she returned to Samir when she was about to give birth to her child?

She felt Thomas's hand on her elbow.

"I suppose this is a lesson to both of us in meddling," he said with a wry smile.

Tiffany returned it. "A lesson that neither of us will take to heart anytime soon."

Thomas threw back his head and laughed. Tiffany felt the bubble of anxiety inside of her chest pop as she joined him in his mirth.

CHAPTER 14

Sundays had once been Tiffany's favorite day of the week. She loved to enter the Lord's house and to feel the faith of ages in its stones. She also loved the sound of the music and adding her own voice to the singing. And her father's deep voice as he read from the New Testament the words of Jesus Christ.

But Mr. Shirley, the rector, made the sabbath the worst day of the week.

"Must we go?" Mary asked, tying the ribbons of her bonnet.

Tiffany put on her own calash bonnet and sighed. "Yes, Mary. Our Lord expects it of us. We must give him one day of our seven."

"It ain't the Lord that I mind. It's Mr. Shirley. All he ever does is tell us we're all going to hell, and he takes a whole bloody hour to do it!"

"Mary, please watch your language."

Her maid grumbled and tugged on her shawl. "I dunna see what's so bad in saying *hell*. The rector says it at least a dozen times a Sunday."

Tiffany cleared her throat. "*Bloody* is a curse word and not at all appropriate for conversation. *Hell* is a place and therefore an apt term."

Mary grinned. "What about *bloody hell*?"

Tiffany pursed her lips together, determined not to laugh at the young woman's naughty joke. But she couldn't quite hold in a smile.

"We'll make a sinner of you yet, Miss Woodall," Mary said, entwining her arm with Tiffany's.

Tiffany closed the door behind them. "I am afraid that I am already a sinner, Mary. But I am trying to be better and repent for my mistakes."

Her maid shook her head. "Ye're a saint, and nobody could convince me t'otherwise."

Tiffany's heart felt full at Mary's words, and she only wished that she were more deserving of them. It was true that she had rescued Mary from an abusive home, but she had also broken one of the ten commandments: *"Thou shalt not covet."* And she coveted another's husband.

Because of Mary's slow pace, they were some of the last worshippers to enter Mapledown Church. Tiffany tried to keep her head bowed as she walked to their pew, but when she saw Evie sitting next to Samir, she stopped walking. Evie was a great deal cleaner than when Tiffany had last seen her. Somehow, she'd been able to scrape off the layer of soot and grime that had covered her skin. Her hair now looked a lot lighter. Tiffany would have categorized it as dark blond before, but now it was nearly white and as finely spun as wheat. She appeared both younger and prettier. Tiffany felt a pang of jealousy, for she had to be at least a decade older than this woman.

Mary tugged on her arm, and Tiffany remembered herself. She continued walking, and her eyes caught another person who made her pause. For half a moment, she'd thought she'd seen Mr. Bernard Coram sitting in a pew on the opposite side.

Her heart stopped beating, but then the man turned his head, and she realized that it must be his father. The face was eerily similar, but lined. Mr. Bernard Coram had been tall and slender, and Farmer Coram looked like a man of fifty whose body had gone to seed. His stomach paunch rested over his breeches. The bruise around Mrs. Coram's eye had healed, but there was a goose egg on her forehead. Beside her, in a perfect row from tallest to smallest, sat ten children. They had all inherited their mother's darker hair color and round face.

Her maid tugged on her arm a second time as Mr. Shirley began to speak from the pulpit. Tiffany and Mary rushed to their seats.

Mr. Shirley's face looked as skeletal as ever. "We read in Proverbs 28:13: *'He that covereth his sins shall not prosper: but whoso confesseth and forsaketh them shall have mercy.'*" His bony white fist pounded on the pulpit. "You must stop covering your sins and confess them to your Lord and Savior that he might possibly show you the mercy that you do not deserve."

Tiffany felt a slight elbow to her side. She looked at Mary, who tipped her head toward the front of the church. Her maid had been entirely right. They were to be called to repentance. She sat up straighter in her seat but did not hear the rest of the rector's sermon. Like Mary, she doubted that she'd missed much. Mr. Shirley never spoke of anything but repentance and hellfire. When it came time to sing, Tiffany opened her hymnal and mouthed the words.

Mr. Shirley returned to the pulpit and cleared his throat loudly before saying, "I am pleased to publish the banns of marriage between Mr. Lawrence Hadfield of Bramble Farm and Miss Caroline Anstey of Mapledown. This is my first time asking. If any of you know a cause or just impediment why these two persons should not be joined together in holy matrimony, ye are to declare it."

Tiffany's head swiveled around the chapel. Her eyes quickly found Miss Anstey. She was hard to miss, with her glorious red hair. She was holding her little brother in her lap. Mr. Hadfield was more difficult to see because of his size and rather unprepossessing features. But his chest was puffed out, and he appeared to be very pleased with the union. Tiffany wished them both joy but couldn't help but wonder why they had announced the banns of the marriage the same week of Mr. Bernard Coram's death.

She wanted to talk to Samir about it after the closing prayer, but he was surrounded by Corams. Evie held onto his arm, which caused a dark feeling in Tiffany's heart. Then Farmer Coram, his wife, and ten other children circled the pair. Passing by, Tiffany did not think it was a pleasant reunion. Evie's face appeared mutinous, and Samir was tight-lipped. Farmer Coram's resemblance to his dead son was even more marked when he sneered.

Mary and she hurried along to the door but were stopped by Mrs. Anstey. "Poor Miss Woodall. I never supposed Mrs. Lathrop would come back. And to come back with another man's bastard. It must be a terrible blow to ye."

It was.

"I am sure it is none of my business," Tiffany lied. "Constable Lathrop and I are merely good friends."

Her maid gave her a strange, disbelieving look as Tiffany pulled her away from the Anstey family and right into the three young Day girls.

"Hello, Jessica," Mary said with a smile.

Tiffany curtsied. "I am Miss Woodall. Do please forgive us for bumping into you. We are only eager to go home."

"My mum says your beau has a wife," Jessica said, twirling a curl around her pointer finger.

"Who is heavy with child," Miss Amelia Day added, her eyebrows raised.

If only Mary could keep her mouth shut! No doubt Mrs. Day and her daughters had learned about Tiffany's feelings for Samir through her maid. Samir's wife was clearly the talk of the town, and Tiffany's connection to him in the gossip did neither of them any good.

"That would seem to be the case," Tiffany said, attempting a pathetic smile and grabbing Mary's elbow once again. "Good day, Miss Day, Miss Amelia, and Miss Jessica."

They left the church, and she tugged Mary all the way back to Bristle Cottage.

CHAPTER 15

The library on Monday was sadly silent without Captain Beau. Tiffany sniffed and barely held back her tears. Her monthly woman's flow had blessedly stopped, but her emotions were still perilously close to the surface. Picking up her handkerchief, she dabbed at her runny nose. If she couldn't spend the day with Beau, she would at least find him the very best children's books. The library at Astwell Palace did not appear to have any at all. She'd requested catalogs from London that Samir had been so kind to get for her.

Samir with Evie on his arm.

Shaking her head at the memory, Tiffany picked up her teacup and took a sip of the black brew. Setting the cup down, she opened the first catalog and studied the offerings. There was a two-volume set of nursery rhymes by Mary Cooper called *Tommy Thumb's Pretty Song Book*. Tiffany was particularly fond of verse, so she circled it. She saw that a Mr. Thomas Boreman had written several books for children and included a great deal of illustrations. Tiffany picked up her quill and circled *Three Hundred Animals*, *Gigantick Histories*, and the two-volume *Curiosities in the Tower of London* about his Majesty's animals in the Tower Zoo. Even though these books were for children, she felt a thrill in her soul at being able to view pictures of animals that her eyes would never get to see in real life. Places her body would never go. So many adventures could be had in a good book.

Even with mathematical pirates.

Sniffing, Tiffany forced herself to focus on the catalog. It appeared that John Newberry was the best known and most recommended author and publisher of children's books. His first, *A Little Pretty Pocket-Book*, seemed to only have been written for pleasure, not learning. According to the advert, it contained rhymes, pictures, and games. She was certain that Beau would love that. And Tiffany knew from the title that they would both enjoy *The History of Little Goody Two-Shoes*. It made her grin just to read it.

She also circled several books of fairy tales, including one of the Mother Goose tales translated from French by Charles Perrault and the Comtesse d'Aulnoy.

Picking up a fresh sheet of paper, Tiffany began to write out her list to give to Samir. He might have one or two of the books at his shop, and the rest he would have to send for from London. She hoped that they would arrive soon. She needed an excuse to speak to Beau, and she was sure nothing less than a new leatherbound book would get her past the studious Miss Drummond. Tiffany massaged the back of her neck. How she missed his sweet little face. His laughter and his smiles.

Tiffany got to her feet and decided to deliver the list to Samir at once. She could only pray that Evie was out visiting her family or the shops. Otherwise, she would not get a word in private with him.

She left the servant's entrance and was pleased to see that the sun had mostly dried up the roads, with only large puddles here and there that she could easily walk around. Tiffany popped into Bristle Cottage, but again, Mary was not there. Sighing, she hoped her maid wasn't getting into any trouble and letting her tongue wag. Or drinking blue ruin at the Black Cauldron. Tiffany was beginning to doubt that she would ever turn the energetic young woman into a proper lady.

The road split, and Tiffany took the shorter path near the church. She wanted to avoid the Corams' farm more than she wanted to avoid the rector. It was a telling choice. Her heartbeat quickened as Samir's bookshop came into sight. She brought her hands to her face and hair, patting to make sure that everything was just as it ought to be. She didn't want Samir to see her in the same state of disarray that Mrs. Ford had. Assured that her curls were set, her hair pillow was in place on top of her head (and not showing), and there was nothing in her teeth, Tiffany stepped forward to the bookshop and pulled open the door.

The villagers of Mapledown were not much for reading as far as Tiffany could tell. In fact, she'd often wondered if the Duchess of Beaufort was Samir's *one* customer. The only other person that she'd seen inside the shop (aside from Evie Lathrop) had been Mr. Shirley, and he had followed Tiffany in there.

Yet today, she saw at least five men in the shop, not including Samir. The bells on the door rang as she walked through the entrance. She recognized the plump and unpleasant face of Sir Walter Abney, the dusty and muscular form of Farmer Thackeray and the sour face of Farmer Coram. The other two men appeared to be servants, for they were dressed in livery and wore finer clothing than either Mr. Thackeray or Farmer Coram. Both Samir and Evie were behind the counter, and it appeared that Evie was trying to constrain him to stay.

"Let go of him, whore," Farmer Coram growled at his daughter. "He's under arrest for the murder of your brother."

Tiffany flinched at the ugly word. It was even worse than *straw damsel*. She felt another involuntary pang of sympathy for the woman who was married to the man that she loved. How awful it must feel to be called such a word. And even worse, by her own father. Tiffany's own father had been cold, but he had never been cruel.

"Sam had nothing to do with it, and ye know it, ye old lech!" Evie shouted back. "He's twice the man ye'll ever be."

While Tiffany agreed with the sentiment, she didn't appreciate hearing it from Evie's lips. With one hand, Evie clutched her round stomach, and with the other she held Samir in place. Tiffany knew that Samir was strong enough to break free, but she also knew that he wouldn't treat any woman roughly. It was one of the many things that she admired about him.

Tiffany cleared her throat and took out the paper. "I am here with a list of books that the Duchess of Beaufort requires immediately." Name-dropping and titles often helped with horrid men like Sir Walter. "I am sure she would be greatly distressed if her order isn't filled immediately."

Sir Walter shifted from one foot to the other, putting both of his hands on his belly, which was quite a bit larger than Evie's, with no baby inside it. "Uh, well, Farmer Coram, I don't see there's any need for an immediate arrest. The circuit judge won't be here for another week, and there can't be a trial until then."

Farmer Coram spat onto the clean wooden floor. "He's a bleedin' foreigner. Ye can't trust him not to run. He needs to be locked up in the prison until the assizes judge arrives."

Tiffany cracked her knuckles. Such hateful words should never be spoken, but the foolish justice of the peace, Sir Walter, seemed to be considering them.

"What proof do you have that Samir killed Bernard Coram?" she asked, turning her eyes to Sir Walter. "It must be substantial for the justice of the peace to issue a warrant and an arrest."

Red splotches formed on his face and neck. He sputtered, "W-well, he is our only suspect since Doctor Hudson exonerated you and your maid."

Tiffany stepped closer to the little baronet, towering over him with her natural height. "And why is he a suspect?"

Farmer Coram spat on the floor again; this time, Tiffany could see that it was a mixture of spittle and tobacco. "I over-heards Bernard threatening to tell m'daughter that Lathrop was fraternizing with Spinster Woodall—unless he gave him ten pounds. Evie is his legal wife after all, no matter where she sleeps. Lathrop refused to give my lad an honest penny. Then Bernard went into the public house for a drink, taking m'three pennies with him. The next morning, the lad is found dead, and my slut of a daughter is back in town. Don't need more proof than that."

Tiffany was pretty certain that her own face had red splotches of color and embarrassment, but she turned her eyes to Evie. "Mrs. Lathrop, the day after I found your brother's body, you told me that you knew I was friends with your legal husband. Is that not true?"

Evie let go of her hold on Samir's arm. "It's true."

"You also told me that your brother Bernard had already informed you of our friendship—is that not correct?"

"'Tis."

"Then if Evie already knew about our friendship, why would Mr. Lathrop pay Mr. Bernard Coram to keep the information to himself? You're not talking about murder, Farmer Coram; you are talking of blackmail and extortion. You should be ashamed of yourself and your son for trying to take advantage of an honest man and then attempting to have him punished for a crime you know that he did not commit."

Farmer Coram, like his daughter, was at least Tiffany's height. Sir Walter stepped aside as the large man came toward her, his right fist raised. Tiffany closed her eyes as she tensed for the impact of his blow. But it never fell.

Blinking, she saw that Samir had his arms around Farmer Coram from behind.

"You will not strike a lady, Coram. Or you will be put in prison yourself."

Farmer Coram struggled free from Samir's hold, but he didn't go near Tiffany except to spit again in her direction. "Miss Woodall ain't no lady. She dressed as a man and carried on with m'daughter's husband."

Sir Walter held up his sausage-like fingers. "Now, now, Farmer Coram, 'tis no call to be insulting a lady. Especially one that is employed by the Duchess of Beaufort."

The older man pointed a roughened finger at her. "She should keep her mouth shut, like all women should. Says so in the Bible, it does."

Tiffany looked at Sir Walter beseechingly. "Then you intend to let the matter rest until the court of assizes judge returns to our city?"

He waved one sausage finger at her. "I cannot do that, Miss Woodall, or I would be failing in my duty. I have received credible information, and I must act on it."

She bit down on her lip and remembered the bite mark on the corpse's thumb. "Have you discussed the matter with Doctor Hudson? He is the one who examined the body, and he believed that the bite mark on Mr. Bernard Coram's thumb was important to identifying the murderer. Should you not have him examine Mr. Lathrop's teeth and compare them to the corpse?"

Sir Walter swallowed, and all of his chins jiggled. "I'll leave such matters to the judge and jury. Mr. Lathrop, would you please come with me and my footmen to the prison."

"Aren't you going to tell Sam to fetch the bloody keys first?" Evie asked. "Or are ye forgetting that he is yer constable and the one that oversees the blasted building."

Tiffany looked at the baronet, who at least had the grace to appear chagrined. The foolish man did not even have keys to the prison.

Samir stepped toward the back of his shop. "I shall go and fetch them."

"Follow him," Sir Walter said to his footmen. "Make sure he doesn't try to escape."

Tiffany's blood was boiling. Samir was being arrested on the gossip of a blackmailing farmer without any evidence at all. She would love to assume that no judge or jury would ever convict him on such thin proof. But she had heard too many slanderous words relating to the color of Samir's skin and his foreignness to believe that he would receive a fair trial. The same judge and jury had nearly convicted Thomas only a half a year ago because of his dark skin. The only reason that they had not was because the Duchess of Beaufort had intervened on both Thomas's and Tiffany's behalf.

Samir walked back into the room, with his coat and hat on, followed by the two matching footmen. He gave Sir Walter the keys to the prison and then turned to Tiffany. His arms encircled around her, and she closed her eyes to enjoy what might be their last embrace. She felt him drop something down the back of her dress.

"It opens the locked drawer in my desk with my financial papers. Please take care of Evie and the baby. There is no one I trust more," he whispered.

He stepped back. "Would you like me to lead you to the prison, or shall I follow you, Sir Walter?"

Samir's green embroidered suit was not quite as fine as Sir Walter's silks, but he looked to be ten times the gentleman as they stood across from each other.

The baronet coughed. "You may lead, Constable."

Samir nodded and turned to meet Evie's imploring eyes. "Miss Woodall will take care of you and the child. You need have no worries on that head. Goodbye, Evie."

He opened the door and held it for not only Sir Walter but his footman. "Perhaps Farmer Coram and Farmer Thackeray will also leave the shop. I do not think that either *lady* wishes for their continued presence."

Tiffany saw Farmer Coram's broad hands curl into tight fists, and she flinched.

Sir Walter clapped. "Come, Coram. Come, Thackeray. You are no longer needed, and I should not wish to have rumors of your ill-treatment of defenseless ladies affect the outcome of the trial. You two had best return to your homes."

Mr. Thackeray left without a word or look at either woman. Farmer Coram sneered first at Tiffany and then at his daughter. "Look fer the jewels he gots from the duchess for helping find the murderer of her maid, and don't expect me to provide for your bastard."

Evie spat at him, and the spittle hit his cheek and ran down his face. "I don't expect anything of ye!"

Farmer Coram's face turned an angry red, and Tiffany stepped forward to pull Evie away from him. But before he could respond, the two footmen had reentered the bookshop, and each took one of his arms. They frog-marched him out the door, and Tiffany ran to lock it behind them. Farmer Coram was a violent man to cross.

Turning, she saw Evie clutching her stomach. "Are you alright? Why don't you go lie down, and I'll make you some tea?"

Evie's face appeared pained, and she only nodded.

Tiffany gently took her by the elbow to the back of the shop, where the stairs led to Samir's apartments above. She helped her into the bed in the smaller bedchamber.

"I'll fetch you a glass of water first, and then I'll boil the tea. Is there anything else I can get for you?"

Evie closed her eyes and shook her head. "I dunno why ye're helping me. If I were ye, I'd hate me."

"There is already too much hate in the world, and I have no intention of adding to it," Tiffany said. "Rest. I am sure both you and your baby need it."

By the time Tiffany returned with a glass of water, Evie was fast asleep. Tiffany could see the steady rise and fall of her chest and the movement of her stomach.

She returned to Samir's kitchen, which was as neat and tidy as his bookshop. Jumping up and down, she tried to dislodge his key that was poking uncomfortably into her back. It did not budge. Pigeon feathers! Tiffany took off her bodice and corset, then folded down her chemise, and finally the metal key fell to the floor. She picked it up and held it in her fist as she put back on her clothes. Whatever was locked inside the drawer was important to Samir, and he had trusted her with it.

She started a fire and then fetched more water from the town well, for the kettle. Instead of watching the pot and waiting for the liquid to boil, Tiffany went downstairs to Samir's desk. It was located in the back room of the ground floor. Her hands were shaking as she put the key into the middle drawer lock and turned it. The mechanism clicked, and the wooden drawer sprang forward an inch. Evie had tried to search through it the night that Tiffany first met her, but it had been locked. With her free hand, she pulled the drawer out as far as it would go.

There were no rubies.

Not even one coin.

Simply papers.

Picking up a leatherbound book, she opened it to see a ledger, and it fell to the last written page. She gasped. Samir had over ten thousand pounds invested in the Funds and at least that same amount in several other speculations. It was a fortune beyond anything she'd ever imagined. Her eyes flew down his tidy columns, and she could see that even before the Duchess of Beaufort had given him the jewels for his diligent efforts in proving Thomas's innocence, Samir had been a steady investor of his profits. He clearly followed the stocks and sales of the London exchange, selecting which speculations he believed would be the most successful—risk versus the reward.

She shut the book and put it back into the drawer. The rest of the papers there were the certificates of his stocks and other financial proofs of his investments. Locking the drawer, she wished that his money could be used to help get him out of prison. But she could hardly summon a London solicitor in time for the arrival of the assizes judge, and even if that were possible, she didn't know to whom she should write.

Tiffany needed a plan.

She must first find incontrovertible proof that Samir was not the murderer, and the only way that she could do that was to find the true killer herself.

CHAPTER 16

Tiffany didn't know where to put the key. Ladies' clothing was never practical. At last she decided on stuffing it down her stocking. It was rather uncomfortable to walk, but it would have to do until she found a more permanent (and safe) location.

She added tea leaves to the whistling kettle and took it off the fire. Then she let the tea steep for several minutes before she poured a cup and brought it to the smaller room. Evie was snoring, and Tiffany thought the poor woman probably needed her sleep, so she returned to the kitchen and drank the cup herself. Her hands finally stopped shaking. She set the kettle near the flames to keep it warm.

Evie did not wake for an hour, so Tiffany took the water off the hearth and doused the fire. She could not afford to waste the entire day sitting around. She needed to go and speak to Doctor Hudson at once. Stealing down the stairs, she left the bookshop by the back door. It felt better than leaving the main door unlocked. Farmer Coram seemed prone to violence, and Tiffany didn't want Evie hurt, or herself.

She knocked on the doctor's door and waited only moments before Mrs. Balogh opened it.

Tiffany curtsied. "Good day, Mrs. Balogh. Is Doctor Hudson by chance at home?"

The housekeeper nodded. "He is. This way, Miss Woodall."

Mrs. Balogh opened the door to the doctor's operating room. Mr. Hudson was sitting at his desk and looking at a series of clay bite-mark disks through a magnifying glass. He set down the instrument when he saw her.

"Miss Woodall, what a nice surprise. I didn't expect to see you today."

"I wish it were under better circumstances, sir, but I am here to inform you that Sir Walter Abney has issued a warrant of arrest for Mr. Lathrop for the murder of Bernard, based on the testimony of Farmer Coram. The farmer overheard his son trying to blackmail Samir, and the foolish justice of the peace has imprisoned him."

Doctor Hudson stood up, rubbing the tip of his pointy nose. "But they cannot put Mr. Lathrop in prison. That is where we are keeping the body."

Tiffany's stomach turned. She'd spent time in prison herself, but at least the only other occupant (Thomas) had been alive. "I don't think Sir Walter knows or would care."

The young doctor nodded, his closely set brown eyes focusing on a jar of fresh clay. He picked it up and passed it to Tiffany. "We shall have to make an imprint of Samir's teeth."

"But where are we going to put the corpse?"

"We can put him in our cellar for at least a week," Mrs. Balogh said. "'Twould be cooler there, and hopefully the body will not decay too far before the judge arrives. Poor Mr. Lathrop will need every possible proof of his innocence."

Tiffany could have hugged the woman. "You are so kind and so wise. Thank you."

Doctor Hudson appeared less convinced (or less thrilled to have a dead body in his cellar). "How are we to carry it here?"

She sighed. The doctor was slender and not at all muscular. Mrs. Balogh was elderly, and Tiffany had slept little the night before. "Why don't you go and take the bite mark, Doctor Hudson? I will go and ask Mr. Day if he and perhaps some other men at the public house might be willing to carry it for us."

"A sensible suggestion, Miss Woodall," the housekeeper said. "'Tis not a job for a lady."

Tiffany thanked them both once more before leaving the doctor's home and heading to the Black Cauldron. Her palms felt sweaty as she turned the knob of the door, and her breath caught as she opened it. The first face she saw was Mary's. She was sitting at a small round table with another young woman, who was trimming a hat. Tiffany's body relaxed, and she smiled at her maid—a familiar countenance in a new place. The entire room was paneled in dark wood that seemed to absorb the light from the windows.

"Miss Woodall, what ye doin' here?"

Tiffany swallowed, but there was still a lump in her throat. "There has been . . . that is . . ."

Her young maid stood up from her barstool and came over to Tiffany's side, taking her arm. The tight knot in Tiffany's chest seemed to loosen a little at Mary's touch.

"Do you need a drink, Miss Woodall?" Mary asked. "Nothing like a cup of Blue Ruin to get the blood movin'."

She shook her head; cheap gin was the last thing that she needed. "I was hoping to speak to Mr. Day. There has been a terrible misunderstanding, and Sir Walter Abney has had Samir arrested and put in prison."

"Isn't that where ye left Bernard's body?"

Tiffany could smell the hops in the air, and it soured her tender stomach. "Yes. Doctor Hudson has kindly offered to keep the corpse in his cellar."

She turned her head to the sound of a firm tread. It was a short woman with a voluptuous, but neat figure. Her brown hair shone like she'd washed it in whiskey. "Are ye here to ask for my husband's assistance?"

"Yes. I know that he is friendly with Mr. Lathrop."

"Aye," the woman said, jingling the coin purse she wore on her waist. "I'll have Mr. Day meet you at the prison." She spat on the floor, which was otherwise very clean and polished. "I'm glad Mr. Bernard Coram is dead. Never paid his tab and couldn't keep his paws off the girls. He were one rotten sod."

Tiffany felt her cheeks warm at the vulgarity, but she entirely agreed with the sentiment. "Thank you so much, Mrs. Day."

The other woman nodded. "Mary, ye walk with your mistress. She looks as if she could fall over at any minute."

"Yes, Mrs. Day."

Mary led Tiffany outside, and she immediately felt better. Together, they walked down the street to the prison. The door was ajar, and Tiffany could see the thin outline of Doctor Hudson's figure. The scent of decay met her nostrils once they stepped through the doorframe. Poor Samir! That he should be subjected to such a place for even a minute was monstrously unfair and entirely prejudiced. Especially with a rotting corpse in a wooden coffin that wasn't nailed shut. At least it was not inside the cell with Samir, but it was in the same room.

Doctor Hudson held up a clay disk. "You'll be pleased to know, Miss Woodall, that we were both right about our friend,

Mr. Lathrop. His bite mark does not match the victim's thumb. You can see that Mr. Lathrop's right lateral incisor is turned slightly outward."

Nodding, Tiffany brought her shawl up to cover her nose. She saw Samir behind the iron bars. The last time they had both been inside the prison, it had been her in the cell. When you loved someone, either circumstance was intolerable. His hat was off and his hair slightly mussed, as if he'd been running his hands through it. He stood up from the cot and walked to the iron bars, holding out his hands to her. She dropped the shawl to give him both of hers.

"You don't need to be here, Tiffany. Mrs. Balogh has kindly offered to bring me my meals."

Tiffany squeezed his hands. "I will get you out of here, I promise."

One side of his mouth quirked up in a small smile. "You make a better constable than I do."

She shook her head, a tear slipping out of her right eye. "Nonsense. You are clever, thorough, and honest. Unlike our abysmal justice of the peace, who wouldn't know justice if it punched him in the nose."

Again, his lips twitched, but his countenance quickly sobered. "How is Evie?"

Tiffany's back stiffened, and her palms went cold in Samir's hands. She didn't want him to care for his wife—a small and selfish thought that shamed her to her very core. "I put her down for a rest. I will go back and check on her after we move the body to Doctor Hudson's cellar."

Samir rubbed the top of her hand with his thumbs. "I am grateful for your kindness to her. Evie's had a hard life. Her father is a brute, and she tried to shield her brother from him.

That sort of violence changes people. I don't think she's capable of caring for anyone else, and now Bernard is dead."

Sighing, Tiffany didn't want to feel sorry for Evie. She wanted to feel sorry for herself. The man she loved was in prison and married to someone else! But Samir was right. Both her mother and her father would have expected her to show Evie all the Christian charity inside of her heart.

The sound of the prison door swinging on its hinges caused Tiffany to jump. She released Samir's hands and turned to see Mr. Day stride into the room. The short but very muscular man seemed to fill the space.

He rubbed the hair on one arm. "The missus said ye needed help movin' the coffin."

"Thank you, Frank," Samir said.

Mr. Day tapped his hat and nodded to him. "I'll takes the head, ye take the feet, Doc. Then neither of us have to smell his stinkin' corpse any longer."

The barman went to the top of the wooden coffin and easily lifted his side with his burly arms. Doctor Hudson set down his clay jar and Samir's bite-mark disk on the floor. Tiffany quickly scooped them up. Such precious evidence needed to be taken care of. She watched the young doctor struggle with his side of the load as he attempted to step backward out the door to the prison. The doctor stumbled over his own feet, and Mary rushed to his side, lifting part of the coffin.

"We don't want to let the lid come off and fill this place with stink," she said, wrinkling her nose.

Tiffany couldn't have agreed with her more. She watched as the three people managed to get the coffin outside of the prison and began to walk it down the street. The prison door was open, but the room definitely needed an airing out.

She and Samir were finally alone.

Tiffany swallowed, feeling lightheaded. She wanted to tell him so many things. Mostly, that she loved him. But her mouth would not make the words.

"Miss Woodall, you're still here?" Mrs. Balogh said from behind them.

Tiffany turned around and saw the housekeeper was carrying a basket of food with a flask in it. She glanced at the door, and her courage failed. "I was just leaving. I need to go and check on Mrs. Lathrop. The arrest seems to have quite overturned her spirits."

The housekeeper nodded, giving Tiffany a look of pity.

Not knowing what to say to either person, Tiffany left the prison through the open door and went through the back alley toward Samir's bookshop. Her fingers were on the knob when she heard a scream.

Oh dear!

She should have not left Evie alone. Her father must be back.

Flinging open the door, she rushed up the stairs and burst into the smaller room. Evie was on the bed, her stomach moving a great deal. Tiffany's eyes searched for someone else in the room, but there was no one.

Evie screeched again, a high-pitched wail of pain.

Tiffany rushed to her side. "What can I do to help you?"

Evie grabbed her stomach, her face contorted in pain. "The baby's comin' and I don't know what to do."

Tiffany did not know either. She could see that there was a puddle of water underneath Evie, but it didn't smell like urine. She had seen her father christen many a child, but she had never assisted with a birthing. She thought first of bringing

Doctor Hudson but then remembered that Mrs. Balogh was a midwife. Personally, she would prefer female assistance. The very thought of a male doctor seeing her anatomy made her face as hot as hellfire. But it was not her decision to make.

"Mrs. Lathrop—Evie—would you like me to fetch Doctor Hudson or Mrs. Balogh, the midwife?"

Evie grabbed Tiffany's wrist in a bruising grip as she screamed, "Get the bloody midwife!"

Detaching Evie's grip from her arm proved more difficult than she expected, but once she was free, Tiffany bounded to the door and down the stairs. She retraced her steps to the prison but found Samir alone there.

"What is the matter?" he asked, getting to his feet.

"Evie's having the baby!" Tiffany said, but didn't wait for his response. She walked as fast as she could to Doctor Hudson's house and pounded her fist against the bright blue door.

Mrs. Balogh answered, still wearing her pelisse and hat. "Miss Woodall?"

"Evie's in labor. Will you please come at once?"

The housekeeper nodded. "Aye. I will. But I need to get my supplies ready. Go and sit with her until I come."

Tiffany hugged herself. "The back door to the bookshop is unlocked. But what do I do?"

"Keep her company," Mrs. Balogh said, shutting the door.

Taking a deep breath, Tiffany turned on her heel and headed back to Samir's rooms at a brisk pace.

CHAPTER 17

"Ye're back," Evie said in between labored breaths. "But where's the midwife?"

Tiffany forced her mouth to smile. "She's coming."

Evie's eyes rolled back into her head, and she screamed. Tiffany rushed forward and took her hand, patting it awkwardly. "Mrs. Balogh will be here at any moment."

Again, Tiffany felt Evie's masculine-strength grip pinch her fingers. She winced but didn't say anything. She had not experienced childbirth and did not know the depth of pain women went through to bring new life into the world. Evie squeezed and hollered several more times before her body relaxed.

She yanked her hand out of Tiffany's and wiped at her sweaty brow. "Ye're the sort of lady Sam deserves."

Biting her lower lip, Tiffany didn't know how to respond to such a statement. She wished that she and Samir could be married, but they couldn't. He was already married to Evie and imprisoned for killing her brother.

"He told me that he loves ye," Evie continued with a whimper. "And the fool even went as far as to say that he hoped that Tate loved me."

Tiffany pinched her own chin and eyed the pregnant woman pensively. "I visited Mr. Tate, and he told me that he never asked you to leave."

"The baby ain't his."

Pointing her knees toward Evie, Tiffany leaned forward. "I know. He told me that too."

Evie shook her head. "Tate's a good'un. Every time my life is goin' well, a child comes along and ruins it."

The baby was certainly not responsible for its mother's behavior, but then Tiffany also thought it would be nice if women could choose when and if they wished to bear children.

Feeling strangely protective of Evie, Tiffany lowered the tone of her voice. "I am sorry that this baby was not planned, but aren't you thrilled with the opportunity to be a mother?"

"Ain't," she said flatly. "I's already took care of me brother and me half siblings. I don't want to take care of another bairn."

The sound of Mrs. Balogh's footfalls on the stairs saved Tiffany from trying to find a polite response to Evie's shocking words. The housekeeper carried a leather satchel and set it down on the bedside table.

"Miss Woodall, would you boil some water? We need to keep our hands and instruments clean."

Tiffany was on her feet before Mrs. Balogh had finished her sentence. Boiling water was something that she *could* do. Again, Tiffany lit kindling and started a fire. She fetched more water from the well and found a drawer in Samir's wardrobe with more clean linens. She was sure they would need them. Tiffany already planned to make a new feather mattress for the bed. The current one was quite ruined from bodily fluids.

The kettle whistled and Tiffany took it off the fire. Using a cloth, she carried the hot kettle into the small room. Evie's skirts were up, and Tiffany could see the baby's head between her legs. The sight was bloody, but it didn't feel dirty. There was beauty in birth. In new life.

Red-faced, Mrs. Balogh took the kettle from her. "The babe's crowning; 'twill probably come in the next contraction."

"Contraction?"

The housekeeper and midwife put down the kettle and placed a pair of scissors in the hot water. Then she took a fresh linen and kneeled below Evie's legs.

"A contraction is nature's way of getting the baby out. Your muscles squeeze and push, helping you get started."

Evie gasped and clutched her stomach. It must be another contraction. Tiffany moved to the side of the bed and offered her hand. Evie grasped it again in her tight grip as she breathed in sharply.

"Push, Evie!" Mrs. Balogh instructed.

Squeezing Tiffany's hand, Evie closed her eyes, gritted her teeth, and appeared to be pushing with every muscle in her body. Tiffany watched her strain and push, but the babe did not come out. Evie collapsed back against the pillow, her hold on Tiffany's hand barely a touch.

"That's alright," the midwife said, nodding her head. "It usually takes a few good pushes to get a babe out. But once we get the head and shoulders, the rest slides out real easy."

Tiffany pulled out her handkerchief and dabbed at the sweat on Evie's face. Despite her earlier nap, the poor woman looked exhausted. "Would you like a drink of water?"

The glass Tiffany had fetched her earlier was still on the bedside table.

Mrs. Balogh shook her head. "No water for her. She'll just cast it up with the next contraction."

Evie's head leaned forward, and her eyes popped open. The next contraction was already here.

Tiffany patted her hand again. "You're doing so well."

The housekeeper shook her head. "Don't mollycoddle her. Push, Evie!"

Screaming, Evie squeezed Tiffany's hand until it turned white with the loss of blood circulation. Then Tiffany saw the back of a head with light hair. She watched as Mrs. Balogh carefully turned the baby around, so that its head was upward, and then helped guide the shoulders and the rest of the body out. A long, thick red cord appeared to be attached between Evie and her child.

The baby was red, wrinkled, and screaming. Tiffany loved him on sight, for his gender was quite easy to see before Mrs. Balogh wrapped him up in the fresh linen. She set him next to Evie's leg and took the scissors out of the hot kettle. Then she cut the cord that connected mother to son, close to his belly. For the first time, Tiffany realized that her belly button had once connected her to her own mother. Once the cord was severed, Mrs. Balogh tried to pass him to Evie.

She shook her head, folding her arms. "I don't want it."

Tiffany let go of Evie's hand. "I'll hold him."

Mrs. Balogh gave the baby to Tiffany, and it felt as if her heart would burst. She brought the babe close to her chest and gently stroked his hair. It was sticky with blood and whatever fluid was inside of a woman's womb. There was also an unpleasant smell, but she did not care. This little life was worth anything. Everything. The babe kept turning his head back and forth and moving his sweet little lips.

"He's hungry," Mrs. Balogh said. "But you can hold him while I deliver the afterbirth and clean her up a bit."

Tiffany pressed a gentle kiss on his forehead and wished that she could give him the nourishment he so desperately wanted and needed. She glanced up at the housekeeper and was shocked to see a great mass come out of the same opening the baby had. It was also attached to the cord.

Oh, how she wished she knew more about the inner workings of her own anatomy! Dropping another kiss on the crying babe's forehead, she wondered why her own mother had not explained to her not only how babies were made but also the changes to expect during childbirth. Perhaps if Tiffany had been married, she would have. But such knowledge was surely needed *before* even courtship. Tiffany resolved to talk to Mary about it. She did not intend to go into great detail, for she herself was still rather ignorant.

If only there were a book about such things that young women (and women not so young) could read. But what male editor would publish it? And what father would purchase it for his daughters?

She shook her head and watched as Mrs. Balogh placed all the bloody, sodden linens in a pile. She folded a small linen into squares and pressed it against the opening between Evie's legs that was growing smaller by the minute. How miraculous! A woman's body expanded and retracted to allow for the baby's birth. Tiffany noticed that the scissors were back in the hot water of the kettle.

Mrs. Balogh held out her arms, and Tiffany reluctantly gave the little boy to her. "Give Evie a drink while I wash him. I don't suppose you've prepared any nappies for him?"

Tiffany blinked in surprise but realized that the second question had been directed toward Evie and not herself.

"No. I didn't want him."

"Whether you wanted the babe or not, he's here and he needs nappies. I'll wrap him up after washing him, but you and Miss Woodall will have to make some tomorrow. New bairns go through nappies every hour or so."

Evie didn't say anything to Mrs. Balogh. Nor did she thank Tiffany for fetching her the glass of water.

Tiffany's eyes turned from the tired and angry new mother to the still crying babe. Mrs. Balogh dipped a corner of the rag into the water and washed the fluids from birth off him. Once she was finished, she wrapped him tighter than a bed with a tick.

"He needs your breast," the midwife said flatly.

Reluctantly, Evie unbuttoned her bodice. She wasn't wearing a corset or a chemise underneath. Mrs. Balogh placed the baby into Evie's arms and helped direct the head onto the nipple. It was a good thing the little lad seemed to know what he was doing, for he received no encouragement from his mother. After a few minutes, Mrs. Balogh moved him to the other breast.

The baby closed his eyes and fell asleep, detaching himself from his mother. Evie relinquished the baby to Tiffany. "Ye hold him. I need to sleep."

"Drink another glass of water first," Mrs. Balogh insisted. "You need water to produce milk for the bairn."

Evie took the glass from the midwife and slowly drank the entire thing.

"Miss Woodall," the housekeeper said, "why don't you take the bairn into another room, and I'll help Mrs. Lathrop into new clothes."

Nodding, Tiffany carried the dear sleeping baby out of the bedchamber and to a rocking chair in the sitting room.

Clutching him close to her heart, she rocked him back and forth. And back and forth.

According to the law, this was Samir's son. Tiffany would have loved him simply for that, but what she felt for this sweet babe was so much more. He seemed as if he belonged to her. Tiffany knew such thoughts were foolish and that Evie would take the baby back. But for now, for these precious moments, he was hers.

CHAPTER 18

The baby boy's wails and whimpers woke Tiffany. She had somehow fallen asleep while rocking him. Tightening her hold on the little babe in her arms, she resolved never to be so careless again. The sitting room and kitchen were both dark. It had to be late in the evening. She stood up, still holding him, and saw that the kettle had been washed and was drying on the counter. There was a small fire in the hearth that gave only the dimmest of light to the room. Once she passed the baby over to Evie for feeding, she would add more logs and stoke it.

Tiffany carried the baby to the small room. The door was closed, so she lightly knocked before opening it. The room was nearly dark, but Tiffany couldn't see Evie or the dirty linens.

"Evie."

No answer.

Perhaps she had moved to Samir's mattress that wasn't covered in childbirth fluids. Tiffany carried the baby to the next door, knocking again before entering. But the larger chamber was just as empty as the smaller.

Where had Evie gone?

Gently, she set the baby on the floor and fumbled for a candle in the kitchen. She lit it in the fire and put it on a candlestick. Returning to the small bedchamber, she opened the doors to the wardrobe and the drawers. All of Evie's effects had been removed. She had not stepped out for a little while. She had abandoned her newborn babe.

The boy's wails grew louder.

He was hungry. He would die without proper nourishment.

Pacing, Tiffany wished that her own breasts had milk to feed him, but they didn't. Her chest felt tight, and her breaths were short and fast. She needed a woman who was producing milk for her own baby. If only she knew more of the mothers in the village!

The only small child she had seen was at the Anstey's home. Perhaps Mrs. Anstey would be kind enough to provide milk for this baby until a more permanent situation could be found. Picking up the baby, she wrapped him a second time in her shawl. Then she grasped the candle and went down the stairs. With every minute, the light was fading. Tiffany could see the moon as she set down her candle and knocked loudly on the Anstey's door.

No one came for several minutes.

The poor baby's wails became louder. Tiffany was near tears herself, bouncing up and down as she tried to soothe the child. She pounded her free fist against the door.

A few more minutes passed, and Tiffany grew desperate, a jittery feeling in her belly. She was about to shout when the door finally opened. It was Mr. Anstey, a wiry man with large hands and a sharp chin.

"Miss Woodall, what for goodness' sake are ye doing?"

"I am so sorry to awaken you," Tiffany said. "But Mrs. Evie Lathrop delivered her child and then abandoned it. I was hoping that Mrs. Anstey would feed the baby. Only tonight, until other arrangements can be made."

Tiffany could see a peep of red hair over his shoulder. His wife stood behind him, holding their little son. She touched her husband's arm, and he moved aside for her.

"I am sorry, Miss Woodall, but our son is weaned. I wish I could help ye."

Tears streamed down Tiffany's face, and she could see tears on the baby's face as well. He was desperate to be fed. "Please. Is there any mother you know who could help me?"

"I do."

The voice was not Mrs. Anstey's, but her daughter Caro's. She was wearing a robe over her nightdress. "I'll come with you, Miss Woodall."

"'Tis a bad idea," Mrs. Anstey said, shaking her head.

Tiffany's wet eyes moved to Mr. Anstey's, but he said not a word. His eyes were only on his daughter.

"The bairn needs feedin'," Caro said. "Let me fetch my boots, and I'll come at once."

"Thank you," Tiffany said through tears.

Caro pulled on a pair of boots and picked up Tiffany's candle on the ground by the door. "Follow me, Miss Woodall."

Tiffany trailed behind Caro on the road, expecting her to lead them to a cottage. But they walked all the way to Tiffany's own home. Caro opened the front door.

"Miss Woodall, is that finally ye?" Mary called out.

"Yes, Mary," Tiffany said, but her voice was hoarse from tears and frustration as she followed her inside the house. Her hair stiffened on the nape of her neck. Why had Caro brought them to Bristle Cottage?

The young maid rushed into the room. "Miss Caro, I didn't expect to see ye. I've got hot water in the kitchen fer tea and a nice fire. Been waiting for Miss Woodall all evenin' . . . What ye doin' with a baby? And why is it crying like that?"

Before Tiffany could find quite the right words to describe the events of the day, Caro took off her robe and Tiffany could see that her dressing gown was wet over her breasts, but the rest of it was dry. She unbuttoned the front of her nightgown.

Caro held out her arms to take the child. "I can feed him now."

Dumbfounded, Tiffany turned the baby over to her. The poor boy was only whimpering now, as if crying took up too much of his depleted energy. With one hand, Caro moved aside her wet dressing gown and brought the baby to her breast. Tiffany could hear his sucking sounds and watched his little fingers move against Caro's chest. Breastfeeding, Caro walked into the kitchen and took a chair near the fire.

Tiffany stood stock still in the doorway of the kitchen. Her mind tried to catch up with what she had seen. How did an unmarried young woman have milk? The only reasonable explanation was that Miss Caro's much younger brother was not her brother at all, but her son. Her parents must have claimed the child to protect both their daughter and their grandchild from the stigma of illegitimacy.

But who was the father of the child?

"I got us a right good cow, Miss Woodall," Mary said, unperplexed by any of the night's events. "She's a real milker. We're gonna have butter and cream and all the best from her. And she only cost ye two pounds. Once ye pay Mrs. Smith for her."

Brought back into the moment, Tiffany nodded her head. "I will give you the coins tomorrow to take to her, and an extra shilling for you if you promise not to tell anyone else that Miss Caro came to our house this evening."

Mary beamed. "My lips is sealed. Ye're a right one, Miss Woodall. Nows, come take a seat and I'll get ye something to eat. I bet ye haven't had a bite of supper."

She hadn't. Tiffany followed her maid into the kitchen and slumped into a chair. She could almost hear her own voice telling Mary to sit tall like a lady, but Tiffany was too tired to follow her own admonitions. Yawning, she gratefully accepted the plate of cold ham, vegetables, and a slice of bread.

"I'll brew ye some ginger tea now, Miss Woodall," Mary said brightly. "'Tis yer new favorite, after all."

Tiffany stole a glance at Miss Caro, but she didn't seem to have heard Mary's comment. She was moving the baby to her other breast. The little boy was moving his arms wildly. Tiffany supposed that he must still be hungry. Being born was hard work. Sighing, she returned her focus to her late dinner and slowly chewed every bite.

Mary presented her with a steaming cup of tea.

"Thank you, Mary. You have been a saint to me this evening. Why don't you go on up to bed?"

"But what about the dirty dishes?"

Turning her head toward the sink basin, Tiffany saw that Mary had not cleaned a dish all day. "I will do them. It's the least I can do after you made me supper and found us a great bargain on a cow."

"Can I name her?"

Tiffany blinked. "The baby is a boy."

Mary giggled and shook her head. "Not the baby—the cow."

She couldn't hold back her own chuckle over her teacup. "Of course, Mary."

"Goodnight, Miss Woodall. Goodnight, Miss Caro. Although I didn't see ye. Not even so much as a glance."

Both Caro and Tiffany returned the salutation, and Mary all but skipped out of the kitchen, no doubt already planning on how she would spend her shilling. Tiffany hoped that it would not be on blue ruin at the Black Cauldron.

Tiffany's eyes moved back to her half-eaten plate, and she took another bite. Her mind was whirling with possibilities. The Ansteys had obviously gone to a great deal of trouble to keep their daughter's name untainted. However, Tiffany couldn't help but wonder why the father of the child hadn't married Caro. Unless, like in her own case, the man she loved was already married. For Mr. Hadfield seemed quite devoted to the young woman, and if the child were his, Tiffany was sure that he would have married her at least a year ago.

She stole another glance at Caro by the hearth, and she saw that the babe's arms no longer flailed about. His eyes were closed, and he seemed blissfully content as he suckled.

"I cannot thank you enough for helping me tonight," Tiffany said slowly. "And I can assure you that neither myself nor Mary will ever breathe a word of it. You should not be punished for saving a baby."

A tear slid down Caro's cheek, and the young woman appeared even more beautiful and very young. "Mr. Hadfield doesn't know. Do you think I ought to tell him?"

Yes.

No.

Tiffany did not know. If Mr. Hadfield had enjoyed any woman's sexual favors, he would not feel similarly compelled to tell his new bride. Women, however, were always held to a higher standard.

"Is the father of your baby living in the village?" Tiffany asked. It could prove quite devastating if someone else told the farmer about the child's true parentage.

Caro shook her head, more tears falling down her cheeks. "He's dead."

Which men from the village died within the last year or so? Her half brother Uriah. No, despite his many flaws, he had not been a seducer of innocents. The only other male to have died in the last year was—Tiffany dropped her fork. Mr. Bernard Coram was the father of Caro's child. When he had called her a "straw damsel" in the public house, perhaps he was referring to the child, or the creation of it.

"Did he know about the boy?" she asked, wondering if Farmer Coram also knew. Trying to choose her words carefully.

Sniffing, Caro shook her head. "Mother and I went to stay with my aunt for the final months of my confinement. No one in Mapledown knows."

Except Tiffany and her dear but very gossipy maid.

"Did Bernard Coram not wish to marry you?"

Caro shook her head again. "I did not wish to marry him . . . He—he attacked me and forced himself on me. And when I begged for him to stop, he told me I was being a flirt and toying with his affections. I had allowed him to kiss me, but I hadn't intended on anything further. I am a good woman, Miss Woodall."

"I never doubted that for a moment, Miss Anstey."

She sniffed loudly. "Bernard would not stop, and when I tried to scream, he covered my mouth." Caro closed her eyes. "All I remember is the darkness and the pain and the shame. And when my monthlies didn't come, I told my mother what had happened. She didn't blame me, but my father . . . he said that I must have behaved wantonly for Bernard to do what he did. But I swear to you, Miss Woodall, I didn't. I didn't."

Tiffany got to her feet and walked to the chair where Caro sat, then knelt before her. "You have done no wrong and no sin. My father was a vicar, and even he would not hold you responsible for being raped. For that is what happened to you. None of it is your fault. Nothing you did caused it to happen. The fault and sin are entirely Mr. Bernard Coram's, and I am sure our Lord and Savior is punishing him now."

More tears streamed down Caro's cheeks, and she let out a little sob. Tiffany patted her shoulder, trying to comfort this poor young woman who was the victim of an unspeakable crime.

"The wise woman in the village I grew up in would suggest that you bring a small vial of chicken blood to your marriage bed," Tiffany said, remembering a shocking detail she'd once overheard as a young girl. "New husbands will expect a bride to bleed, and therefore you can place some on yourself and the sheets."

Caro wiped at her eyes. "Would you do that, Miss Woodall?"

Tiffany exhaled slowly and began to rub instead of pat Caro's shoulder. "Marriage is a long time, and hopefully, your husband will be your greatest friend, your most ardent lover, and your dearest confidant. I would tell Mr. Hadfield the truth in all of its terrible detail. A good man will not hold you to blame for the violent actions of another. You are a victim of rape, not of sin."

"Lawrence is a good man. I think he will believe me."

"And if he doesn't, he is not worthy of you. For you, Miss Caro Anstey, are a woman of great worth, with a heart second to none."

The young woman nodded; she looked as if she were too overcome with emotion to speak. Tiffany sincerely prayed that she'd said the right things: words of comfort and solace.

She saw the babe detach from Caro, clearly asleep. Tiffany got to her feet and held her arms out for the baby. She pulled him close to her and held him tightly. Even in a terrible world there was still innocence and beauty.

Caro buttoned up her slightly damp nightgown. "I can probably feed him a couple of times before morning. I am afraid ye'll have to raise him by hand or get a wet nurse tomorrow. I have nearly finished weaning my own baby."

"What does 'raise him by hand' mean?" Tiffany asked, woefully unprepared for motherhood.

"Feed him with a bottle of milk. Some babes tummies can tolerate cow's milk, and others can't."

Tiffany hoped this little boy's tummy was strong, for she wasn't acquainted with any wet nurses. Perhaps Thomas might know someone among one of Beau's tenants. "Why don't you come upstairs and sleep for a little while? I have a spare, clean nightdress."

The young lady got to her feet. "I should appreciate wearing it, Miss Woodall."

Turning to locate a candle, Tiffany saw that one was already lit. Mary was a very thoughtful young woman, even if she had difficulty completing a task. Cradling the baby in one arm, Tiffany picked up the candlestick and led Caro up the stairs to the room that had once been her own. She set the candle on the bedside table and pulled a clean nightgown out of the bottom drawer of the wardrobe. And then it hit her. The drawer would make the perfect bed for the baby. At least for this night.

Kneeling down, she placed him on a soft, folded linen sheet. He made a sweet little sound but didn't open his eyes.

"Is it alright if he stays here with you?" Tiffany asked in a whisper.

Caro nodded.

"I'll leave you the candle and give you privacy." She touched the doorknob and stopped. "May I ask you one more question of a personal nature?"

"Yes."

"Do a mother's breasts always leak before she feeds a baby?"

The young woman smiled and even gave a soft laugh. "No, Miss Woodall. But sometimes the sound of a cryin' babe, particularly yer own baby, can bring in yer milk. Most of the time, yer breasts don't leak all over yer dresses."

Sighing, Tiffany said, "Thank you."

She left the room, closing the door gently behind her, and went to her own, just adjacent to it. She didn't need a candle to make her way around the familiar space, nor to take out her own nightdress and put it on. Once she was tucked up in bed, she couldn't help but think Mr. Bernard Coram's death might have something to do with the rape of Miss Anstey. Perhaps Bernard told Mr. Hadfield that Miss Caro had laid with him willingly. Or maybe Mr. Anstey had finally defended his daughter.

Closing her tired eyes, Tiffany had to admit that the list of suspects was not narrowing, but getting larger.

CHAPTER 19

Twice in the night, Tiffany heard Caro feed the baby. The poor young woman was not getting much rest. And neither was Tiffany. She woke just before the sunrise and quickly dressed. Knocking quietly on Caro's door, she waited for the young woman to say, "Come in."

Tiffany entered the room. "Would you mind feeding him once more, and then I will walk you home?"

Caro threw off her coverlet, yawning. "Ye don't need to do that."

"It's the least I can do," she said. "Mary can watch the baby for a little while until I get back. I'll go and make you a cup of tea. Is there anything else I can get for you?"

"Nothing, Miss Woodall."

Closing the door behind her, Tiffany started a fire in the kitchen hearth and added a few more logs. She boiled two kettles of water, the first for washing dishes and the second for tea. Again, she made ginger tea, even though her guest would have probably preferred black. Tiffany's cramping tummy insisted on ginger as she scrubbed all the dirty dishes and left them out to dry.

Tiffany carefully carried a full cup of tea up to Caro's room. The young woman was sitting up in the bed, still feeding the baby.

"Just set it on the bedside table there," she said. "I don't want a drop to fall on him."

Tiffany set down the saucer and cup. "Would you like to borrow one of my gowns, or will you walk home in your robe?"

Caro smiled. She was an extraordinarily beautiful young woman. "Ye're so much taller than me, Miss Woodall, I don't think any dress of yers would work. Yer nightgown goes all the way to me ankles."

Smiling, Tiffany nodded. She was very tall for a woman. The only other woman she'd met that was as tall was Evie Lathrop. But any sympathy she'd felt for Samir's wife had been replaced with anger at her abandoning her baby to starve. She went down the stairs and brushed off Caro's boots and prepared her robe. Then she did the same to her own boots and cloak.

Tiffany walked back up the stairs, clutching her side, and knocked on Mary's door. "Can you wake up, dear? I need you to watch the baby while I walk Miss Caro home."

There was no verbal answer, but Mary swung open the door in only her nightdress. "Does that mean I gets to hold the baby?"

"Yes. Now put on a robe or get dressed, Mary."

"Faster than two spits in an urn," she said, slamming the door.

If the baby had been asleep, he was no longer.

In only a few minutes, Mary had possession of the baby, and she was smothering the lad with kisses. Tiffany folded up

Miss Caro's nightgown into a bag and helped her put on her robe and boots. Then they set off together to the village. The sun was still not up, but it was light enough to see the road and the golden tendrils of the sunrise spreading over the farmers' fields.

The glow of the sun was always more glorious after the rain and the mud, Tiffany thought as she and Caro walked both quietly and quickly. Even with Tiffany's escort, it was still very scandalous for the young woman to be out in only her robe. Hopefully, no one would catch them. They took the shortest path to Mapledown Village, and Tiffany's heartbeat did not slow until Caro was safely inside her parents' house.

Tiffany went to the bookshop, where the back door was still unlocked. She went inside and was relieved to see that nothing had been stolen during the night. What a poor friend she would be to Samir if she didn't take care of his business and home. She found a set of two keys on his desk that she assumed were to the building. She tried the first and it didn't fit in the lock, but the second did. Assured that Samir's livelihood was safe, she began to walk back to Bristle Cottage. This time she took the longer path, to lessen the chances of someone seeing her twice before breakfast. By the time the road passed the Corams' farm, the sun was easily visible in the sky, its rays shining on all the world beneath.

A glimmer of gold on the road caught her eye. At first, Tiffany thought it was only a shiny rock. But coming closer, she could see that it was a button. And not just any button. She stooped down to pick it up, brushing off the dirt. It was a golden button with a unique design on it. It was about the size of a farthing and had four columns with little lines on each pillar. The expensive button must have fallen off in the rain or mud. Whoever dropped it would be very sorry. If it was some-one in the village, she would return it to them.

Mary was sitting in the kitchen in the same chair Caro had sat in the night before. She was talking to the baby as if he were old enough to understand every word that she said.

"Ye're back already, Miss Woodall. 'Tis a good thing. Matilda needs milking."

It took Tiffany a few moments to realize that Matilda must be the name of their new cow. She reached out her hands for the baby—who needed a name much more than a cow did—but they came away feeling wet. The baby needed a change.

Standing, Mary shook her hands off. "Oh, I forgot about that. Dunno how to change a nappy."

"First, let's set him down and wash up with soap and hot water. Then, before you visit Miss Matilda, perhaps you will be good enough to help me get a trunk down from the attic."

The maid's eyes widened. "What's in the trunk?"

Tiffany wished for Mary's sake that it was a pirate's trea-sure, but it was really her hope chest. "Linens and things for my trousseau, but also, nappies, blankets, and baby dresses. Our boy needs something fine to wear."

"What are we gonna call him?"

Sighing, Tiffany placed him on the floor. The baby did not like being set down, and began to cry. Tiffany longed to com-fort him, but she needed to get him clean first. "I am not sure yet. I do not know if he is mine to keep."

Evie was his mother. Samir, his legal father.

"Course he is. Ye are the one who has him and who loves him. Ye're his mum. He's our baby to keep."

A surge of love for Mary warmed Tiffany's heart. "Come, I shall hold the ladder and you can crawl up there."

"How will I know which one it is?"

"It will have my name on the lid, with painted flowers," Tiffany said dryly. For many years she'd hated the very sight of it. The hope chest stood for everything that she had wanted in life but didn't have.

Mary scurried up the ladder faster than a sailor up a rigging. Less than a minute later, she called down, "I's found it, Miss Woodall. Should I push it to the opening?"

"Yes, please, Mary. I'll help you carry it down the ladder."

Tiffany slowly climbed up the rungs as she heard the sounds of scraping. Mary had pushed the chest all the way to the opening, and together, with a little finagling, they managed to get it down to the floor. The top of the wooden trunk was covered with dust, like Tiffany's dreams. But it wasn't too late for her.

Opening the chest, she saw that the items inside were not at all dusty. The cedarwood had kept all the linens in good order. She passed Mary a stack of nappies, then picked a pretty white dress for the baby to wear and a blanket that her own mother had knit. In all the ways that mattered, this baby was hers.

She bid Mary to fetch more water from the well, and she carefully washed the baby, who had managed to cover most of his back and legs with a noxious yellowish-brown liquid. He did not appreciate the lukewarm water and screamed as loud as he could. She dried him off with a fresh towel and showed Mary how to put the nappy on and secure it. Then she pulled the dress over his head. By now, her sweet baby was furious with her. She picked him up and held his face against her cheek, crooning to him.

"It's alright, Mama Tiffany's here. You're clean now."

Mary wrinkled her nose. "Looks like we're going to be doin' washing every single day."

Tiffany smiled and felt her baby's tears on her cheek. She was sorry that it had taken her so long to get him nappies and to clean him. His cries were now whimpers, and hopefully he would calm down in a few moments.

Her maid picked up the egg basket. "I'll go fetch the eggs and milk Matilda. At least with a cow you don't have to change nappies."

Tiffany laughed again as Mary left the kitchen. She continued to bounce on her feet and keep his face next to hers. She loved the feel of his soft fresh skin against her cheek. What was she to name him?

Her initial thought was to name him for her own father. She had loved him, but he'd been strict and cheerless. No, she would not name her baby after him. First babies were usually named after their grandfathers, but Samir had already named his first son William after his father. She would not take away the name or anything from the love he'd felt for his dead son. If a boy wasn't called after his grandfathers, he was given his father's name, and since Tiffany did not know his exact parentage, she would refer to the babe after his legal father: Samir.

For a moment, Tiffany allowed herself to dream of a family with Samir and herself as the parents of a beautiful baby for them to love. It would be confusing if both Samir and the child were called Samir. Perhaps, it would be better to have that be his middle name. And for his given name: *Nathaniel*.

Her old friend and fiancé's name popped into her head. Nathaniel had been a good man. A kind and strong one. And she adored *Nat* as a nickname.

Nathaniel Samir Lathrop was a strong name. She would have him christened that.

CHAPTER 20

Armed with a bag of nappies, blankets, and two extra baby dresses. Tiffany carried Nat, all wrapped up in her mother's blanket, to the palace. It probably would have been better for her to stay at Bristle Cottage, but she needed to save Nat's father and talk to Thomas about a wet nurse. She wondered how she could tell him to look into Mr. Anstey and Mr. Hadfield without mentioning Caro . . . perhaps she would only hint about Bernard Coram's slander of Miss Anstey in the public house the night that he died.

Then there was the button in her pocket. Perhaps it was silly, but she thought it might have something to do with the murder. It could have easily fallen off in a scuffle and been lost in a puddle of mud and sleet.

Tiffany fully expected to meet Mr. Ford at the door of the servant's entrance, for she was late again. But the person who opened it was none other than the Duchess of Beaufort. She wore a beautiful silk sack dress of sapphire blue. Her face was painted, but today she wore no wig.

"What are you carrying, Miss Woodall? And why must you always be late?"

Before Tiffany could answer, Nat began to cry. It had been a couple of hours since his last feeding, and her poor boy was hungry again.

The duchess's eyes widened. "Surely, that baby cannot be yours."

"Um, not precisely. I did not give birth to him, but he is mine until someone takes him from me. Your Grace, may I present Nathaniel Samir Lathrop, the son of Evie Lathrop, the legal wife of Samir, who is nonetheless not the father of the child."

The duchess's already painted white face paled. "Fie! The bookseller is already married?"

Tiffany breathed in deeply. "I was not aware of it either. Samir and Evie have been separated for nearly ten years, but she returned the day after I found Mr. Bernard Coram's body. He was her brother."

Saying the words aloud, Tiffany couldn't help but realize that the date of Evie's return to Mapledown was extremely suspicious. Had she had something to do with her half brother's death? Tiffany could not think of anything Evie would have to gain from it. But judging from the bruises on Tiffany's wrists this morning, Evie certainly had the strength to deliver a killing blow. Her years working in a blacksmith's forge had made her strong.

"How do you get yourself into such scrapes, Tiffany?"

The Duchess of Beaufort had called her by her given name. She'd never done that before.

"I-I don't mean to."

She held up one hand. "La! Never mind. Let me have the baby, and see if the chef can make him a warm bottle of milk. I suppose we shall need a wet nurse."

"W-we?" Tiffany stammered as the duchess took Nat from her arms and carried him into the servants' quarters.

Walking inside and taking off her cloak and boots, Tiffany glanced around and saw that she was not the only employee surprised by the duchess's presence there. All the servants were standing still, their backs straight, like an army at attention.

"Bonne, a warm bottle of milk for the baby. Ford, please inform Thomas that his presence is required at once in the library. Miss Woodall and I will be there."

Mr. Ford, usually the pattern card of perfection, did not move. His eyes widened and he looked at the baby, then at the Duchess of Beaufort, then at Tiffany, and then at all three of them again, as if trying to understand a particularly thorny problem.

"At once!" the duchess said, and then everyone in the room finally moved.

Tiffany followed her through the servants' quarters, to the hall to the library, wanting her baby back, but not knowing how to get him. The duchess sat down on Tiffany's favorite sofa and unwrapped Nat from his covers. He was wearing a white lacy cap and a long white dress, and looked positively adorable.

"Oh, aren't you the sweetest little thing," she crooned, and then to Tiffany's even greater surprise, she kissed his little cheeks. She placed Nat back on her lap and proceeded to count his fingers and toes, something that Tiffany hadn't thought to do. She was relieved to see that there were ten of each.

The door to the library opened, and Thomas burst into the room, out of breath. "Whatever is the matter, Mother?"

The duchess held up the baby. "Miss Woodall has acquired a baby."

Like Mr. Ford, Thomas appeared to be so stunned that he couldn't move. Monsieur Bonne walked through the door and around him, to deliver a glass bottle with a rubber nozzle at the end of it on a tray.

He offered it to the duchess like it was an exotic dessert. "Shall Your Grace require anything else?"

The duchess took the bottle and placed it inside Nat's open, wailing mouth. The baby quieted instantly as he began to suck. "That will be all for now. See if you can find or have someone purchase several bottles and ask if anyone on the staff knows of a wet nurse. A mother's milk is better than a cow's."

Monsieur Bonne bowed. "Yes, Your Grace."

He left the room, passing Thomas again, and closed the door behind him.

"Mother, what are you doing with Evie Lathrop's baby?"

Instead of answering the question, the duchess's sharp eyes turned to Tiffany in accusation. "Fie! You told Thomas, but not me?"

Tiffany felt her face go red, and she glanced at Thomas in confusion. "I am sorry. I didn't know how to."

The duchess's sharp eyes softened as she looked down at the baby. "I see that you were in a rather awkward spot, but how are we to be friends if you don't share your confidences with me?"

Tiffany felt gawkier and more miserable than she had at her first dance. "You wish to be my friend, Your Grace?"

"You may call me Catharine when we are alone."

"Th-thank you," Tiffany said, glancing again at Thomas in confusion.

His hands were on his face. "It has only been a day since I talked to you, Tiffany, but I feel that there is a great deal of information that I am not in possession of."

Nodding, she exhaled. "Yes. Samir has been arrested on a warrant from Sir Walter Abney. Farmer Coram said he heard his son Bernard try to blackmail Samir, and he claims that is why his son is dead."

Catharine's sharp eyes swiveled to her son. "Isn't Coram one of our lease tenants?"

"Yes, Mother. His family has been our tenant farmers for over a century."

The duchess sniffed. "Well, if he would like his family to continue to be our tenants for the next century, he must withdraw his testimony against Mr. Lathrop."

Thomas fiddled with his hands in his lap. "I can put pressure on him, Mother, but there is a chance that even withdrawing his complaint will not change Sir Walter's mind. The justice of the peace is greatly prejudiced against Samir and felt that Samir embarrassed him last year at my trial."

Catharine gritted her teeth, and Tiffany thought for the first time that they might actually be able to be friends. For she could see that the duchess was just as angry as herself about the injustices done to her son and Samir because of their skin color.

"We must put pressure on Sir Walter. My late husband said that he was perpetually in debt. Write to our man of business in London and have him acquire all of Sir Walter's notes and the mortgage on his Maplehurst estate."

"Isn't that blackmail?" Tiffany asked.

"Of course, it is," Catharine said, in a singsong voice as she gently jostled Nat in her arms. "If the justice of the peace doesn't follow the law, neither shall we."

Thomas nodded his agreement, and Tiffany couldn't help but feel they both had a valid point. Not an ethical one, though. But she would do anything to see Samir freed.

"After Samir was arrested," Tiffany explained, "Evie went into labor, and Mrs. Balogh delivered the baby, Nathaniel. I call him Nat. I was rocking Nat, and I'm afraid I fell asleep. When I woke up, they were both gone. All of Evie's belongings were too. I assumed that she had abandoned the baby, so I took him home late last night."

She would keep Caro's name clean.

This time Thomas exhaled slowly. "What a mess we find ourselves in. I will first send an express to our man of business. Then I will go and speak to Farmer Coram. And lastly, I'll see if I can locate Evie Lathrop. Her behavior throughout has been most suspicious."

"Do you think she went back to Mr. Tate?" Tiffany asked.

"That's a great place to start," Thomas agreed. "I will come and fetch you before setting off for Bardsley."

"What about the baby? Who will take care of him?"

"Me, of course," Catharine said.

"But you're a duchess."

Catharine sniffed. "Before you say another word, I have two sons of my own, and I am completely qualified to take care of a newborn. I will also see what can be done about finding him a wet nurse."

Thomas got to his feet. Leaning down, he dropped a kiss on his mother's cheek. "Thank you, Mama."

The duchess blushed a pretty pink, and she grinned fondly at her son. "Thank you, Thomas. It is so nice to have a man about the house to take care of the business."

Or blackmail.

After Thomas left the room, Catharine said, "You look terrible, Tiffany. Go and find an empty guest room, and take a long nap. I daresay you got next to no sleep last night."

"Very little," she admitted. "Thank you, Your Grace."

"*Catharine.*"

Tiffany stood up on her wobbling legs. "Thank you, Catharine."

CHAPTER 21

Opening her eyes, Tiffany did not recognize where she was. She felt like a heroine in a fairy tale, magically transported into a beautiful palace. The bed she slept on was spacious enough to fit six people and had four large posts and a canopy over the top. Everything she touched seemed to be made of satin or silk. This featherbed was the softest she had ever laid on.

Her stomach groaned and then cramped.

She remembered where she was: Astwell Palace. She also remembered that she had not eaten in hours. Pulling off the coverlet, she located her boots. She put them on and attempted to tidy her cotton gown of Indian embroidered calico with little red birds and flowers. Then she tugged up her bodice and retied the fichu around her neck. Touching her hair, she could feel that more than half of it had fallen out of her coiffure. Tiffany sighed and took out the rest of the pins, before making a simple chignon at the base of her neck.

Satisfied that she was presentable, Tiffany left the guest room and went to find the duchess. *Catharine.* It would be strange to think of the fashionable and formidable duchess by her first name. She did not find her in any of the parlors or the library. She opened a door that she had never been through and saw a large and empty ballroom. The tiles on the floor were a light gray–veined marble, as were the pillars. The ceiling was coffered and each square painted in a different pastoral scene. Where the woodworking beams crossed, there were countless crystal chandeliers hanging from the ceiling. Tiffany had never dreamed that a room could be so ornate and sumptuous. It was truly a room out of a Mother Goose fairy tale.

Closing the door, she went to the nursery and found Catharine holding Nat and showing him to her little son.

"I was never that small."

"But you were."

Beau shook his head. "Impossible."

Tiffany's lips twitched into a smile. Her little charge was certainly willful, and if he didn't want to believe something, he wouldn't.

"Miss Woodall, your color is much restored."

The duchess's words caused Tiffany's cheeks to flush with heat. "I am sorry if I overslept."

Catharine shook her head slightly. "No, but Thomas has returned from seeing the tenant and is ready to go with you to Bardsley."

"I will go and find him."

"Go to the kitchens first and get something to eat. You're still looking peaky. Beau will fetch his brother and have him meet you there."

Tiffany thanked Catharine and reluctantly left Nat with her. The duchess was proving to be a very efficient and very bossy friend. On her way to the servant's area, Tiffany's stomach groaned three times. Perhaps the duchess did have a point after all.

Monsieur Bonne was only too happy to make Tiffany a plate of food and a steaming cup of tea. By the time Thomas arrived, she was feeling much more like herself and quite able to travel in the carriage to Bardsley.

The horses pulled up in front of the blacksmith's house and shop. Thomas helped Tiffany down and then knocked on the front door. She saw a glance of someone in the window, but then the face was gone. She thought it had been Evie, but she couldn't be sure.

He knocked one last time before saying, "Let us go around to the shop."

Offering his arm, he walked her around the house and to the blacksmith's forge. Like their previous visit, the two double doors were open to allow fresh, cool air inside. Today, however, Mr. Tate was wearing a shirt, or rather, a smock. He swore underneath his breath when he saw them.

"'Tis the Spanish Inquisition back?"

Tiffany felt Thomas's arm tense underneath her hand.

"Sir, we are not here to cause any problems. Or to meddle. We are simply here to assure that Evie Lathrop's needs are being met."

Mr. Tate spun the hammer he was holding. "And why should the likes of ye care about Evie?"

Taking a deep breath, Tiffany stepped forward. "We only want to make sure she is in health. She left so soon after the birth of the baby."

The blacksmith wouldn't meet Tiffany's eyes. His focus was on the hammer he was playing with. "Is the bairn thriving?"

"Yes, the baby is a boy, and I have named him Nathaniel Samir Lathrop. And unless someone with a greater claim wishes to take him, I mean to raise him as my own son."

Mr. Tate shook his head. "She dunna want him."

"Well, I do."

The blacksmith tugged at his beard with one hand before finally meeting Tiffany's eyes. "Then I'd say the bairn is yers to keep."

Mr. Tate shuffled to his feet and pulled open a drawer. There was a small box inside it. "I suppose the only business ye have left wi' me is the matter of the ring."

He presented her with the box, and she opened it up. Tiffany had expected a simple gold band, but what she saw in her hand was intricately lovely and anything but simple. It was a weave of four different golden bands moving seamlessly over, under, and through. Her diamond cluster ring was a beautiful work of art. She slipped it on the fourth finger of her right hand and was surprised that it fit perfectly.

"How?" she asked the blacksmith. "You never even measured my finger."

"Ye talk with your hands. T'weren't difficult to guess the size."

Nodding, she thought he must be a very talented blacksmith. Or he knew a woman with a similarly sized hand. And if that were so, he would have seen Evie since Tiffany gave him the diamond pin.

"We do not expect you to break a confidence, Mr. Tate," Tiffany said slowly. "Nor would we wish you to. However, perhaps you can tell us if we should continue our search for Evie to make sure she is safe and well, or if we should trust she is with friends."

The gruff blacksmith didn't speak for several moments. Thomas gave Tiffany a questioning stare, but she held up her hand with the ring on it to silence him.

At last, Mr. Tate said, "I believe she is with friends. Ye need not continue to look fer her."

Tiffany nodded. "Very well. Thank you for your intricate and beautiful work, Mr. Tate. We shall bid you good day."

Again, Thomas cast her a glance of surprise, but he did not contradict her. They walked side by side to the carriage, and he helped her into it. Thomas did not speak until he was inside with her and the door had been closed.

"I feel as if I did not understand the second half of the conversation."

Sliding off her new ring, she gave it to Thomas. "I do not doubt that Mr. Tate is a skilled and talented tradesman. But no savant could look at a *gloved* woman's hand and know her precise ring size . . . He must have measured the ring on Evie."

"Then why did he not tell us outright that she had returned to him?"

Tiffany swallowed, a lump in her throat. "I know that I am not entirely unbiased when it comes to Evie Lathrop; however, I think it is safe to assume that she was somehow involved in her brother's death. Why else would she be hiding from us?"

"You think she killed her own brother?"

"I think she knows more about his death than she's letting on."

Thomas nodded slowly. "If that is the case, why did you not insist on speaking to her? Demanding the truth?"

She slid the ring back on her finger, then she pulled her glove over it. "I didn't think it would do us any good. I don't believe she will admit to anything without proof. She's proven too wily for that."

"Why would she want to kill Bernard? Not that I don't understand the sentiment, but as far as I have heard, she was the only one who loved him unconditionally."

Tiffany wished she knew. From her reading of the London newspapers, most murders seemed to be committed over money. The second biggest reason was infidelity, typically between husbands and wives. But Evie and Bernard were brother and sister. Bernard Coram had been without employment for several months and continued to drink and make merry. Could there have been a financial argument between them?

"The only reasonable conclusion I have so far come to is that they must have fallen out over money."

"But is Evie Lathrop strong enough to kill a man with only one strike to the back of his head?"

Pulling up her sleeve, she showed Thomas the five perfectly rounded bruises on her wrist—one for each of Evie's fingers. "Mr. Tate said that Evie worked in his shop. When I first met her, she was covered in a layer of grime and soot. I thought she was a slattern, but I realize now that it was only from working in the forge. If she can wield a hammer and bend iron to her will, I think her arm strength is more than a match for a human skull."

Thomas blew out a puff of air. "We have no proof. Without a murder weapon, all we have is conjecture. No judge or jury would believe us over her. I am a man of color, and you are a woman who has been apprehended for masquerading as a man."

"I confess, some days I miss the breeches," Tiffany said, attempting to lighten the mood in the carriage. "But you're right. We need indisputable proof. We must discover not only the murder weapon, but the location where the murder took place and the motivation for it, if we are to free Samir."

Thomas briefly touched her knee. "My mother was right. Farmer Coram recanted his testimony against Samir faster than a fox in a hen house when I threatened to end his farm lease. I took him over to Maplehurst, and Sir Walter kept us waiting for over an hour before he deigned to meet with us. Farmer Coram told him that he must have misunderstood the conversation between his son and Samir, and withdrew all complaints against him. I asked for the prison keys to release Samir, but Sir Walter refused to withdraw the warrant. He merely repeated that if Samir was truly innocent, the jury and judge would find him so."

Tiffany's hands clenched into tight fists. How she hated that small-minded man. Gritting her teeth, she no longer felt even a little bit guilty that Catharine wished to coerce him by his debts. "I hope your man of business ruins him."

Thomas laughed softly. "Don't let my mother's words fool you. She is the true manager of all the estate's affairs, and she doesn't need a man to do her work. If the baronet is ruined, it will be my mother who does it."

Tiffany laughed too, the tension in her face and back lessening. Thomas looked at her and then guffawed. Tiffany's laughter turned to hysteria. They laughed until they could no longer breathe.

Once they sobered, Thomas said, "I stopped in at the prison to bring Samir some food and a change of raiment, and he is being well taken care of despite the terrible circumstances. He would like to speak to you."

She longed to see him but needed a little more rest to regain her courage. "I'll go first thing in the morning."

When they arrived back at Astwell Palace, Tiffany and Thomas went straight to the nursery. Catharine had Beau sitting on a small chair and carefully holding Nat in his arms. Tiffany's heart warmed when she saw the pride and happiness in the little boy's face.

"First Mate Woodall, we have a new sailor for our crew!"

Beau shifted a little in his seat, and Catharine reached to carefully hold the baby securely on his lap.

Exhaling slowly, Tiffany smiled. "I am sure he will prove an excellent addition to our piracy."

Beau wiggled again, and his mother picked up the baby. He sprang to his feet, ran over to Tiffany, and wrapped his arms around her middle. She hugged him back tightly. Oh, how she had missed him these last few days. Usually, she had been the one to give him comfort, but this evening, it was he who was comforting her. And she needed it.

Tiffany dropped a kiss on his head. "I have missed you, Captain."

He hugged her again. "Well, you did have a baby."

Her ever-ready blush was back. Tiffany touched her cheek and could feel the heat coming through her glove. "Actually—"

Catharine handed Nat to Tiffany. "Yes, she did. And we must let First Mate Woodall get some rest. Why don't you challenge your brother to a game of jack straws? You might even be able to persuade me to play."

Beau grabbed his mother's arm and grinned up at her. "Please, Mama. No one is better at jack straws than you."

The duchess patted his cheek with her free hand. "Flattery—excellent weapon of choice. I should be delighted to play with my sons."

Thomas encircled Beau's shoulders, and they made such a beautiful portrait of a family.

"I suppose, I should head back home."

"Nonsense," Catharine said. "You are still dead on your feet. You and the baby must stay the night; besides, I have yet to have a moment to tell you that I have found a suitable wet nurse. Mrs. Able has been hired and paid for the next six months. You will find her in the servants' quarters when baby Nat is ready for his next feeding."

"I—you-you didn't have to do that."

The duchess sniffed. "La! Someone had to take charge."

And Catharine was obviously very capable of doing just that.

Tiffany held Nat closer to her chest. "But what about Mary? I cannot leave her alone, and I don't think she'll come without Matilda."

"Who is Matilda?" Beau asked.

"Our new dairy cow."

The little boy grinned. "I love cows!"

Catharine sighed. "Very well. I shall send Jones to invite your maid, who doesn't seem to do much work, and your cow to stay at the palace."

They left the room, and Tiffany spied a rocking chair near the fire. She sat down and rocked her baby.

CHAPTER 22

Tiffany left Nat with Mrs. Able the next morning. She was a widow around thirty years of age and made her living by being a wet nurse. Her only child was a boy of seven, who was making himself useful in the kitchens. Her light blond hair was braided in a coronet around her head, and her eyes were a dark blue, almost gray. She had been recently employed at the Bardsley Rectory, but the Duchess of Beaufort had persuaded both her and her employers that their babe of thirteen months was ready to be weaned. Tiffany believed that coins were exchanged. Mrs. Able was both clean and kind, and Tiffany didn't think she could have found a better wet nurse for her baby.

Both Thomas and Catharine offered to call her a carriage, but she politely declined. She had missed her daily walk yesterday, and she needed the time and space to choose her words for Samir. She desperately wanted to keep Nat. She had always wished for a child, and the Good Lord certainly worked in mysterious ways.

She passed by her cottage and remembered finding Bernard Coram's body there. It made sense that Evie would try to incriminate Tiffany if she was upset on learning her legal husband cared for her. But the former footman weighed at least seventeen stone. It would have taken a person of extraordinary strength to drag or carry him that far. Tiffany didn't think that Evie could have done it alone. Someone must have helped her.

But who?

Tiffany was clutching at the stitch in her side by the time she reached Mapledown Village. Passing the church, she thought of sweet Nat. He would need to be christened soon. As much as she did not wish to, she needed to stop and speak to Mr. Shirley and schedule it. If only the Duke of Beaufort's former chaplain hadn't retired after the death of his patron. That visit would prove to be most uncomfortable to say the least.

She walked by the Anstey's home. Mr. Anstey was a wiry man, but he must have been strong enough to carry the coffins he made and perform his duties as the village undertaker. Aside from Caro, he had the most motive for killing Bernard Coram. He or Mr. Hadfield, Caro's fiancé, who was also a smaller man, but a hard worker. Running a farm took a great deal of physical strength, and no one could vouch for his whereabouts after his altercation with Bernard at the public house, besides his mother.

How did Evie fit into this?

Or the Queen Anne's lace?

Who had Bernard Coram intended to give it to?

Tiffany turned to go to the prison, leaving the road that she and Samir had taken to Mr. Hadfield's farm and where they had seen Sir Walter Abney's estate. She spit in its direction. Such a hateful man. For Tiffany could only assume that it was prejudice and spite that drove his actions to persecute Samir.

She continued to walk. It felt like she was trying to put together a puzzle, but missing pieces of it. The picture it created was not yet clear. When she reached the prison, she knocked on the door.

"Come in," she heard Samir call.

Taking a deep breath, she opened the door, prepared for the terrible smell of decay. Instead, she inhaled sandalwood and plumeria in the air. Samir was still in his cell, and there were the remnants of a fire in the hearth. Someone had had the forethought to keep him warm, and she was certain that it had not been Sir Walter. Samir stood up. His clothes were a little rumpled, but otherwise he looked well and unbearably handsome, with the beginnings of a beard on his chin. Lining the iron bars were baskets of food and drink. Tiffany wished that she'd had the forethought to bring him something.

She gestured to the baskets. "Mrs. Balogh is taking very good care of you."

He smiled and for the first time, Tiffany could see the slight turn of his tooth. How grateful she was for this little imperfection that had saved him from earlier suspicion.

"She has been very kind, but only one of the baskets is from her," Samir said. "Sometimes it is easy to focus on the people who treat me poorly, but being in prison, I realized how many good people there are in the village. Many who brought baskets thanked me for my work as constable."

"May I ask who they were? For such actions will certainly raise them in my estimation."

He walked to the edge of his cell. "This one was from Mrs. Anstey. The one with the bottles of spirits is obviously from Mrs. Day. This basket and the incense were brought by Mrs. Canning, the apothecary's wife. I am the most grateful to her for ridding me of the noxious smell. The next two are from Thomas, and the last, but not least, from Mrs. Balogh."

Tiffany took a step closer, but she was still too far for Samir to touch her through the bars. "I wish I had brought something with me."

"From what Thomas told me yesterday, you have been quite busy taking care of things for me."

"You have another son," she said, tugging at the lace collar around her throat. "He will never be able to replace your first, but he can carry on your name and the memory of his brother."

"Have you given the babe a name?"

Tiffany did not know where to look as she said, "Nathaniel Samir Lathrop. I hope that you don't mind that I've called him after an old friend. I didn't want it to become confusing as to which person we were referring to by naming him Samir as well. The choice is ultimately yours, but you must decide quickly, for I am going to make an appointment with the rector to christen him."

Her eyes were on the floor, but she could feel Samir's gaze on her face.

"I am honored to be included in his name, and I hope that I will be able to see him grow up."

Tiffany's control of her emotions slipped, and she let out a little sob and then some odd sounds from her throat.

"I remember the first time that I saw you," Samir continued.

She laughed and pulled out a handkerchief from her apron to dab at her wet eyes, stealing a furtive look at him. "I think it would be very hard to forget. You tried to save me from drowning in the lake when I was only washing, and you saw me without a stitch of clothing on."

He shook his head. "That was not the first time I saw you."

"But you demanded to know my name."

"I didn't want you to know that the reason I walked around the lake was for the hope of catching a glimpse of you when I was coming or going. There are other paths of beauty nearer the village, but I walked the path around the lake because I wanted to see you."

Forcing her eyes to meet his, she sniffed and stepped closer to the bars that contained him. "You never so much as spoke a word to me."

"How could I?" he asked gently. "I was not free to court you, and I was not sure that you would accept my friendship . . . The first time I saw you, you were entering the chapel behind your brother. The light from the door highlighted your golden hair, giving you a halo, and I thought, there and then, that you looked like an angel in an illuminated manuscript."

Her father's chapel had an illuminated Bible with illustrations of the characters in it and she had thought it was the most beautiful book in the world. There was something magical and mystical about the colors and images near the sacred text. This was a unique but beautiful compliment from a bookseller.

"Why did you not introduce yourself to me?"

Samir shook his head. "I made the mistake of trying to befriend your half brother first, and he made it more than clear that there would be no social interaction between myself and the Woodalls."

Tiffany took the last step forward and reached for Samir through the bars. His hands engulfed hers. All of her doubt and fear seemed to drain away. She felt the familiar spark of warmth and desire in his touch. The need to be closer to him.

"And yet you still came walking by my cottage."

He brought one of her hands to his lips and lightly kissed it. "You had made quite an impression on me."

Samir turned her hand over and kissed her wrist and then pressed his lips against her palm. Her knees wobbled underneath her gown, and she felt a burning deep in her belly. Then he brought her other hand to his lips and repeated the same delicious steps. Tiffany closed her eyes and focused all of her senses on his caresses. The soft glancing touches. The shape of his mouth.

He released her hands, and her eyes popped open.

"I was wise enough to stay away from you then, but once you noticed me, I could not. Tiffany, I knew it was wrong. I kept trying to convince myself that you only felt friendship for me. I knew that I should tell you everything about my past, about my son and Evie, but I was a coward. I knew that I couldn't marry you, so I tried to keep my distance from you. But it was impossible. I am drawn to you. My heart is entirely yours, and if I am acquitted, I want nothing more than to be at your side for the rest of my life. I wish I could offer you my name, but all I can give you is my heart."

They were no longer touching, but Tiffany could feel him all over her skin. This was the love she had waited her entire adult life for.

"Your heart is all that I ever wanted," she whispered, and Samir leaned forward, his face against the bars keeping him in place. "I love you with all that I am . . . And we already have a son."

Samir shook his head incredulously, a small smile on his lips. "A baby."

"I will bring little Nat to see you tomorrow. It doesn't matter who made him. I knew as soon as I held him in my arms that I was his mother. And I love him with all my heart."

Samir kissed the tip of her nose and then lightly brushed her lips. "Then I shall love him with all of mine. But Tiffany, it does not look good for me. I do not know if I will ever walk out of this cell a free man."

Through the bars her hands moved to his cheeks, and her fingers tangled in his hair. "Farmer Coram has recanted his testimony, thanks to pressure from Thomas, but Sir Walter Abney refused to release you."

"He can't."

"Why not? He should not have arrested you in the first place."

Samir pressed his forehead against the bars, and Tiffany rested her head against his skin.

"It is my fault, Tiffany. I thought I was protecting myself, but in the end, I practically signed my own death warrant."

Her fingers tightened in his dark curls. "What? How? I don't know what you mean."

"With the rubies, I purchased one of the mortgages on Sir Walter's Maplehurst estate. I thought I could use it as leverage to keep him off my back, but instead he is trying to kill me rather than repay the debt. He knows that I had nothing to do with Bernard's death."

Tiffany's mouth hung open. She had never liked Sir Walter, but she had not thought he could stoop so low. He was the vilest of villains. Much worse than any fictional foe she'd ever read about.

"What happens to the mortgage if you were to . . ." She could not bear to say that word alive.

"Die?" Samir said. "I think he assumes nothing. I have been long separated from my legal wife, and I had no heirs. And I have foolishly never written a will."

"Until now," Tiffany said. "Even if you do not have a will, you have a legal son. Nat would inherit all you possess without a will, as your next of kin."

He shrugged. "I do not think Sir Walter foresaw that my estranged wife would reappear and bear a son that is legally mine."

"I will tell Catharine all about this. She will know how best to pressure Sir Walter."

"Catharine?"

Tiffany gave a short laugh. "The Duchess of Beaufort. I think she means for us to be friends, whether I wish to be or not. She has quite taken me under her wing and has been wonderful with Nat. I had no idea she was so good with babies and children. I fear that I have greatly misjudged her personality."

Samir cupped Tiffany's cheek as he lightly caressed her through the bars. "She is like a porcupine: all sharp quills."

"But with a good heart."

He continued to lightly stroke her cheek. "Speaking of good hearts, how is Mary?"

Tiffany shook her head. "By chance, I have discovered another young woman's secret, and I fear that Mary will not keep it. My maid is never at the cottage when I stop there during the day, and I have learned that she is to be found enjoying an afternoon pint and a bit of gossip at the public house."

Samir pressed a kiss to her forehead. "She's young and merely lonely. She isn't used to being left by herself for hours on end. I think Mary is greatly devoted to you and will not say anything purposely to harm either this young woman or you."

"I wish I could stay here all day with you, but I need to take care of Nat and discover who really killed Bernard Coram before the assizes judge arrives on Monday for the trial."

He took her hands in his, through the bars. "Take care of yourself and our son, Tiffany. And don't worry about me."

Tiffany shook her head, a tear falling down her cheek despite her best efforts to control her emotions. "Our son needs a father, and I mean to see that he gets the very best. No one but you will do."

She pressed her face against the iron bars one last time for a kiss. Samir's warm lips brushed against hers slowly, over and over. Then Tiffany opened her mouth slightly and felt his tongue enter her lips. He tasted sweet like honey and more intoxicating than any wine she'd ever drank. She lost herself in the kiss, and it was as if the bars, the prison, and even Maple-down Village faded away. Only she and Samir existed in the entire universe. Lips. Tongues. Hands. And teeth.

A knock at the door caused them to break apart in confusion. Tiffany compulsively straightened her gown and touched her falling hair.

Samir cleared his throat. "Come in."

A young woman entered the prison, carrying another basket. It was Jessica Day. Like her mother, she was a short, curvy woman, with a great deal of shining brown hair. She had brown eyes, a little round nose, a dark mole on her chin, and a too generous mouth, which should have detracted from her beauty, but instead only added character to it. The full lips were a bright red, and Tiffany wondered if she used carmine on them. It was hard to guess her age, for she had the figure of a woman, but there was a softness to her cheeks that seemed to speak to her youth. The young woman could have been any age from fifteen to twenty.

"Miss Jessica," Samir said, bowing his head. "Your mother is too kind, but I have still not eaten her last basket. I could not in good conscience take another charitable offering from her."

She placed the basket next to the first one the Days had brought. "Mum said to bring it, and she dunna take no for an answer. Not even from Pa."

He gave her a small smile. "Then I won't decline it, but please assure her that I am well cared for. Miss Jessica, may I introduce you to Miss Woodall?"

Jessica turned her head, and Tiffany saw the remnants of bruises on the back of her neck. They had to be several days old, for they were yellow with a tint of green. She bobbed a schoolgirl curtsy. "I've already met Miss Woodall. Good day to ye."

Tiffany curtsied back. "Delighted to see you again, Miss Jessica. Mary speaks so highly of you."

"She's my best friend. Mary's a good'un."

Smiling, Tiffany said, "I agree whole-heartedly."

The young woman glanced at the door. "I've gots to go. Mum expects me t'help clean this morning."

"I shall come with you," Tiffany said, opening the door. "I also have much to accomplish this morning. Good day, Mr. Lathrop."

"Good day, Miss Woodall."

Jessica passed through the door, folding her arms around herself. Tiffany closed it behind them and walked a step or two. The yellow bruising was more obvious in the sunlight. Tiffany wondered if one of the patrons of the Black Cauldron had become rough with her. She would have thought that Mr. Day could have protected his daughter better. However, there was the chance that her father had given her those bruises. Tiffany shook her head. There was too much violence in the world.

The young woman slipped down an alley and to the back of the public house without a word to Tiffany. She seemed a little discomposed by Tiffany's presence or her class. Tiffany may have been a gentlewoman by birth, but her life had been anything but gentle. Nor did she think her parentage made her better than Miss Jessica Day or her family. As far as Tiffany could tell, aristocracy and gentry were merely people who were lucky enough to be born to wealthier parents who could afford fine clothing and an education for their children. Nothing about Sir Walter Abney made him special or more worthy of his title. And not all gently born folk were well educated. The more books Tiffany read, the more she realized how much she didn't know.

She arrived at the rectory all too soon. She had not paid a visit to it since she'd broken her engagement (that she'd never agreed to) with Mr. Shirley. A servant opened the door.

"May I speak to Mrs. Shirley?"

The rector had married Widow Davies shortly after Thomas's trial and Tiffany's pardon for wearing men's clothing. She was roughly the same age as the rector, around fifty, and had snowy white hair.

The maid bobbed a curtsy. "This way, Miss Woodall."

Tiffany was pleased to see that the rectory appeared to be less austere under the new Mrs. Shirley. There were decorations on the walls and new curtains on the windows. The maid led her to a parlor with fine furniture. Tiffany wondered if the widow had brought it with her as a part of her dowry. Knickknacks and doilies covered the mantle and tables. It felt like a different house.

Mrs. Shirley and her eldest stepdaughter stood to greet her. They were both wearing new dresses. Miss Shirley's celestial blue gown helped soften her rather sharp features, and her new stepmother must have taught her how to arrange her hair; for it was no longer scraped back like butter over bread, but left soft and curly around her face.

Curtsying, Tiffany smiled. "Thank you so much for taking time for me today, Mrs. Shirley, Miss Shirley."

"But of course, you are a member of my husband's parish," Mrs. Shirley said, gesturing to a chair. "Won't you sit down?"

Tiffany took a seat and tucked one foot behind the other. "I am actually here on parish business. Mr. Lathrop is now the father of a fine son, and I would like to set a date and time for the christening."

"Such matters are usually handled by my husband directly."

Tiffany cleared her throat. "I felt that it might be better going through you because of the unfortunate misunderstanding the rector and I had last year."

Instead of taking affront, Mrs. Shirley nodded. "A sensible idea, Miss Woodall. I believe my husband is available tomorrow morning, shall we say ten o'clock?"

"That would be perfect."

"And may I ask who the godparents are going to be? I presume you will be the godmother."

Exhaling, Tiffany shook her head. "Actually, no. The Duchess of Beaufort will be the godmother, and Mr. Thomas Montague will be the godfather. I know it is a little odd to have a mother and son for those roles."

Mrs. Shirley shook her head. "Not as odd as having a duchess be the godmother to Evie Coram's illegitimate child."

Tiffany blinked. "You've heard."

"Everyone from Mapledown to Bardsley knows about Mr. Lathrop's wife returning to town to bear a bastard child and then abandoning it," the rector's wife said.

"For shame!" Miss Shirley added, covering her mouth with her hand.

The young woman's clothing may be brighter, but she is still a pious prig, Tiffany thought.

"Technically, the baby is legitimate because Mrs. Evie Lathrop was married at the time of the birth. Although, you have a valid point. We are unsure of the father."

Mrs. Shirley stood, her hands on her hips. "And Mr. Lathrop is going to acknowledge the child as his own?"

"Yes," Tiffany said with a forced smile. "The babe will be named Nathaniel Samir Lathrop."

"Am I to assume that you are to be this child's mother?"

Tiffany didn't like being in a conversation where the other person was standing. It felt too much like being looked down on. She got to her feet, still gritting her teeth into a painful smile. "Yes. I am Nat's mother. Thank you so much for your time. I will be sure to have the payment for the christening with me tomorrow."

"Very good, Miss Woodall."

"Good day to you, Mrs. Shirley, Miss Shirley."

CHAPTER 23

When she passed Bristle Cottage, Tiffany checked to see if Mary was there. But neither her maid nor her cow were anywhere to be seen. Tiffany assumed they were safely at Astwell Palace. She opened her hope chest and found the prettiest dress in it. Nat had to look his best for the christening and for meeting his father. Tiffany wrapped the dress in an extra blanket; this one, she herself had sewn from old dresses. It would be sweet to wrap her baby inside the clothes of her childhood.

The clouds were gray when Tiffany started her walk to Astwell Palace, but darkening by the minute. She felt a few stray raindrops hit her face, and she quickened her pace. She didn't want to be caught out in the rain, nor have Nat's christening gown ruined. Larger drops of rain fell, and Tiffany broke into a run. She'd barely reached the door to the servant's entrance when the rain began to fall like sheets from the sky. The sound of the rain hitting against stone, glass windows, and even rocks covered all other noises.

Exhaling slowly, Tiffany took off her pattens and cloak, grateful to have barely missed the worst of the storm. She passed the kitchens, where she saw Monsieur Bonne standing at the counter with a young boy with a mop of wheat-colored hair. He was showing the lad how to cut a carrot. Such a menial task would typically be done by a kitchen maid, but the French chef had a smile on his face and seemed genuinely happy to be instructing the young boy on how to hold a knife properly. The child must be Mrs. Able's son, Tiffany realized.

She glanced around the servant's dining room and the sitting room and did not see the wet nurse or her baby. She left the servants' area and went to the library. No one was there, so she set down the blanket and dress on her desk. Next, she went to the nursery. Catharine was holding Nat and rocking him as she sang softly.

"How is the constable this morning?"

Tiffany sighed. "Better than I expected. His prison is covered in basket offerings from the village."

Catharine nodded. "He's a good man and a good constable. I am pleased that so many commoners realize this."

"He's happy to be a father. Although the circumstances are not ideal."

"That's putting it mildly."

The duchess got to her feet and transferred the baby from her arms to Tiffany's. The familiar warmth and love filled her chest as she received him. She kissed Nat's forehead and cheeks, but he didn't wake.

"Mrs. Able just fed him, so he'll probably be good for two or three hours," Catharine said. "I have estate business to attend to, and I wish to see if our solicitor from London has arrived."

She walked across the room and was nearly to the door before Tiffany found her tongue. "Would you . . . would you like to be Nat's godmother?"

Catharine turned, pointing a finger at her chest. "Me?"

Tiffany felt her face go hot. "If you'd rather not, I understand." She wished that she hadn't assumed the duchess would say yes, and had already told Mrs. Shirley.

"I would be delighted to be his godmother. I assume that Thomas will be his godfather."

Her face grew even hotter. "I have as well, but I should probably ask him first."

The duchess smiled. "He will say yes. You and Mr. Lathrop are his two closest friends. I will mention it to him."

"The christening is scheduled for tomorrow at ten o'clock, if that is agreeable to you?"

Catharine nodded. "I'll order a carriage for half past nine, so we may all go together. Do you have a suitable gown for the babe?"

"I sewed it myself nearly twenty years ago."

"Then it is well past time for the gown to be worn," she said with her lips slightly upturned. "I'll see you at dinner. Do not worry—I've had Mary fetch your dresses, and Emily is teaching her how to take care of them better."

Nodding, Tiffany smiled. Catharine's version of friendship was rather managing, but very thoughtful.

CHAPTER 24

Tiffany had to admit that her gown that morning had never looked better. Whatever concoction Emily and Mary had used to wash and press it had made the bottle-green taffeta look brand new. Mary also insisted on dressing Tiffany's hair for the first time. It wasn't perfect, in fact, one side drooped a little, but it was a start. Mary beamed and looked prodigiously proud of herself, and Tiffany couldn't help but feel a bit proud of her too.

The Duchess of Beaufort, Mr. Montague, and the young Duke of Beaufort were all ready to go precisely at half past nine. The fancy carriage had the Beaufort coat of arms on the doors, and two footmen helped everyone in. Thomas and Beau sat with their backs to the driver, and Catharine and Tiffany, holding Nat, sat forward. As an employee and as a member of a lower class, Tiffany should have had the worst seat, but all of the duchess's family treated her as an equal. For the first time since her mother's death, she felt as if she were a part of a family again.

It was Thomas and not a footman who helped everyone out. The ground was still wet from yesterday's downpour, but at least there were no clouds this morning. A footman opened the door to the church, and light streamed in through the stained-glass windows. Mr. Shirley stood at the front of the chapel, dressed in his white and black ceremonial robes. His face looked longer and more skeletal than ever underneath his curly white wig.

Thomas walked by Tiffany's side as they went down the aisle, followed by Catharine and Beau, holding hands. She saw that Mrs. Shirley was sitting on the front pew. Tiffany assumed that she'd come to see the duchess; and Catharine was well worth seeing in her gorgeous gown of painted Chinese silk. She wore her most tremendous wig and even a dual string of pearls. Such a costume would be normal at the king's court, but it was certainly out of place in Mapledown Church.

Mr. Shirley laced his long, bony fingers together. "Your Graces, ladies and gentleman, welcome to the christening of this child." He took a deep breath and then picked up his Bible. "I shall read a few verses about what a baptism means."

Tiffany couldn't help but cringe. Surely Nat was too young to be told about the fires of hell?

The Duchess of Beaufort tapped her cane on the stone floor, and it echoed in the empty chapel. "Skip the verses and get to the ceremony, Rector."

Tiffany had to bite her lower lip to contain both her smile and her laughter. Thomas was not quite as quick, for he grinned at both his mother and Tiffany.

"Very well, Your Grace," Mr. Shirley continued, adjusting the wig on his head. "People of God, will you welcome this child and uphold him in his new life in Christ?"

Thomas stepped closer to Tiffany and Nat. "I will with the help of God."

"As will I, with the help of God," Catharine said.

"Me too!" Beau said.

Tiffany couldn't keep back her grin this time. The little Duke of Beaufort didn't realize that this part of the ceremony was only for the godparents, but she certainly wasn't going to correct him. And after a sharp glance from the duchess, neither was the rector.

"Your Grace and Mr. Montague," Mr. Shirley said, pointing, "if you would come stand in front of the child."

Catharine and Thomas did, with Beau standing between them. Tiffany felt as if her cup was overflowing with happiness.

Mr. Shirley poured a little water on Nat's head from the chapel's font. "Nathaniel Samir Lathrop, I baptize you in the name of the Father and of the Son and of the Holy Spirit. Amen."

The rector had barely said "Amen" when Nat began to wail. He apparently did not appreciate having his forehead soaked with cold water. Tiffany kissed his head and bounced him in her arms.

Thomas gave the final prayer.

Mr. Shirley presented Tiffany with a candle. "Nathaniel Samir Lathrop, shine as a light in the world to the glory of God."

Tiffany's eyes went up to the stained-glass window over the north transept, and she saw the Virgin Mary, with a golden halo, illuminated above them. The sun shone brightly, spilling a rainbow of colored light into the chapel and onto Nat, who lay in her arms. And Tiffany knew, despite her many mistakes, sins, and shortcomings, that God was there in the little details of her life.

Somehow Catharine ended up with Nat, and Tiffany was forced to follow the dour Shirleys to the rector's office to add Nathaniel's birth information to the Mapledown chapel's registry. Tiffany half wondered who Mrs. Shirley was protecting, Tiffany or her husband; either way she stood as a buffer between them.

Mr. Shirley placed a heavy book with yellowed pages in front of her and then provided a quill and ink. He turned it more than halfway to an open page. "You need to enter the babe's parents' names. His birth date and his christening date."

Tiffany nodded and was relieved when both Shirleys left the small antechamber. Picking up the quill, Tiffany dipped it into the ink: *Nathaniel Samir Lathrop, born April 4, 1785, to Samir Lathrop and Evangeline Coram. Christened April 7, 1785.*

She was more than half tempted to write her own name as mother, but she decided that someday Nat deserved to know the full truth of his parentage. Besides, writing a lie in a church was practically blasphemy.

Blowing on the ink, Tiffany waited for her words to dry. She ran her fingers against the well-worn spine and the edge of the pages. How many births, christenings, marriages, and deaths did it contain? Ten years' worth? One hundred?

Once the ink was fully dry, she couldn't resist peeking at the previous entries. It wasn't long until she found the entry for Samir's marriage on August 29, 1774, to Evangeline Coram, daughter of Mr. Zedekiah Coram. The registry listed his mother's name, Priya Singh, and his birth date: he was five years younger than Tiffany at only thirty-five. Mary's curse word combination came to her mind, but she contented herself with an *alas*. She wished that she weren't so much older than him. Then she read Evie's age and saw that she had been nineteen when she married, which would make her thirty now. There was no mention of her mother, which was curious. Tiffany continued to turn pages and saw Farmer Coram's marriage to his second wife. Then even further, the birth of Bernard and then Evie. Their mother's name was Ludmilla Phelps.

Tiffany did not see her death date. She flipped back through the entries and poured over each one. She saw his new marriage and numerous entries for his second family, but nothing about when and how his first wife died. Turning the page, Mr. Ford's name caught her eye. She opened the page and saw that Mr. Simeon Ford espoused Ludmilla Phelps Coram by purchasing her at the local fair from her husband, Mr. Zedekiah Coram, May Day 1761.

"Good heavens!" she whispered.

She had never heard of such a thing. She wondered if it could possibly be legal for a husband to *sell* his wife to another man at a fair and then marry again in the church as if he'd never been married in the first place. Tiffany could well believe that Farmer Coram would be that callus, but it surprised her that Mr. Ford would be a party to such an exhibition. Her heart went out to poor Ludmilla Phelps Coram Ford.

How humiliating it must have been to be sold at a fair like cattle!

"Are you quite done, Miss Woodall?" Mr. Shirley asked sharply.

Startled, Tiffany slammed the registry closed. "Yes. Sorry. I happened to see an entry where a wife was auctioned at a fair. Is such a thing legal? Does the Church recognize those marriages? Or divorces?"

The rector's eyes narrowed on her. "The Church does not condone taking holy matters into one's own hands; however, it is not unheard of for the *lower* classes to end an unhappy marriage by the husband putting a rope around his wife's neck and selling her at a fair to a more willing man."

Her hand stole to her own throat, which constricted painfully. Oh, the indignities women were forced to put up with! And with no legal recourse. Not even the church seemed willing to defend them.

"Thank you, Mr. Shirley."

He held out his hand to her, and Tiffany pulled out a little coin purse, placing it in his palm. Then she went back to the vestibule to meet with her friends, who had become her family.

CHAPTER 25

Wife-auction.

Tiffany was still trying to comprehend such an idea when she entered the prison. Catharine had said that she and her sons would wait in the carriage. At first, Tiffany thought this was because duchesses didn't go into prisons, but then she realized that Catharine was giving her a little privacy with Samir.

There were fewer baskets today, or their contents had been combined. The room smelled of freshly burnt incense and had been recently cleaned. Samir immediately stood up from his cot and came to the bars of his cell. Tiffany met him there, holding Nat's face up for Samir to see. Samir reached through the bars and gently caressed Nat's forehead and then his downy, soft light hair.

"Our son," he whispered.

A tear slipped out of Tiffany's eye, but she was smiling as she reiterated, "Our son."

Being a new mother had made her a watering pot of tears.

Samir took Nat's little hand into his own. "He's got a good grip."

Nat's eyes were wide as he looked up, not necessarily at either of them; but Tiffany was glad that her sweet little glutton was awake. Her baby seemed to prefer to sleep during the day and stay awake at night. The only times he awoke in daylight were for feedings and the cold water at christenings.

Tiffany grinned. "Isn't he beautiful? Does he remind you of your first son?"

Samir continued to caress Nat's head. "Both he and his brother inherited Evie's eyes. Our son had dark hair and darker skin."

He was right. Tiffany had seen those exactly shaped eyes twice before. Evie had inherited them from her mother, Ludmilla Ford. Why had Evie not gone to her own mother for help when she found herself in a predicament? Mr. Ford had his own house and appeared to be doing well for a butler. It was also a great deal closer to Bardsley than Mapledown. Why had Evie come to Samir, the husband she had scorned, a stranger for ten years?

Unless.

Unless, she knew about her brother's murder and didn't want suspicion to come on her mother. As far as Tiffany recalled, she'd never once seen Mrs. Ford in Mapledown. Not at church and not shopping.

"Samir, what is Evie's relationship like with her mother?"

He looked up from the baby to meet her eyes. "Evie hates her stepmother. She beat both Evie and Bernard."

Tiffany shook her head. "Not her stepmother—her mother, Mrs. Ford."

"I don't know what you're talking about, Tiffany. Evie's mother is dead."

Except she wasn't.

She was not going to argue with Samir, but it was strange that Evie had never confided to her husband that her birth mother was still living.

Nat's face went red and he started to wail. It had been nearly two hours since his last feeding from Mrs. Able, and he liked his meals regularly. Tiffany bounced him a little in her arms and tried to soothe him, but her baby continued to cry.

Samir's hands moved from Nat's face to hers, cupping her cheeks gently. "Thank you for bringing our son to see me, Tiffany."

She twisted her head to place a kiss in Samir's palm. "I love you and I promise you will get out of here. And we will be a family."

Leaning forward, their lips briefly met between the bars before Nat reminded them loudly that he was really hungry. Reluctantly, Tiffany left the prison, and a footman helped her into the carriage.

Catharine shook her head. "What have you done to the baby?"

Tiffany sat down beside her on the seat. "I think he's hungry."

"I'll hold the lad," Thomas said, and he gently took Nat from her arms. Perhaps it was his deep voice, or his strong arms, but Nat calmed down and watched Thomas's face with wide eyes.

"Look what a natural Thomas is with children," Catharine said. "How it would make his mother happy if he gave her grandchildren to hold."

Tiffany couldn't help but smile at the duchess's not so subtle hint to her eldest son.

"You've got me to hold," Beau reminded her.

Catharine grinned at her sons. "A fact for which I am most grateful."

Thomas shook his head, his expression turned grave. "I am not contemplating matrimony anytime soon."

"Oh, we'll see about that."

Tiffany knew from her own experience that the duchess was a person to be reckoned with. It wouldn't surprise Tiffany if she heard that Thomas was courting a young woman very soon. No doubt, Catharine would make a list of proper candidates. After Thomas's unfortunate engagement to the late Miss Sarah Doddridge, his mother wouldn't leave him to his own devices in the selection of a wife.

CHAPTER 26

Tiffany felt rather embarrassed to ask a duchess to watch her baby while she went on an errand, but she needed to speak to Mrs. Ford immediately. Catharine didn't seem at all offended. She took Nat from her son's arms and told the footman to summon Mrs. Able at once. Young Master Nat was clearly ready for his next meal. Beau trailed after her, leaving Tiffany and Thomas alone in the carriage.

"Will you come with me to speak to Mrs. Ford?" she asked.

Thomas gave her a penetrating look. "I am always happy to pay a call on Mrs. Ford, but I am wondering why you would wish to."

Exhaling, Tiffany explained about finding her name in the chapel's registry and the entries for her marriage to Mr. Zedekiah Coram and then to Mr. Simeon Ford.

"I don't believe it. Mrs. Ford couldn't be Bernard's mother. He was pure evil and the woman is a saint."

Tiffany swallowed. "I don't wish to offend Mrs. Ford, but merely, to ask her some questions, and since you are her particular friend, I was hoping that it might be less awkward if you were there."

"Of course, I will come," Thomas said, and then called out directions to the driver.

Subsequently, the short journey between Astwell Palace and the hamlet of Dee was a quiet one. When they arrived in front of the Ford cottage, Thomas opened the door and helped her out. His manner was stiff and disapproving. Tiffany was sorry to offend her friend, but Samir's life was on the line, and she couldn't afford to be polite.

Thomas knocked on the door, and Mrs. Ford answered it. Tiffany noticed that she opened it with her left hand and that her right arm hung limply at her side. She grinned at Thomas, but her smile faded when she saw Tiffany standing behind him.

"To what do I owe the pleasure of this visit?" she said, her voice slightly trembling, but the cadences were that of an educated woman. Quite unlike Evie's own common tongue.

A doubt rose in her throat, but she swallowed it back down.

"May we come in? Miss Woodall has some questions for you," Thomas said.

Using only her left arm, Mrs. Ford opened the door all the way and ushered them into the cottage. It was small, but the selected pieces of furniture were all very fine. There was a small sitting room at the front of the house, with a sofa and two chairs. Mrs. Ford asked them to sit there. Thomas and Tiffany each took a chair on opposite sides of the sofa.

"May I offer you some tea?" Mrs. Ford asked.

Tiffany shook her head. "I am afraid that we are not here on a social visit, but rather to learn what you were doing the night of your son's murder."

Mrs. Ford blinked. "Ex-excuse me?"

"We know that you were once married to Farmer Coram and that you bore him two children: Evangeline and Bernard.

We also know that Bernard visited you the night of his death." Tiffany was pretty certain on the first bit of knowledge; the second was merely a guess to catch the woman out.

Mrs. Ford's left hand moved to her neck, where there was now only a hint of the bruise that Tiffany had seen there. "Bernard wanted money, but I had none to give to him. He grew angry and violent . . . my son tried to choke me, but I was able to bite his thumb, and he let me go."

Thomas's expression turned murderous, but Tiffany knew his anger was not directed at either lady, but at Mr. Bernard Coram's corpse. What sort of man tried to strangle his one-armed mother? She studied Mrs. Ford's teeth and saw that they were straight and even. They would probably match the indentations on the body's thumb.

How did Evie fit into all of this?

Tiffany took a deep breath. "What caused him to leave if you didn't give him any money? He was found with only three pennies on his person, and Farmer Coram claims that his son received those from himself."

Mrs. Ford visibly flinched at the mention of her former husband's name, but kept her mouth closed.

"Your daughter Evie was there," Tiffany said, figuring it out as she spoke the words. "And she was strong enough to make him stop hurting you and leave."

"She didn't kill him," Mrs. Ford said, outstretching her own good hand beseechingly. "I swear it on my soul. She didn't kill him. All she did was force him out of the house. He was more than half drunk and swung at her a few times, but she managed to push him out the door and lock him out. My son was still alive when he left this house. I swear it."

"Then why did you not come forward when Doctor Hudson and Mr. Lathrop were taking teeth indentations of all the female servants? Surely, Mr. Ford would have known that the bite mark had come from you."

Mrs. Ford nodded her head slowly. "Mr. Ford arrived home soon after my son left. He said that Evie could stay a night or two at our house but that she needed to go back to her lawful husband, Mr. Lathrop. Mr. Ford believed that her unborn child was legally his."

Nat.

"But Mr. Lathrop was not the father."

The older woman hung her head. "Evie doesn't know who the father is. Nor did she want the child. Her own childhood was marked by violence and grief."

The words were out of Tiffany's mouth as she thought of them: "Why did you not protect her?"

Mrs. Lathrop picked up her limp right arm with her left. "I tried to. I took beating after beating to protect my children until one day Zedekiah knocked me out, and I fell on my arm. I fainted for so long that by the time I awoke, it no longer functioned correctly. My husband would not fetch the doctor—my face was more bruises than skin. He said he didn't want a broken woman for a wife, so he put a rope around my neck and dragged me to the village square on May Day. He said he wanted to sell me and would take as little as a farthing to be rid of me. Simeon—Mr. Ford—happened to be there. He took pity on me and paid an entire pound. He removed the rope from my neck, and I have never known the smallest act of violence from him."

"But your children?"

The older woman sniffed, and tears began to stream out of her eyes. "According to the law, children are the property of their father. There was nothing that I could do. Mr. Ford offered Zedekiah money to take the children, but he wouldn't part with them. It might have been to punish me, and if so, he could not have chosen anything crueler. My children grew up as strangers, believing I was dead. Evie tried to protect Bernard, but in the end, he became a brute like his father."

Thomas stood up and passed the older woman a handkerchief. She dabbed at her eyes and nose.

"Why did you never visit them?" Tiffany couldn't help but ask.

"Mr. Ford and I tried once, and that is when he got his limp. Zedekiah is a violent man, and his second wife is not much better. He threatened to hurt my children if I ever showed my face in Mapledown again."

Tiffany could only shake her head at the unfairness of the laws that protected violent husbands and not innocent women and children. "When did you reconnect with your children?"

"When Bernard became a footman at the palace, Mr. Ford invited him to dinner at our house. After several meetings, I told him the truth. I thought he would be happy to be reunited with his mother, but he wasn't. All he could see was a lame old woman. He didn't come back to our house until after he lost his position at the palace. And then he only came for money. I gave him all that I could, but Mr. Ford forbade me to give him so much as another farthing."

"And Evie?"

Mrs. Ford brought Thomas's handkerchief back to her nose with her good hand. "After her first baby died, she fled to Bardsley and took up with the blacksmith. It was rumored he couldn't father children, and she had never wanted to be a mother. I have visited her there for many years, but Mr. Ford does not allow her here. He does not approve of her choices."

Tiffany had to admit that Evie's morals were rather lacking. At least, conventionally. And the butler, if anything, was conventional.

"But Mr. Ford is good to you?" Thomas asked, his gaze penetrating.

She nodded, more tears slipping from her eyes. "I do not deserve it, but he is very kind to me."

Tiffany got to her feet. "I am sorry to have upset you and to force you to recall terrible memories, but I must ask: If I need your testimony to clear Mr. Lathrop, will you tell the court what happened that night?"

Her hand went back to her neck. "I–I don't know if I can."

"Mr. Lathrop is prepared to take care of your grandson. To be a father to him. But he cannot be if he is hung for a crime he did not commit," Tiffany said sharply. "Will you or will you not help an innocent man and your own grandchild?"

Mrs. Ford sniffed. "I will ask Mr. Ford."

At least it wasn't a direct no.

Tiffany pitied the woman, but she couldn't help but feel angry at her for allowing Samir to take all the responsibility for her children's choices. She left the parlor and the house. As she closed the door, she heard Thomas comforting Mrs. Ford.

Life was not fair.

Especially if you were a woman.

CHAPTER 27

Nat kept Tiffany and poor Mrs. Able up most of the next two nights, but she still decided to go to church for the Sunday services. Not that she thought her soul needed to be reminded by Mr. Shirley of its eminent stay in hell, but church was one of the few places where people of all classes mingled together.

Arriving early, Tiffany was only the second person to come into the chapel, not counting the impressive clan of Shirley children.

Pulling out the golden button that she'd found in front of the Corams' farm, she rubbed her finger over the distinct pattern: four columns with countless little line notches on each of them. It was an expensive button. Not something one would lose and forget. She was desperately hoping that she would find it's match on a man's coat or a woman's pelisse.

Several families came into the chapel and filed into pews in the back. Tiffany was surprised how many people she did not recognize. But none of them wore clothes fine enough for such a button as the one she held.

Sir Walter Abney paraded into the church like he was the king. His clothing was as fine as five pence. He shook a few of the men's hands and waved to several of the women. He behaved as if he were a public benefactor for putting Samir behind bars. Hate for that man burned hotter in her heart than any fire in hell. Sir Walter tipped his tricorn hat when he passed Tiffany, and she gritted her teeth. His coat was indeed fine, but the golden buttons were etched with a flower and leaves. Oh, how she wished that the button matched his.

Turning her head, she saw Mr. and Mrs. Day enter the church, followed by their three daughters. Tiffany was surprised to see them there two Sundays in a row. The family didn't usually attend. Mr. Day's scarred face appeared grumpy and disgruntled. Mrs. Day smiled and waved, much like Sir Walter, as if she were putting on a show. Behind their parents, the three daughters all wore bright red cloaks. Their arms were linked together, and they made a very pretty trio. Tiffany would have guessed that Miss Jessica was the youngest of the three, seeing her next to her sisters. The family resemblance was certainly marked among them. They all had milk-and-cream complexions, lustrous brown hair, and curvy figures. The necklines of their dresses were cut a little low for church, but they made such a bonnie picture, Tiffany was sure that no one minded.

Farmer Coram and his second wife came in next, trailed by their children. Tiffany was rather shocked to see both the farmer and his wife had black eyes. She remembered Mrs. Ford's words about the second Mrs. Coram being just as abusive as her husband. Tiffany could only assume that they were both hitting each other, and felt a surge of pity for their children. All boys and girls deserved to grow up in a home where they were safe and loved. She could only be relieved that Nat would not be raised in such a violent family.

The last two people to straggle into the church were Mr. Hadfield and his mother, Widow Hadfield. She supposed that they had come to hear the banns read for the second week. Tiffany tried to get a good view of them, but Mr. Shirley was already at the pulpit, beginning the meeting. If she continued to stare, it would cause remarks. Sighing, she focused her attention to the front of the chapel and prepared to listen to yet another sermon on how they were all in dire need of repentance.

The last thing Tiffany recalled was the rector reading Isaiah 13:6: *"Howl ye; for the day of the Lord is at hand; it shall come as a destruction from the Almighty."*

She thought that she had only closed her eyes for a moment, but she must have slept through the rest of the sermon. All the late nights with Nat were catching up to her. Someone was shaking her shoulder.

Tiffany blinked her eyes open and saw Mrs. Shirley. "Time to go home, Miss Woodall."

Blushing, Tiffany pulled her shawl around her shoulders. "Do forgive me. I meant no offense."

Mrs. Shirley shook her head, a kind look on her face. "You don't get much sleep with new babies, and you're older than most mothers."

Tiffany smiled. The rector's wife had managed to be both polite and offensive in one speech. Cleverly done. Standing, she heard the clatter of the button fall to the floor. She must have dropped it in her lap while she was sleeping. She stooped down to pick it up from underneath the bench.

"What is that, Miss Woodall?"

Opening her hand, Tiffany held it out to her. "I found it in the road and hoped to return it to its owner, for the button appears to be very fine."

Mrs. Shirley took it from her and brought it very close to her eyes. Tiffany wondered if the woman was severely short-sighted. She examined it for a few moments and then gave it back to Tiffany.

"I can't say that I recognize it, but I did notice that Mr. Hadfield was missing the lowest button on his coat. Perhaps it is his."

Tiffany could not keep in another smile. If the button was Mr. Hadfield's, then it would place him at the Coram farm the night of the murder, and not back at his own property, Bramble Farm. Both his and his mother's stories would be proven false.

"I shall see if I can catch up to them and return it. Good day, Mrs. Shirley."

"Good day, Miss Woodall."

With the button gripped tightly in her hand, Tiffany all but bolted from the church. Once through the double wooden doors, she brought her free arm up to cover her eyes from the sun. She saw that Mr. Hadfield had not yet returned home, but was walking next to Miss Anstey. His mother was trailing behind them, speaking to Mr. and Mrs. Anstey, who was carrying the small boy. In the light of day, Tiffany could see not only his true mother, Caro, in the lad's face, but the father, Mr. Coram, as well. The little boy had Bernard's blond hair and nose.

Holding the stitch in her side, Tiffany jogged to catch up with the group and arrived out of breath (and no doubt red-faced). She stopped nearer Mr. Hadfield and Miss Anstey.

"Sorry to interrupt," she said, out of breath, "but I was wondering if you had lost a button, Mr. Hadfield?"

Tiffany held out the golden button and saw that it indeed matched the other nine small gold buttons on his coat. Only a blue thread marked the place where it should have been.

Mr. Hadfield took the button from her. "Thank you, Miss Woodall. I misplaced it and thought it was lost for good."

Taking another deep breath, Tiffany said, "I found it in the mud outside of the Coram farm, Mr. Hadfield, shortly after the death of Mr. Bernard Coram. You told Constable Lathrop and myself that you went home after your altercation with Bernard in the public house. Would you like to amend your statement now?"

Mr. Hadfield swallowed, and his neck and face were a blotchy red and white. His fiancée, Caro, moved her hand from his arm but then interlaced her fingers with his, a sign of support and trust.

With his free hand, Mr. Hadfield pulled at his cravat, as if trying to get more air to his lungs. "Forgive me, Miss Woodall. Ye have caught me out in a lie, but I can assure ye that I never saw Bernard Coram alive or dead after being thrown out of the Black Cauldron. As I said, I did start the journey home, but I could'na let his words stand. I saddled a horse and road back to Mapledown and to the Coram place. I knocked and Farmer Coram answered. He said that his son were not home. But I dinna believe him and made rather a fool of myself by searching the house. Bernard were not there. I apologized to Farmer Coram and his wife but stayed in the road, waiting for him to return home. I waited until well past midnight, but I finally gave up when it started to rain and snow. I were wet through. I assumed he were spending the night with someone."

The Queen Anne's lace!

The last thing Bernard had been holding was a packet of Queen Anne's lace, which was used to prevent childbirth. But whom had he intended to give it to?

Mr. Hadfield's story did corroborate with what Tiffany already knew about that night. Mr. Bernard Coram had not returned home, but instead went to Mrs. Ford's to demand money. He even attacked his mother, and his sister forced him out of the house. Where had he gone next? According to Mr. Hadfield, it was not home.

"I believe you, sir," Tiffany said, even though it would be much easier if she didn't. "Did you see no one walking on the road?"

The farmer shook his head. "Nothin'. I heard the sound of a wagon, but dinna see who was driving it. 'Twas too dark, and they dinna have a lantern on their buggy."

A wagon. It made more sense that whoever had dropped Bernard on the road in front of her house had brought him in a carriage. Still, it would have taken strong arms to lift the body both in and out of it.

Tiffany cleared her throat. "May I ask what caused your button to come loose?"

He fingered the buttonhole that was missing a button. "Must've been during the fight in the public house or when Mr. Day threw me out on my face."

Sighing, she nodded. "I know that it is a most indelicate question, but do either of you know who Bernard Coram may have been visiting that night?"

Miss Anstey buried her face into Mr. Hadfield's shoulder. Tiffany wondered if she had told her fiancé the truth about Bernard's violation of her.

He shook his head. "Bernard was all too free with his favors. I couldna say who he was hoping to tup that night."

Mr. and Mrs. Anstey and Widow Hadfield had caught up with them.

The widow all but growled at Tiffany, her expression menacing. "Do ye imagine yerself to be the constable, Miss Woodall?"

Tiffany touched her own hot cheek. "No indeed, Widow Hadfield. But I do consider myself a friend of Constable Lathrop and wish to see his name cleared of all suspicion."

She grimaced at her. "Ye'd best clear it quickly. Sir Walter was telling everyone that the assizes judge arrives tomorrow, and he's hoping for a quick and speedy trial on Tuesday."

Blast. It was sooner that Tiffany had expected. Criminal trials rarely lasted more than one day, and sentencing was required by law to be carried out in only two days. She had run out of time. Tiffany could no longer afford to be tactful in her interrogating.

"Mr. Anstey, may I ask what you were doing the night of Bernard Coram's murder?"

The older man flinched. "Excuse me, Miss Woodall. What can you mean?"

"Only that your daughter had been insulted—worse than insulted—and you did nothing?"

Mrs. Anstey surrendered their young son (grandson) to her husband. "Now, Miss Woodall, like Widow Hadfield said, 'tis not yer place to go about questioning folks. My husband were home with me like the good Christian man he is."

"He was, Miss Woodall," Caro said, letting go of Mr. Hadfield's fingers. "I come home immediately after and told m'parents what happened. They said that we should do nothing. Say nothing. They dinna want anything to stop my marriage with Lawrence."

The young woman stepped away from her fiancé and toward her parents. "But I am tired of doing nothing. Of saying nothing. Mr. Bernard Coram hurt me and violated me, and ye did nothing. Ye said it were my fault." Caro pressed her fist into her chest. "It weren't my fault. I fought. I cried. But nothin' I did stopped him, and then ye blamed me for it happenin'."

"A lass should be more careful wi' her smiles," Mr. Anstey said, his eyes lowered.

"And a father should defend his daughter's honor." Caro turned to face her fiancé. "I am so sorry, Lawrence. I should've told ye when ye asked to marry me, but my parents swore ye'd never have me if ye knew that I bore Little Luke. But I tell ye, I was raped. And Miss Woodall says I ain't guilty of any sins, and I hope ye'll still marry me."

It felt like an eternity to Tiffany before Mr. Hadfield held open his arms to Caro. She walked into them, and he wrapped her into a tight embrace.

Mr. Hadfield patted Caro's vibrant copper hair. "I only wish I would've killed him for hurtin' ye."

Tiffany glanced back at their parents who all had the grace to appear chagrinned. They would not meet her eyes, but looked at the ground. Tiffany had caused enough misery today. She curtsied and left without another word.

CHAPTER 28

Pulling the key from her pocket, Tiffany unlocked the back door to Samir's bookshop and home. She wanted to go through his financial documents one more time, alone. She knew Nat was in the capable hands of Catharine, and although she missed him so much that her heart ached, she needed to free his father—the love of her life.

Taking out another key, Tiffany unlocked the drawer in Samir's desk. She set aside his accounting book and slowly read each and every document. Halfway through the pile, she found the note on the Maplehurst estate. Sir Walter Abney had taken a loan for ten thousand pounds on the demesne— the land where the house was built. Tiffany found an addendum to the sale. Samir had purchased the note from a Mr. Reardon in London. According to Mr. Reardon's letter, he had not been paid the quarterly fees in nearly two years. It was of little wonder that the man was eager to sell the mortgage to Samir.

Tiffany put all the papers she found regarding Sir Walter Abney or his Maplehurst estate in one pile. She would bring them all to Astwell Palace to discuss them with Catharine, Thomas, and their man of business, who was supposed to arrive from London this afternoon. She fervently prayed that the man had secured enough leverage to stop Sir Walter.

She put the documents in a satchel and was about to leave when she remembered the list of children's books that she had brought the day of Samir's arrest. Moving to the front of the building, where the bookshelves were, she picked up the list. She wanted to find at least one book to bring home to Beau. He'd been such a great help with Nat. He was always happy to fetch a blanket or a nappy. Tiffany hadn't realized how much the young duke had craved children for playmates.

Searching the spines, she located a little section on the bottom shelf of children's titles. She found *The History of Little Goody Two-Shoes* and *The Original Mother Goose's Melody*. She hoped that Miss Drummond would allow her to read both books to Beau. Tiffany was the librarian after all. When the severe governess didn't appear to be in awe of a duchess, she could hardly be expected to show deference to a mere librarian.

Tiffany made a note for Samir that she had taken both books. That way he could charge Astwell Palace *when* he got out.

Not *if.*

Never *if.*

CHAPTER 29

Rocking Nat all afternoon calmed Tiffany's nerves. There was something indescribably wonderful about holding a newborn. His sweet little noises and grunts. The way he snuggled against her chest and made her feel whole, even when the rest of the world was falling to pieces.

Beau came into the nursery with one of the new children's books she'd brought from Samir's shop. "Will you read it to me, First Mate Woodall?"

Heat radiated through her chest, and her hands tingled. How she had missed reading to him.

She smiled, her eyes watering. "Of course."

Still holding Nat, she pulled Beau onto her lap. "You must turn the pages, but the book is small. Just the right size for your hands."

The little duke turned the pages, and Tiffany could see an illustration of a little girl. A book with pictures—how delightful!

Rocking back and forth, Tiffany began to read:

All the World must allow, that Two Shoes was not her real Name. No; her Father's Name was Meanwell; and he was for many Years a considerable Farmer in the Parish where Margery was born; but by the Misfortunes which he met with in Business, and the wicked Persecutions of Sir Timothy Gripe, and an over-grown Farmer called Graspall, he was effectually ruined.

Tiffany couldn't help but think that Farmer Coram was certainly a *Grasp-all* and that Sir Walter Abney was wickedly persecuting Samir, and if she didn't do something, he would be ruined. She continued to read the tale of Margery, now an orphan with only one shoe until a rich gentleman gives her a complete pair. Margery tells everyone that she has "two shoes," and through her pious behavior becomes a teacher and then marries a rich widower (clearly her reward for being "goody").

Beau turned the final page, and Tiffany read the moral:

Remember this Story, and take Care whom you trust; but don't be covetous, sordid and miserable; for the Gold we have is but lent us to do Good with. We received all from the Hand of God, and every Person in Distress hath a just Title to a Portion of it.

"*Take care whom you trust.*" Those were words that Tiffany needed to read. Someone she trusted must not be telling the full truth. Otherwise, Samir would not be in prison, and Tiffany would know who the murderer was.

"Did you like the story, Beau?"

He nodded, his little fingers touching the last illustration. "Very much, and I am glad that I have two shoes. It would be very hard to walk with only one and be a pirate."

Tiffany gave a soft laugh. It would be very difficult indeed. "That reminds me of a story that I read in French when I was at school, called "Finette Cindron," by Comtesse d'Aulnoy. It is about a young woman who loses one of her shoes. Shall I tell it to you?"

Beau leaned his head back against Tiffany's chest and held Nat's hand. "Please do, Miss Woodall."

"The Comtesse d'Aulnoy called her stories *contes de fées*. In English we would say *fairy tales*. Now this particular fairy tale is about Cunning Cinders. Her parents were a king and a queen, but they lost their kingdom and became very poor. Her mother, the queen, wanted to abandon Finette and her two elder sisters somewhere. This made Finette very sad, so she went to see her fairy godmother, Madame Merluche. It was a long walk, and her feet became very sore, but a beautiful Spanish horse gave her a ride to the house. When she told her fairy godmother that her parents wanted to lose their children, the old woman gave her a ball of thread to fasten to the door of her home, so wherever her parents left them, she would be able to find her way back. Her fairy godmother also gave her a bag full of fine dresses of gold and silver."

He shook his head. "Her parents are very bad."

Tiffany had always thought so, but then she thought of Evie and little Nat. Perhaps not all women were meant to be mothers. Some, like Evie, did not wish to be. Not that Tiffany condoned leaving a newborn or abandoning three daughters; she understood that there was perhaps more to the queen's story and other women's stories that were not told in moral tales.

"But Finette was very good."

She continued to tell the story of Finette and the beautiful Spanish horse that helped her. Using the thread to find their way back home. Visiting the castle of an ogre. Working hard and becoming covered in cinders and soot. Burning the ogres. Finding a key that opened a magical chest full of beautiful clothes. Going to balls. One night staying too late and leaving one red velvet slipper, embroidered with pearls. The prince finding the slipper and promising to marry whoever fit the shoe.

"That's a silly idea," Beau interjected. "What if it fits someone he doesn't like?"

The young duke did have a very good point, but points were rarely the purpose of fairy tales. "But Finette Cindron's feet were particularly small and delicate; therefore the slipper couldn't fit anyone else."

"I bet it would fit a child."

Tiffany laughed and Nat woke up, fussing. He was probably ready for another feeding. She was about to tell Beau that they must finish their story later, when the door opened and Mary bounced in. "Miss Woodall, Mrs. Wheatley says that ye've been summoned by Her Grace."

Beau hopped off her lap and she got to her feet. "You may tell the housekeeper that I will come shortly. I have to first take Nat to Mrs. Able."

Mary bobbed a curtsy and bounced back out of the room with an energy that Tiffany could only be envious of.

"Captain Beau, would you like to come with me to the servants' quarters to bring Nat to Mrs. Able?"

He shrugged one little silk-clad shoulder. "I suppose. Why Miss Woodall?"

"Mrs. Able has a little boy about your age. His name is Peter. I thought perhaps you would like to play with him."

Beau's eyes widened and he grinned. "A boy my age?"

"Yes, and I am sure he would be just as happy to play with you as you are to play with him. The only person he's had to talk to is Monsieur Bonne, who has put him to work cutting vegetables."

Tiffany was reasonably sure that both the boy and the chef had been having a lovely time with basic food preparation, but the little duke didn't need those details.

"We must go rescue him from the French pirates!"

She bounced the baby in her arms. "Yes, and if I were you, I would also plunder some French pastries from the pantry while I was at it."

"Do you think I need my sword?"

Even though it was wooden, Tiffany did not think it was a particularly good idea for him to be wielding it in the servants' quarters—or, heaven forbid, at any of the servants.

"Perhaps next time."

Together they left the nursery as Nat began to fuss. Tiffany's own stomach rumbled. Like her son, she liked to eat her meals at regular intervals. When they reached the servants' sitting room, Tiffany handed Nat over to Mrs. Able.

"Would it be alright, ma'am, if your son played with Master Beau?" Tiffany didn't want to call him the Duke of Beaufort. It was much too severe a title for a six-year-old boy.

"I am sure Peter would be happy to, Miss Woodall," Mrs. Able said. "Shall I go and find him?"

Tiffany shook her head. "Oh no. I do believe the only person who could successfully accomplish such a difficult and dangerous adventure is Captain Beaufort."

Beau beamed up at her before laughing. "Where should I look?"

Tiffany turned to Mrs. Able.

"The kitchens. The lad has taken quite an interest in cookin'."

"The perfect place to plunder pastries," Tiffany said, glancing down at Beau. "Captain, can you handle this raid on your own? I need to speak to your mother."

Beau saluted her. "Sure I can, but then you won't get any of the spoils."

Touching her brow, Tiffany sighed theatrically. "Alas."

As she made her way back to the main hall, she didn't hear any screams of terror and assumed Captain Beaufort's attack on the kitchens had been accomplished without bloodshed. She saw Mr. Ford walking toward her with his limp, caused, she knew now, by an injury given to him by Farmer Coram.

"Mr. Ford, do you know where the duchess is? I should like to speak with her."

The butler gave her a ceremonious bow. "She is in the crimson drawing room. I should be most happy to escort you there."

"Thank you," Tiffany said, and moved to walk beside him.

They passed several paintings and the door to the library.

"Mr. Ford, may I ask, did you see Mr. Bernard Coram the night of his death?"

The butler breathed in deeply through his long beaklike nose. He looked over it, down at her. "I did not. I am afraid that I stayed later that evening than usual. I only wish that I had been there to spare my wife the injuries she received at his hands."

His tone was cold, but his eyes were not. Tiffany truly believed that he cared for his wife, even if his marriage to her had come about in the most unlikely of circumstances. "Then he'd come to your wife before asking for money?"

"Yes, Miss Woodall. Mr. Bernard Coram stopped by frequently for money and requested that I give him a letter of reference. I did give him several pounds, but he never used it to find a new position. He wasted it on drink, gambling, and wenches. I told him that I would not pay for such a life. I did not realize at the time that he would take those words out on my wife."

Tiffany nodded. She didn't blame the butler. Bernard Coram seemed to have been taking money from everyone who knew him, but not working or attempting to find employment. "I am sorry for the pain she has suffered."

Mr. Ford shook his head, and the older man looked tired. "Ludmilla's life has been almost all suffering, and her two children only added to it. There was bad blood in Bernard, and no matter how hard we tried to help him, he didn't change."

"And Evie?" Tiffany prompted.

"She wanted to leave the babe with Ludmilla, but there was no way my wife would be able to take care of her grandchild. It is hard for her to perform the most basic of tasks with only one arm, and she is not getting any younger."

"So, you told Evie to go to Mr. Lathrop."

For the first time in her acquaintance with Mr. Ford, he appeared uncomfortable and out of countenance. "I did. I was protecting the woman I love. Not unlike what you are doing now to protect Mr. Lathrop. He's a good man, and I hope that you are able to clear his name."

Tiffany felt speechless. She'd never expected such a sincere confession from the older man. Nor his own observances of her feelings for Samir. One sometimes did terrible things to protect those they loved.

"I cannot deny that I am glad that Evie left Nat with me. I love him as if he were my own son, and I am pleased and able to take care of him. However, both of my parents are deceased.

And if either yourself or Mrs. Ford would like to visit Nat as his grandparents, you would be most welcome."

Mr. Ford sniffed. It was the most emotion she'd ever seen him display. "I shall tell Mrs. Ford."

"And will *you* visit Nat?"

The older man nodded. "I should like that very much, Miss Woodall."

He opened the door for her, and she left him in the hall.

CHAPTER 30

"Where have you been?" Catharine demanded from her chair at the table. She was surrounded by several documents that she appeared to be going through.

Tiffany gulped. "To church and then in the nursery with Nat. Has something happened?"

"I have learned that the London assize courts have sent the same intolerable man, Judge Phineas Faulkner, who would have hung my son merely because he is African."

"The twelve jurors found Thomas guilty—the judge was not the only one to blame."

Catharine waved that aside. "It would be better for us not to allow Samir's case to even go to trial, but to have the judge throw it out because it lacks evidence."

Sighing, Tiffany couldn't help but agree. She assumed that it would be the same twelve jurors as it had been six months before. The only one of the twelve she was certain was on their side was Doctor Hudson. The apothecary's wife had brought Samir a basket of food in prison; perhaps her husband, Mr. Canning, would give Samir a fair trial. She didn't know Mr. Wesley, the shop clerk well enough to guess which side he would take. But for the rest—the butcher, the carrier, the farrier, the clothier, the candlemaker, the baker, the miller, the weaver, and the tanner—Sir Walter Abney had certainly been currying for their favor at church.

Pointing to the seat across from her, Catharine said, "Sit. We have much to go over unless you've already discovered the true murderer."

Tiffany perched on the edge of the chair. The documents on the table were all bills or mortgages signed by Sir Walter Abney. The entirety resulted in a fortune of debt.

"Do you own all of these notes?"

The duchess smiled viciously, and Tiffany was glad they were friends. "Yes. I am only missing one mortgage, but it is the most important one."

"The one for the demesne with the house on it."

Catharine's eyes narrowed. "Precisely. My man of business tracked it to a Mr. Reardon, who recently left for the American colonies. It could take months or even a year before we track him down."

"I have it."

She blinked. "*You* have it."

"Or rather, Samir had it," Tiffany explained. "He purchased it from Mr. Reardon. He thought of it as a sort of protection from Sir Walter Abney, but it proved to be quite the opposite."

The duchess laughed, a light, high sound. "La! Clever bookseller."

"It's up in the nursery with my things. Shall I go and fetch it?"

"At once," Catharine demanded in her most duchess-like voice. "I need all the pieces to spring my trap."

Tiffany scurried from the room like a scullery maid and easily found the satchel with the documents. She brought everything back to the crimson drawing room and passed it all off to the Duchess of Beaufort.

Catharine gave another vicious smile as she glanced at the legal note and the documentation. "This couldn't be more perfect. Sir Walter Abney is in arrears."

"Excuse me?" Tiffany asked, sitting down again.

"He hasn't paid on his loan. Not even the interest. I don't think any judge in England would fail to declare Sir Walter bankrupt. He hasn't paid in over two years. We shall be well rid of him at last."

Tiffany folded her arms and furrowed her brow. "But the mortgage is on the land of the demesne, not the house. Surely, the judge can't foreclose on the land, but not the house?"

The duchess laughed again, soft and haunting, like a villain in a Gothic romance. "Sir Walter is welcome to try and carry what he can, but you can't move brick and stone. And the land where the house resides belongs to the owner of that note."

"Samir can hardly defend himself while in prison."

Catharine picked up the document. "I'll pay you for this mortgage."

"The full ten thousand pounds?" Tiffany asked. She could tell that the duchess was a cutthroat businesswoman, and she didn't want to do Samir a financial disservice by selling the note at a loss.

Catharine set the paper back down. "I will offer you thirty thousand pounds for it. Three times its face value."

Tiffany's jaw dropped. "Why?"

Her friend twirled a ringlet around her finger. "I will admit that it is not out of friendship for you or for your besotted bookseller. I have long thought it was time for Thomas to have an estate of his own; but I didn't wish for him to move far from me. The Maplehurst estate is but two hour's walk, and less than half of that time in the carriage."

"Are you sure that it is a fair price? I would not wish to take advantage of you."

"Oh, Tiffany, only you would worry about cheating a duchess. In my opinion, the house is worth at least thirty thousand pounds, probably closer to fifty or sixty thousand pounds; but you would find few purchasers, since I already hold the mortgages and deeds for the rest of the estate. Few buyers at this level want only a house."

Biting her lower lip, Tiffany had to admit that tripling Samir's investment seemed like a very good plan to her. Particularly since Sir Walter Abney had not paid the quarterly interest. But if the duchess was correct, when the judge foreclosed on the loan, he would be the owner of the house. Tiffany tried to picture herself and Samir at Maplehurst. She shook her head. It was too grand for a librarian and a bookseller. And how were they to pay for the servants needed to maintain such a house and its gardens? It would require a steady, continuing source of income that neither of them had. Although Tiffany did think they would need to expand Bristle Cottage at the rate their family and servants were growing. Bristle Cottage was home. Maplehurst was not, and she could think of no better neighbor than Thomas.

"Very well, I will sell you the note for thirty thousand pounds."

Catharine gave her a sharp-toothed smile. "Excellent. As the sole possessor of all Sir Walter Abney's debts, I will have my man of business begin his petition to the judge for immediate foreclosure and bankruptcy. Thomas should be able to move in by the end of the month."

"Will Sir Walter be left with nothing?"

"Yes. And no, I don't feel even a tinge of guilt. The odious little man would have hung my eldest son. And now he is trying to frame the constable for murder, instead of paying his debts. One can only hope that our next justice of the peace will be an honest man."

Tiffany nodded pensively. "Thomas would make an excellent justice of the peace. Do you know who selects the position?"

"The Lord Lieutenant, the main estate holder of the area who is a member of parliament."

Tiffany raised her eyebrows. "And that is?"

"The Duke of Beaufort."

This time it was Tiffany who laughed. It was a six-year-old boy. "I am sure Beau would be more than happy to select his elder brother as a justice of the peace."

Catharine twirled the same curl on her finger. "Yes. I will have to have my solicitor check about the legality of it since Beau is a minor. In that case, as his sole guardian, I should be able to select the new justice. If I can get Thomas instated before the trial, he can release Samir. Judge Faulkner is to arrive tomorrow. Thomas, my steward, my man of business, and my solicitor will be in Mapledown main square to meet him."

Tiffany brought her hands to the sides of her face. "If Samir could be spared the humiliation of a trial, I would be forever indebted to you."

"Nonsense. I owe you thirty thousand pounds."

Tiffany smiled and then laughed again. Catharine chuckled with her, and for the first time it felt like they were truly friends.

CHAPTER 31

Despite sleeping in the enormous bed, Tiffany got very little rest. And it wasn't just because she woke up every time Nat fussed in the room next to hers. Although, it was Mrs. Able who fed him. No, Tiffany tossed and turned with fear that Judge Faulkner would not dismiss Samir's case as being without any proper evidence. Burying her face in the pillow, she tried to stay calm. The Duchess of Beaufort was her friend. She had already helped Tiffany find a wet nurse, let her stay in her home, and purchased all of Sir Walter Abney's debts. Catharine was a force to be reckoned with.

Mary helped Tiffany dress in a somber gown of gray. Tiffany did not wish to wear or do anything that would cause censure from the judge. Her breakfast was brought on a tray, but she felt too nauseous to take even a bite. Mary happily ate it for her.

"They serves you much better food than us," she said, holding a piece of bacon between her fingers. "This is a right luxury, it is."

Tiffany felt her brow furrow with concern. "Have the other servants been treating you well?"

Mary popped the rest of the bacon into her mouth and answered with it still full. "Yeth. They seem in awes of m'sister Emily."

Miss Emily Jones worked as the Duchess of Beaufort's lady's maid, an esteemed position among servants, and she was a very beautiful young woman. Emily had a bit more polish and better manners than Mary. Tiffany knew she should reprimand her more, but she felt that young women were like flowers: too much rain, or criticism, could drown them. So, she tried to sprinkle her conversation with little suggestions to help her maid behave in a more genteel manner.

"It is no wonder. She is a very well-behaved young woman and never speaks when she has food in her mouth."

Mary nodded, obviously missing the gentle hint.

Tiffany went to the room adjacent to hers, where Mrs. Able and Nat were staying. The wet nurse bobbed a curtsy and handed her baby over. Nat looked well fed and smelled wonderful. His little cheeks were round and full. Tiffany kissed them both. It seemed as if everyday something about him changed. She could not afford to miss any more moments with her son. Her only heartache was that Samir had only seen him once and had not yet had the time to create the father–son bond that she knew would grow between them.

Returning to her room, Tiffany did nothing but lie on her bed and snuggle her baby against her chest. It was the greatest peace she had ever felt. Nat mostly slept, but she didn't mind. Holding him was enough.

A couple of hours later, Tiffany heard a gentle knock on her door.

"Come in."

Emily opened it. She had been Tiffany's first friend in the palace. "Miss Woodall, Her Grace requires your presence in the crimson drawing room."

"Thank you, Miss Jones," Tiffany said, getting to her feet. "I will come as soon as I've given Nat back to Mrs. Able."

The lady's maid held out her arms. "I can take him."

Tiffany was about to demur that it wasn't necessary, but she saw that Emily looked as if she wished to hold the baby. And as much as Tiffany would like to be selfish and keep all of Nat's cuddles to herself, she knew that it took a village to raise a child, and she very much wished for Emily to be a part of that village. Carefully, she passed her son over.

She shook her head. "I wish I could let Mrs. Able know when I will return, but it all depends on the assizes judge."

Emily smiled down at the baby. "You don't need to worry about that, Miss Woodall. There is practically a queue in the servants' quarters to hold him."

Her lips twitched into a smile. It would seem that Tiffany was not the only person fond of holding babies.

The lady's maid glanced back up at her. "And I am to tell you that we found Her Grace's missing jewels."

Tiffany's curiosity couldn't help but ask, "Where?"

Snorting, Emily gave a small laugh. "They were in a chest in the attic, Miss Woodall. The young duke certainly knows how to hide his treasure well. Her Grace had every servant in the house searching for her jewels."

Sighing, Tiffany felt greatly relieved as she left Emily and Nat to walk down the grand staircase. With each step, a sense of dread filled her stomach. Samir's life and freedom would depend on what was said and done today. She touched her neck, feeling the pulse. If he were hung for murder, he would not see his son grow up. And their baby would never know the great man that was his father.

Thomas stood at the bottom of the stairs, as if waiting for her. He offered his arm and Tiffany gladly took it. She was feeling none too steady on her own two feet.

He patted her back. "Don't worry, Tiffany. Samir will be here to raise your child with you."

Her friend couldn't know if his words were true, but they comforted her all the same. She rubbed her thumb against the diamond cluster ring she'd placed on the fourth finger of her right hand. Married women wore rings on their left.

"But he cannot marry me."

Thomas stopped and turned to face her. "If something happens to Samir, I promise that I will marry you myself."

Sniffling, Tiffany tried to hold back the flood of emotions she felt for her dear friend. "If I were fifteen years younger, I would hire a carriage to take us to Gretna Green at once. But you are young, Thomas. Your whole life is before you, and even though your first love was false, it doesn't mean that you will not find a life partner who is worthy of you."

"I would not be here if it weren't for you, Tiffany. Believe me when I say that I will do anything for you."

She touched his cheek and saw age spots on her own skin and the thin wrinkles of time. "And your mother saved me. I believe that we are even, although there is no tally or scales between friends. I cannot tell you how much your offer means to me. That you would be willing to sacrifice so much. Thomas, you are an even better man than I thought, and I already thought you were a very good man."

Thomas smiled, his white teeth a sharp contrast to his dark skin. His smile faded almost as quickly as it came. "I should not wish for any child to grow up without a father."

Tiffany dropped her hand. She knew that Thomas was speaking from personal experience. Catharine had adopted Thomas from a slave captain and loved him as her own child. But her late husband had not treated him as a son. He'd even made Thomas be a servant in the house—a footman with the odious Bernard Coram.

"Then we will have to get Samir freed. You are much too young to be a father yet."

He offered her his arm again, and they entered the crimson drawing room. Catharine was sitting at the table, with a row of documents in neat piles. On either side of her sat a man.

She glanced up at Tiffany and Thomas. "Miss Woodall, this is my man of business, Mr. Giffin, and my solicitor, Mr. Sanger. Mr. Giffin informed me that Judge Faulkner has arrived and is willing to hear my petition of foreclosure at two o'clock at the Middlesex sessions house. He also informed me that Mr. Lathrop's trial is tomorrow at nine o'clock in the morning with a full local jury of twelve members. Hopefully, it will not be necessary after today."

Tiffany nodded, unable to speak. The thought of Samir hanging had haunted her dreams. She could hardly close her eyes at night.

"Everything looks to be in order, Your Grace," Mr. Giffin said.

The man of business looked to be about Tiffany's age. He had extremely curly black hair and a swarthy complexion. He wore leather breeches secured to his knees by brass buttons. The buttons made her think of Mr. Hadfield and Miss Anstey; however, she was now all but certain that they had nothing to do with Bernard's death. The solicitor on Catharine's other side was dressed somberly in all black and wore a robe that reminded her of a rector's. On his head sat a curly white wig with a ponytail in the back. His face and figure were round, but his countenance appeared congenial.

"If it pleases, Your Grace," Mr. Sanger said, bowing, "Mr. Giffin and myself will order the documents together to match the prepared speech I have written for the judge."

"Very well." Catharine moved from the table. "I will go and change my dress. I want to appear commanding, particularly since the judge will probably not give me an opportunity to speak. My sumptuous clothing must do the talking for me."

A clever move. But Tiffany was discovering how clever Catharine was—and conniving, now that she didn't have a duke in her way.

CHAPTER 32

Thomas summoned two carriages, and Tiffany and Catharine took the first. Or to be more accurate, Catharine's dress took the first carriage and Tiffany was squeezed tightly into a corner of the opposite seat. Thomas, Mr. Giffin, and Mr. Sanger followed in the second carriage.

Tiffany tried not to breathe. She had never seen a gown so fine. Or so tremendous in size! Tiffany would have guessed the panniers on Catharine's waist were at least a foot and a half on each side of her hips. The embroidered silk felt softer than the petal of a flower to the touch. Catharine's wig and hat were equal to it. Catharine wore gloves, but she had slid ruby rings over them. She had matching ruby earbobs and a necklace that would have been more appropriate at a ball. However, Tiffany did not doubt that Catharine was making a strong impression with her clothing—of power, wealth, and prestige.

It took the assistance of both Thomas and two footmen to get Catharine and her gown out of the carriage. Tiffany followed behind her, aware of how she was eclipsed by the splendor of the duchess. Sir Walter Abney was already in the Middlesex sessions room with Judge Phineas Faulkner when they arrived. The baronet strode forward to bow over Catharine's hand. He looked as if he would have kissed it if Catharine had given him any encouragement, but the expression on her face could have frozen a lake.

"Your Grace, you honor us with your presence," Sir Walter said obsequiously.

Catharine responded with only a slight nod of her head. She held out her hand to Thomas, who escorted her to a seat on the front row of the room. The plain wooden bench appeared incongruous with a bejeweled duchess on it.

Sir Walter took a seat on the opposite bench. He was powdered, painted, bewigged, and silked. His appearance was that of a fine gentleman, but Tiffany knew that he was a dishonorable man.

Tiffany's eyes turned to the judge who sat behind a table. The Honorable Judge Phineas Faulkner's eyes narrowed as he looked at her. His mouth formed a grim line. Clearly, he remembered her from six months ago, and he had not forgiven her masquerade. She moved to take a seat beside the duchess on the end of the bench. Catharine's gown took up nearly the entire seat.

Glancing around the dimly lit room, Tiffany saw that there were no men sitting in the jury seats. There wouldn't be until tomorrow at the trial. If there was a trial. Tiffany was surprised to see that the party from Astwell Palace were not the only people in the audience. It appeared that every major tradesman in Mapledown had come.

Mr. Giffin and Mr. Sanger bowed to the judge.

Straightening his black robes, Mr. Sanger said, "Permission to approach and address your honor?"

A small smile lingered on the judge's thin lips. He appeared to enjoy the power that he held over people. He straightened both sides of his long, curly white wig, which reached past his shoulders and halfway down his black-robed chest.

"You may come and speak, sir."

Mr. Sanger bowed again before walking to the head of the room where the judge sat. He pulled a stack of documents from his satchel and placed them in a neat line on the table in front of the judge.

"As you can see from these mortgages and notes, Your Honor," the solicitor began, "Sir Walter Abney, Baronet, has not paid the interest on any of his loans in over two years. The sum of interest combined is sixteen thousand pounds."

Sir Walter Abney stood, his face red. "What is the meaning of this? We are not here to speak about my debts, but to see that justice is done for a young White man named Mr. Bernard Coram, cut down in his prime."

Tiffany winced at the reference to Bernard's race. She knew it was to remind the judge that Samir was Indian. Guilty of being different. Of having a foreign mother.

The judge held up a bony finger. "Sir Walter, you did not have permission to address myself or the members of this room. I was approached by Mr. Giffin to take the case this morning, and I accepted. He led me to believe that justice could not be served if the matter of these debts was not first addressed."

"Debts are not for the courts, but for the moneylenders," Sir Walter Abney blustered.

Judge Faulkner picked up his gavel and banged it twice. "Silence. If you cannot hold your tongue, Sir Walter, I shall have you removed from the room."

The baronet's bovine face looked mutinous, but he returned to his seat on the opposite bench from Tiffany's.

"You may proceed, Mr. Sanger."

The solicitor squared his shoulders back. "Your Honor will see that the entire amount of the debt is just shy of ninety thousand pounds."

Tiffany heard low whistles from the tradesmen in the room. Such a sum was unimaginable to her.

Mr. Sanger touched the last mortgage. "As you can see from the newest mortgage, Sir Walter Abney gave the demesne of his estate as the security on the loan. The loan was originally created with Mr. Richard Reardon, but he sold the loan to Mr. Samir Lathrop."

Turning to see the crowd's reaction, Tiffany saw gasps and looks of surprise on more than one face.

"Your Honor, Sir Walter is in the arrears on all of his mortgages and should go into default. However, as justice of the peace, Sir Walter decided to clear his debt by placing the blame of a murder on Mr. Samir Lathrop. If Mr. Lathrop were dead, then Sir Walter would not have to repay a shilling."

Tiffany heard someone yell, "Cheat!"

And another: "Thief!"

More words were said, but Tiffany could not discern what or by whom, through the murmur.

The judge pounded his gavel three times before the room became quiet. "If Mr. Lathrop was in possession of this loan, how did it come to be in your charge, Mr. Sanger?"

Tiffany felt a blush begin at her neck and grow into her face. Her connection with Samir, even their friendship, was scandalous. Bringing it up would not help his case.

The solicitor cleared his throat. "After Mr. Lathrop was wrongfully incarcerated, he sold the note to the Duchess of Beaufort. Indeed, Your Honor, the Duchess of Beaufort now owns all of Sir Walter Abney's debts and requests that you free

Mapledown's constable and remove Sir Walter Abney's authority as the justice of the peace. A role that he will no longer be able to hold since he will not have a home in our county."

Sir Walter Abney stood up, puffing out his chest. "The mortgage is on the land, but not on the house. You cannot take my home."

The judge hit the gavel again. "Sir Walter, this is the third time that you have spoken in this court out of turn. There will not be a fourth. Sit down or be removed from the room." Faulkner picked up the mortgage for the demesne and read it carefully. "Mr. Sanger, despite the unfortunate nature of Sir Walter's outburst, he does make a valid point: the house is not included as a security for this mortgage."

Mr. Sanger bowed to the judge. "My client is well aware of that fact, Your Honor. However, she is the owner of the land on which the house stands. If Sir Walter would like to move it off her property, the Duchess of Beaufort will kindly give him one hour to do so."

There were several guffaws and hoots from the crowd.

The judge's lips made a wry, twisted smile. "Her Grace makes an excellent point. If Sir Walter Abney cannot repay the loans, he must forfeit his lands. And if the Duchess of Beaufort owns the land where the house stands, then it is lawful and reasonable that she would also own the house. Sir Walter Abney, are you able to pay the entire sum owed?"

He shook his head. "I may be able to raise enough money for the back interest, Your Honor. But I would need my belongings, the possessions that have been in my family for generations."

"Mr. Sanger," the judge addressed the solicitor, "would your client be content with the amount owing on the interests?"

The solicitor shook his head. "No, sir. The Duchess of Beaufort is foreclosing on Sir Walter Abney's Maplehurst estate. She is fully aware that Sir Walter cannot move the house but could perhaps transfer furniture, paintings, silverware, and other goods. However, she has requested that Sir Walter first settle all of his bills with local tradesmen. Her Grace fears that not even the proceeds from an auction done by a bailiff for all Sir Walter's belongings will bring in enough to fully repay his creditors."

Tiffany could only watch wide-eyed. Catharine was going to leave Sir Walter with nothing. Only the fine clothes on his back.

Judge Faulkner exhaled slowly. "Before I can agree to your terms, or Her Grace's, I must know the amounts for which Sir Walter Abney is in debt."

Mr. Giffin stood and bowed again. "If Your Honor permits, I would like to introduce the local tradesmen and have them present to you their unpaid bills."

The judge nodded.

Mr. Giffin held a list. "Would Mr. Wesley please come forward?"

Tiffany watched the clerk walk to the table and set down his note. "Sir Walter has not paid his tab at my shop in three years, Your Honor. The entirety of his bill is three hundred and six pounds."

"Would Mr. Grove please come forward."

The candlestick maker doffed his hat to the judge and placed a wrinkled paper before him. "The Maplehurst estate owes me one hundred and fifty pounds. The bill is more than four years outstanding, Your Honor."

Mr. Giffin continued to call names: the grocer, the butcher, the farrier, the baker, the miller, the weaver, the tanner, the blacksmith, and the wine seller, whose unsettled tab was nearly seven hundred pounds.

The man of business shifted on his feet. "Your Honor, these are only Sir Walter Abney's bills in Mapledown. He has more unpaid creditors in London, and a house there. The Duchess of Beaufort suggests that a bailiff auction off Sir Walter's goods from Maplehurst House and if any remaining debt is owed to Mapledown tradesmen, she will settle it with her own money. The Duke of Beaufort is the Lord Lieutenant for the area, but since he is a minor, Her Grace sees it as her duty to ensure the livelihood and well-being of those in her care."

Judge Faulkner nodded his head slowly. "Admirable. Admirable. Sir Walter Abney, the choice is before you: secede all of your property and belongings to the Duchess of Beaufort, or go to debtor's prison. What is your choice?"

The baronet's face had turned from red to purple. He stumbled to his feet. "I will not go to debtor's prison."

The judge carefully stacked all the bills into one pile and the mortgages into another. "Mr. Sanger, your client, the Duchess of Beaufort, is now the legal owner of the Maplehurst estate. Please fill out the proper deeds, and I shall sign and witness them. Sir Walter Abney is no longer the justice of the peace, and any warrant that he signs from today forward will have no validity."

The solicitor bowed his head to the judge obsequiously. "May we also request, Your Honor, that Sir Walter not return to his former estate, but go directly to London on tonight's mail coach? A ticket has already been purchased for him."

Tiffany bit her lower lip. Catharine was certainly thorough.

"But what about my clothes and my servants?" Sir Walter whined, sounding like a spoiled child.

Mr. Sanger looked at Catharine, and she shook her head slightly. He turned back to the baronet. "No, Sir Walter. Neither have been paid for. Your clothes will be sold like the rest of your belongings to pay the tradesmen's bills."

The baronet turned to look at the Duchess of Beaufort. "You will hear from my solicitors!"

Thomas and Mr. Giffin each took one of Sir Walter's arms to restrain him.

Catharine only smiled. "Certainly, but if I do, prepare to spend a long time in debtor's prison."

Sir Walter tried to break free of their hold, to get closer to the duchess.

Mr. Sanger cleared his throat. "Permission to remove Sir Walter from the room, Your Honor?"

Judge Faulkner struck his gavel once. "Permission granted."

Mr. Giffin and Thomas frog-marched the baronet from the room. They were followed by several tradesmen. Tiffany only wished that Sir Walter could experience the humiliation of prison like Samir had.

Mr. Sanger straightened his wig. "Your Honor, since we have proven that Sir Walter Abney acted out of his own best dividends, and not in the interest of justice toward Constable Sam Lathrop, we respectfully request his immediate release from prison and that all charges against him be dropped."

For the first time that afternoon, the Middlesex sessions room was completely silent. Tiffany would have been able to hear a pin drop. She watched Judge Faulkner, praying fervently that he would release Samir.

The assizes judge breathed in deeply and shook his head. "The trial will continue tomorrow. If Constable Lathrop is indeed innocent, then the facts will prove him so to the jury. You are all dismissed."

Tiffany winced with each sound of the gavel hitting the table. Her worst fears had been realized. The judge had no proof that Samir *had* murdered Mr. Bernard Coram; but he also didn't have any proof that he *hadn't*. And in the sight of the law, one was considered guilty until proven innocent.

She was under the burden of proof, which she didn't have. Tiffany had failed Samir, the man she loved, when he needed her the most.

CHAPTER 33

Catharine forced Tiffany to eat dinner, even though she still had no appetite. Their meal was a quiet one—only Tiffany and Catharine. Thomas had stayed behind in Mapledown, to ensure that Sir Walter got on the mail coach that evening.

"I wish I had words of comfort for you," the duchess said, dabbing at her mouth with a napkin. "I wish I could assure you that the law was impartial or fair. But as women, we both know that it is not. We also know the anguish of loving someone of another race and knowing that they will be judged more harshly for the color of their skin."

Tiffany toyed with the vegetables with her fork. "At least Judge Faulkner will not get the final choice in verdict—only in the punishment. The jury members from Mapledown may find Samir innocent. Surely they know him better than to believe he could be a murderer? He has been an exemplary constable, and he defended Thomas so beautifully last year."

Catharine's eyes went to her plate, and she didn't answer. Her silence was answer enough. Samir was a part of the town, but he was also not. As a bookseller, he was more educated than most of the men. Not quite a gentleman. But not in the same class as a farmer or laborer. They might know Samir, but that didn't mean that they *knew* Samir.

After dinner, Tiffany accompanied Catharine to the nursery.

Pausing at the door, the duchess said, "I am afraid Judge Faulkner refused to show Mr. Sanger and Mr. Giffin 'the written record of evidence' against Mr. Lathrop before the trial. Mr. Sanger is prepared to defend Mr. Lathrop, but he can only guess at what Sir Walter Abney has written. We assume that Farmer Coram will be called as a witness, and even if he recants his accusation, his previous testimony, if written, will still stand."

"What are you saying, Catharine?"

The duchess placed her hand on Tiffany's arm. "You should hope for the best but be prepared for the worst."

Catharine opened the door to the nursery, and Tiffany could hear Beau's excited voice from the hall. She needed a few more moments to compose herself. She would not prepare her heart and mind for the worst; rather, she would have to find the true killer . . . before the trial in the morning.

Such a task seemed impossible.

Entering the nursery, she was surprised to see Catharine sitting on the floor with Beau on her lap and Nat in his arms. The image was so sweet it took her breath away. This—this was what she was fighting for. A family with Samir. Loving friends like Thomas, Catharine, and Beau. Her own little corner of the world.

"I'm holding him all by myself!" Beau said loudly.

Nat moved his head and wrinkled his nose before whimpering.

"Hush, baby," the little boy said. "I am a duke."

Tiffany grinned. "I am afraid Nat is too young to know what a duke is yet, Captain Beau, but someday he will."

That day the distance between her children and the Duke of Beaufort would be too great to compass, but she would not think of that now. Children were allowed greater freedoms than adults. They could be friends with those of different classes, until they grew up.

Nat continued to fuss.

Beau huffed. "You can have your baby back, Miss Woodall. All he does is cry, eat, and poop. Besides, Mama promised to play jack straws with me again."

Catharine chuckled, and Tiffany fought hard not to smile, pressing her two lips together in a thin line.

"A gentleman never mentions excrement," Miss Drummond said from the corner of the room. The governess was a somber presence in the otherwise playful nursery.

"What's *excitement*?" Beau asked.

Miss Drummond raised her thin eyebrows. "Bodily functions."

The little duke shook his head. "But I didn't mention bodily functions. I said that all he did was cry, eat, and poop."

Turning her head, Tiffany could no longer hold in her smile.

"Master Peregrine, a gentleman does not say *poop*."

"Then why didn't you say that in the first place, Miss Drummond?"

Finally gaining control of her facial features, Tiffany knelt down and took the fussy baby from the little boy. She bounced Nat gently in her arms and he stopped crying.

"I don't see why I shouldn't say *poop*," Beau continued, climbing off his mother's lap. "I mean everyone poops. Horses do all the time; they don't even go somewhere private. Dogs don't either."

Unable to hold back her laugh, Tiffany left the nursery with Nat before Beau could name every creature he knew that pooped.

Besides, she needed time to think. She must be missing an important detail about Bernard Coram's demise. The very detail that could be the difference between Samir's life and death. She brought Nat back to her guest room and sat down in the rocking chair. She rocked him back and forth until his little eyelashes fluttered and he fell asleep.

Once her baby was sleeping, Tiffany went through what she knew about the night of Bernard's murder.

Bernard threatened to tell Evie about Samir's attentions to herself. Samir refused to pay the blackmail money. Farmer Coram overheard this and gave his son three pennies, which were later found in the corpse's pocket.

Then the braggart tried to force his attentions on Miss Caro. She scratched his face. He got into a fight with Mr. Hadfield at the Black Cauldron, and they were kicked out at nine o'clock by Mr. Day. Caro's father, Mr. Anstey, had not protected her when she was violated. He would not defend her now.

After the fight, Bernard went to the hamlet of Dee to demand money from his birth mother. She refused and then he tried to strangle her. Mrs. Ford bit his thumb and then Evie forced him to leave and barred the door. Tiffany assumed that it had taken him at least a half an hour to walk there. Mrs. Ford had not said anything, but Tiffany was sure that Bernard had gone through with his threats to Samir. She believed he had told Evie that her legal husband was fond of a spinster librarian. The conversations could not have been very long, for according to the various reports, he was drunk and violent.

Tiffany guessed that it must have been sometime between ten and ten thirty in the evening when he'd left Dee. There was no mention of him seeing Mr. Ford, who'd arrived home close to eleven that evening. Two hours later than his normal time.

Bernard did not return to his father's farm. Mr. Hadfield waited for hours in the darkness until it began to rain. Bernard would not have gone to Astwell Palace. All the doors and windows would have been locked by that time of night, and whatever Mr. Ford's views were on his wife's children, he was a very efficient butler. Tiffany was sure that Bernard hadn't stopped there. But he had not passed the Coram farm on the way to the village, so he must have taken the shorter path by the church; therefore entirely missing Mr. Hadfield.

Wherever and to whomever Bernard had gone with the Queen Anne's lace, he had been killed and his body brought to Tiffany's home.

Why Bristle Cottage?

Shaking her head, Tiffany was back where she started. Why did the person or persons bring the body to her?

Queen Anne's lace was to prevent pregnancies. It made the most sense given Bernard's dubious character and the time of evening, that he had gone to have sexual congress with someone.

Not Caro Anstey.

No maid from Astwell Palace would have let him back in, or she would have lost her position.

Could it have been one of the Day's daughters? They were all three very pretty young women, and Bernard seemed to prey on the prettiest of girls. Tiffany shook her head. It was terribly judgmental of her to assume that just because these young women worked in a public house and wore low-cut dresses that they had loose morals.

But Miss Jessica Day had brought at least one basket, possibly more to Samir. She'd said at the time they were from her mother, but what if they weren't? What if Miss Jessica was trying to soothe her own conscience? What if Bernard Coram had given her the bruises on the back of her neck and her father had killed him for it? Mr. Day had his own wagon. He'd allowed Tiffany and Samir to borrow it to go see Mr. Hadfield. Mr. Day was a large man and more than capable of lifting the corpse of Bernard Coram in and out of it.

What she needed now was proof of the Day family's involvement with Bernard's death, and she had no idea how she would obtain it.

CHAPTER 34

Tiffany returned to her room after entrusting Nat to Mrs. Able for the night. There was no need for them both to wake every time the baby needed to be fed. Besides, Tiffany was running out of time. She had less than twelve hours to find evidence to exonerate Samir.

Mary knocked on the door and came in to help Tiffany undress.

"How is Matilda?" Tiffany asked.

Her maid began to unbutton the back of Tiffany's dress. "She's a superior heifer, Miss Woodall, and a looker. Monsieur Bonne says that her milk is practically cream out of the tit."

Tiffany pursed her lips together. Now was not the time to tell Mary that *tit* was not a proper word to say in polite conversation any more than *poop*. She remembered that Samir had told her that Mary was lonely at Bristle Cottage.

"Are you liking staying at a palace?"

Mary shrugged her shoulders. "I like seein' m'sister, but I miss havin' my own room. I'm bunked up with Emily now, and she snores somethin' dreadful."

"Then you don't mind being alone at Bristle Cottage?"

"I like the chickens and now Matilda, but there's not much to do in the day, Miss Woodall," she admitted. "I'm not a bad girl, but I often go over to the public house because there is always someones to talk to, and Jessica is my best friend."

Tiffany turned around, holding her unbuttoned dress up. "Is she the youngest of the Day's daughters?"

"Yes. She's fifteen like me. She's the one who told me about Matilda."

So young.

At least ten years Mr. Bernard Coram's junior. The thought made Tiffany's stomach turn, but it wasn't unusual for the man to be older than the woman in a relationship. Even a great deal older if money was involved.

Miss Jessica Day appeared much older than Mary because of her curvaceous figure. Mary was still all knees and elbows. Her face open and trusting. Mary was so innocent and Tiffany was going to use her.

"Have you ever been inside the Days' home?"

"Only once, Miss Woodall, and all my chores was done. It's only down the street a little from the public house."

Mary walked behind her to pull down Tiffany's dress.

"I don't think I'm ready to undress yet, Mary."

Her maid let go. "'Tis after nine o'clock, Miss Woodall."

Tiffany yanked up one sleeve and then the other. Mr. Ford was right: sometimes one had to do terrible things to save the person they loved. "Button me back up, Mary. We are going to break into the Days' home."

The young woman blinked. "Have you gone mad?"

"I do not think so," Tiffany said, taking a deep breath and exhaling. "Won't all the Days be at the Black Cauldron? No one will ever know that we were there."

"But why, Miss Woodall? It doesn't make no sense."

Sighing, Tiffany slumped her shoulders. Her maid was not as malleable as she thought. "Mary, I know that Miss Jessica is your friend, but I think she knows more about what happened to Bernard Coram the night he died than she has said."

The young woman shook her head back and forth. "Jessica didn't have nothin' to do with his death, Miss Woodall. I swears it. He was her sweetheart. He used to bring her wildflowers. I saws him do it. He were often in the public house in the middle of the day too, when everyone else were at work. He used to tease and flirt with her."

"Did she let him kiss her?" Tiffany pressed.

She could see Mary's cheeks turn pink in the light of the fire. "Not in the Black Cauldron, Miss Woodall. Mrs. Day would never have allowed it. But sometimes they would meet and go on walks n' such. She told me that she let 'im kiss her and that she dinna like it at first. It were too wet, but she grew to likes it better. I dunno the difference, Miss Woodall, I's never been kissed."

"Did Bernard ever do more than kiss Miss Jessica?"

"What more is there?"

Tiffany could only be grateful for Mary's innocence, but she also needed her maid to understand how to protect herself and others.

"In a fortnight, when we are back at Bristle Cottage, I will tell you, but we simply do not have the time tonight. We must put on our cloaks and boots. I shall see if Thomas can call us a carriage. I don't care to walk unescorted at night after recent events."

Mary still looked doubtful. "We're not going to steal anything, are we?"

Tiffany shook her head. "We won't take a single thing. What we are looking for is evidence that Bernard Coram was murdered there."

"What sort of evidence?"

"Blood."

Guiding Mary by her shoulders, Tiffany led her down to the servants' quarters. They were nearly empty except for Mr. Ford. He had his hat and coat on and appeared to be leaving.

The butler took off his hat. "Is something amiss, Miss Woodall?"

She swallowed. "You're probably on your way home, but would you mind first alerting Mr. Montague that I have need of him. It would be quite untoward for me to go to his rooms, and I don't know where they are."

His eyes searched her face before he answered. "Very well."

Mr. Ford limped back toward the hall; meanwhile Tiffany and Mary put on their boots and cloaks. Tiffany opened the door to the servants' entrance. She felt a cold gust of wind run over her face and a few sprinkles of rain on her skin. Shutting the door, she locked it again. Rain. That's the last thing she needed tonight.

A few minutes later, Mr. Ford and Thomas appeared. Her younger friend's clothes were a bit rumpled, as if he'd hurriedly put them back on. The butler, even prepared to go home, was still neat as a pin. Not a wrinkle or a spot to be found on his raiment.

"Thank you so much for your help, Mr. Ford," Tiffany said, bowing her head. "I am afraid that I need to ask one more favor from you. Could both you and your wife attend Mr. Lathrop's trial tomorrow morning?"

The butler stiffened, his back straighter than a board. "My wife had nothing to do with Bernard Coram's death."

"And neither did Mr. Lathrop. I am not attempting to accuse her or you of anything other than being victims of his violent temper and increasing demands for money. But if the need should arise, I would like you and your wife to tell Judge Faulkner what happened that night. Preferably, Evie too."

"You ask too much, Miss Woodall."

Tiffany straightened her own back and lifted her chin. "I ask for everything I must to save the man I love."

Mr. Ford touched the brim of his hat. "I will think about it."

"You need not fear missing your work, Mr. Ford," Thomas said. "Both my mother and myself intend to be at the trial."

The butler gave a curt nod and left the palace. Tiffany heard the scraping of his key as he locked the servants' entrance behind him.

Spinning on her heel, Tiffany turned to face Thomas. His eyes looked red and tired. "I am sorry to pull you from your bed, but I think I may know who killed Bernard Coram."

Thomas touched her arm. "Who?"

"Mr. Day. Mary told me that Bernard was flirting with Miss Jessica Day, and I think he must have . . . attempted to have . . . intimate relations with Miss Day. I think she tried to fight him off, for she has bruising on her face and neck. My guess is that Mr. Day hit Bernard in the back of the head, in anger, but without the intent to kill. Either way, Bernard died. Mr. Day must have loaded the body up into his gig and dropped it off in front of my house. Mr. Hadfield told me that he heard someone driving on the road that night."

He sighed, releasing his hold on her arm. "Your theory is based on a great deal of conjecture."

"I know, but we are out of time and I cannot think of anyone else who it could be," Tiffany said, a note of hysteria in her voice. "In addition, the Day family have brought more baskets to Samir than anyone else. One basket is a sign of support and friendship, but they have come daily. I think it is guilt that drives them, for they know he is innocent."

Thomas breathed in deeply, shaking his head. "What is your plan?"

"You're going to call a carriage because it's raining and dark," Tiffany said. "Then you will go inside the Black Cauldron and order something to drink. You need to ascertain that all five members of the Day family are there, and then come out and tell us. Mary and I don't want to alarm anyone when we enter the Day home."

"Ye mean break into their home, Miss Woodall," Mary interjected. "We ain't invited to enter."

Tiffany shrugged her shoulders. "When we break into their home."

Thomas ran his fingers through his thick curls. "I will go and wake up the grooms and carriage driver. Stay here."

"Very well."

It felt to Tiffany as if an hour passed before Thomas opened the servants' door and escorted them into the carriage, but it was probably not more than fifteen minutes. The rain was falling heavily now. It sounded loud from inside the carriage, where it was hitting all four sides and the roof. Tiffany felt terrible for the carriage driver who was not protected by walls or windows. She would not have asked it of all of them if her need had not been so dire.

The carriage came to a stop and Tiffany assumed that they must be in front of the public house. The night was too dark

CHAPTER 35

Tiffany followed Mary down an alley behind the public house and over a street. They walked with arms outstretched to keep from running into fences or walls. The rain was falling so heavily that Tiffany could barely see two feet in front of her.

Mary grabbed her wet, cold hand. "This is it, Miss Woodall."

They stopped in front of a two-story stone house that was completely dark. Tiffany tugged Mary forward to the front door. She attempted to turn the knob, but it was locked. She thought it would be. Pulling Mary behind her, they went around the house to the back kitchen door. It was locked too.

How were they to enter it? There was a window above them that was slightly ajar. If only she were taller . . . But perhaps she could lift Mary up. Her maid would not be able to hold her weight.

Wiping the rain from her face, she asked, "Can you climb through the window?"

"Yes."

Tiffany cupped her two wet hands together, and Mary put her muddy boot into them. With as much strength as she could muster, Tiffany lifted her maid up. Mary's arms clung to the window frame, relieving some of the weight. She watched Mary pull and twist the window open, but she wasn't high enough yet to get inside.

Pressing herself against the wet stone, Tiffany said, "Climb on my shoulders."

She couldn't hear Mary's reply over the rain, but she felt one boot and then another stepping on her shoulders. Tiffany had to brace herself against the house. Mary pushed off her shoulders, and Tiffany could see her legs dangling in the rain. She was half in, half out of the house. Her maid continued to kick and squirm until her whole body fit through the window. Tiffany heard a clunk and a thud and hoped that Mary was not hurt and had not broken any of the Days' possessions. Especially if they were innocent. Resting her head against the rocks, Tiffany took a few steadying breaths before Mary opened the kitchen door. Tiffany walked into the tidy kitchen dripping mud and rain. She had hoped that the Days would not know of the break-in, but it would be obvious. Still, she slung off her wet cloak and pulled off her muddy boots.

Meanwhile, Mary had found a candle and lit it. "Miss Jessica's room is this way, Miss Woodall."

Tiffany followed her up a narrow staircase to a small landing. Mary opened the first door on the right. She held her candle up to illuminate the space. It was a very small room with a sharply angled roofline and only space for a narrow bed. Tiffany had to duck her head to enter the space and she was shorter than Bernard had been. There wouldn't have been much room in there for a man his size. Mary held the candle and Tiffany crouched down to look underneath the bed. There was only dust and a wooden box. She moved the trunk over, but there was nothing underneath it.

The room was cold. There was no fireplace. No source of heat.

"Like I's told ye, Miss Woodall," Mary said. "Jessica 'ad nothin' to do with it."

Exhaling, Tiffany swallowed. "Let's check the other first floor rooms."

Her maid blocked the door. "But ye said we were only lookin' at Jessica's room. We can't go riflin' through all of their things just for a foreigner."

Tiffany winced. "What does Mr. Lathrop's nationality have to do with anything?"

The young woman's eyes moved from Tiffany's face to the candle, and then to the floor. "Miss Woodall, the folks in town can't trust him because of his dark skin. He's a foreigner and everyone knows that foreigners are no good. It's no wonder his wife left him. We're all better off if he's dead."

A raw anger spread through Tiffany's veins and reached her heart, which was beating twice as fast. Prejudice. Blind and ugly prejudice. Over something so silly as the shade of a man's skin. Mary and the rest of the villagers in Mapledown were willing to condemn Samir on no other evidence. She clenched her teeth together to stop herself from saying something harsh to Mary. It wasn't her maid's fault that she had been raised by ignorant parents. Tiffany hadn't known Mary thought this way or she would have tried to explain her own feelings. She had taught her maid the alphabet and basic words, but not basic humanity.

Taking another steadying breath, Tiffany said, "Mary, please give me the candle."

The maid shook her head. "I can't let ye look nowhere else."

Mary *knew* something. She might have known it the entire time that Tiffany was searching from Bardsley to the Bramble Farm looking for evidence of Samir's innocence. And her maid had not told her.

"Whether you give me that candle or not, Mary, I will be searching this entire house. And if you would like to keep your place in my home, you will let me have the candle."

Mary's eyes widened and she looked younger than ever. "Ye would throw me out, Miss Woodall?"

"Yes. I would. I care for you. I have clothed you, educated you, and protected you. But I could not allow you to remain in my home if you've protected a murderer and condemned an innocent man to death."

A tear fell down Mary's cheek. "Friends protect each other. No matter what."

"Samir Lathrop is my friend, and I will do anything to protect him," Tiffany said, stepping closer to Mary so that their wet stockings touched toe to toe. "This is your last warning, Mary. I am larger than you and stronger. I will move you out of my way."

The younger woman stepped onto the landing, but did not give Tiffany the candle. Clenching her teeth, Tiffany went back down the stairs and lit a smaller candle that was nearly burnt down to the nub. She wouldn't have much time to search.

Tiffany saw Mary holding her candle; tears falling down her cheeks. She moved past her and went back up the stairs to the next door. This room was nearly triple the size of the first and had a large bed in the middle across from a small fireplace. Tiffany assumed that this was Mr. and Mrs. Day's room. She got onto her knees with the candle and looked for any stains on the wooden floor. She saw a few burn marks, but nothing

that led her to believe that a crime had happened here. Tiffany
rifled through the wardrobe and the drawers, looking for any
item that Mr. Day could have used to kill Bernard Coram, or a
bright yellow gown. But she found only linens. She felt about
in the hearth, but it was cold. No fire had been lit since the
previous night or that morning.

Tiffany got back to her feet and went to the final door.
Like the middle room, there was a large bed that could have
held two or three people. Instead of being in the center of the
room, it was pushed awkwardly to one side and was perilously
close to the flame of the fireplace. If she were going to push the
bed to the side, she would have done the opposite wall. The
third wall was not a possibility because it had the only window
in the room and a stone chimney. The rocks on the hearth
appeared to be the same as on the outside of the house.

Setting down the candle on the side table, she lifted up
the rag rug on the floor. She couldn't see anything suspicious
underneath it. Tiffany went through this wardrobe and the
trunk at the end of the bed. Nothing that could have been
used for a weapon and no proof that Bernard had met his end
there. Picking up the candle, Tiffany was about to check the
two other trunks when she saw a small red spot on one of the
rocks of the fireplace. The rock's edge was rather sharp and jut-
ted out a bit. Tiffany hadn't been able to see that side when she
entered the room. She brought the candle closer to it and saw
three other small red spots. They looked like splatters of blood.

Bernard Coram had died in this room. She was sure of it.
Setting the guttering candle back on the bedside table, Tiffany
pulled on the bed's corner frame. She yanked again and then
again, until it was far enough from the wall, that she could get
behind it. Using her back against the frame and her feet on the

wall, she pushed the bed into the center of the room. There was another rag rug, more worn, underneath the bed. Tiffany lifted it up slowly and saw a telltale large spot, darker in color than the rest of the wood. The stain reached all the way to the fireplace. That was why the bed had been placed so close to it.

"I wish you hadn't seen that, Miss Woodall."

Dropping the rug, Tiffany turned to see the form of Mr. Day fill up the entire doorframe, illuminated by the candle he held aloft.

She struggled to her feet; her knees shaking. "Did Bernard violate your daughter? Is that why you killed him?"

Mr. Day entered the room, stepping closer to Tiffany. Looming above her. "He preyed on young girls. He got what he deserved. If it weren't me, t'would've been someone else."

Tiffany gulped. "He was a rapist. I agree that Bernard Coram met the fate reserved for such a man. But why did you bring his body to my house? My cottage? What have I ever done to you?"

The large man clenched his fists and Tiffany feared that he was going to hit her. "I meant to take 'is carcass back to 'is father's farm. But I saw someone in the road, so I's took the t'other road and pushed him out. I dinna realize how close I were to yer cottage."

She nodded. Mr. Day must have seen Mr. Hadfield on his horse. The timeline of Bernard Coram's death was coming to a close.

"You dropped Bernard's body away from your own house and then waited for it to be found by someone else. If the placement of the body was not purposeful, you must have known that something had gone wrong when Mr. Lathrop was arrested for murder. Did you intend for him to hang for you?"

He stepped even closer until Tiffany could smell the hops on his breath and clothes. "I never said that. He's got ye and the duchess in his pocket with her fancy London solicitors. There's no need to assume that Sam would be found guilty."

"Are you going to come to the trial tomorrow and tell the truth?"

"No, Miss Woodall. And neither are ye. Ye should have kept your nose out of other folks' business."

Tiffany wrapped her arms around herself. "What are you going to do to me?"

"Nothin'. I ain't a bad man. I'm a father, protectin' my family. Ye'll be locked in this room until after the trial."

Mr. Day had to be twice her girth. She would never be able to overpower him, like she would have her maid.

Mary.

"There is no point in locking me up, sir. My maid will tell Mr. Montague where I am and he will come for me. You are only implicating yourself further."

He stepped back into the doorframe. "I dunna understand yer fancy words, but I know Mary Jones. She were the one who came and got me. She told Mr. Montague that ye'd decided to go back to yer cottage. Ain't no one gonna come lookin' fer ye until after the trial tomorrow mornin'."

Mr. Day closed the door and locked it.

CHAPTER 36

Tiffany shivered, her wet dress clinging to her arms and legs. What was she going to do? How was she to save Samir? The small window in the room looked over a cobblestone back alley and was at least ten feet to the ground. She would not survive such a fall without becoming grievously injured.

Rubbing her arms, Tiffany could feel the hairs on them standing up. The best thing she could do for now was get out of her wet things. Peeling off her stockings, she thought of Mary, who wanted to become a proper lady's maid like her sister. She'd thought the girl was as devoted to her as Tiffany was to Mary. Clearly, this was not the case.

Tiffany took off her gown, petticoat, and chemise. Opening the bureau, she located a clean, dry nightdress. She pulled it over her head. It barely reached over her knees—she was so much taller than the Day sisters. Picking up her sodden clothing, Tiffany went to hang them up over the cold hearth. Shivering, she felt goose bumps cover her arms and legs. Her body needed more than dry clothing. She needed a fire.

Kneeling down, she found there was a little bit of kindling in the hearth and one log. It would not last her the night, but it would be a start. As she took the candle off the table to light the fire, her foot caught on the second rug and she fell hard to the floor. Her face narrowly missing a sharp stone that poked out from the side of the fireplace. Grabbing the candle that had turned on its side, she flipped it back up before the hot wax could put out the flame. Carefully, Tiffany picked up the last sliver of the candle and placed it inside the kindling of the hearth.

The wood shavings quickly lit, and Tiffany could feel the warmth of the fire. The orange flames died down a little as the only log caught fire. The flame wasn't as bright or as large as it began, but it would burn steadily through the night. Tiffany reached out her arms toward the heat. Her fingers were wrinkled with water and cold, as if she were a woman twice her age. Yet her hands couldn't stop from moving to that pointy stone. It wasn't terribly sharp, but if Bernard had fallen backward. If he had tripped on the rug as she had and he hit his head on it, with the force of the fall, it could have killed him. She pulled up the older rug again. It was covering a puddle of blood stain near the hearth.

What if Mr. Day had not struck Bernard with a hammer or a weapon? Perhaps his death had been an accident?

Mayhap Miss Jessica had changed her mind about intimacy? She had obviously invited Bernard into her house and room; but she could have asked him to stop. He would not have stopped. He would have tried to force her, willing or unwilling; causing the bruises on her face. He had not given her the Queen Anne's lace, or she had not taken it. Tiffany's mind spun. If Miss Jessica pushed him away from her while he was standing near the bed, he could have tripped over the rug and his head might have hit the fireplace. He would have bled out within minutes and the young girl would have had a body to deal with—with three coins in his pocket and the Queen Anne's lace.

Tiffany rifled through the remaining two trunks until she found a bright yellow gown with a ripped bodice. It was the same shade as the thread caught in Bernard's index fingernail. He must have snagged his nail when he tore the gown. Tiffany had been right; Miss Jessica had not given herself freely to Bernard Coram.

Jessica Day had four people who loved her. Mr. Day would have removed the body and her mother and sisters must have cleaned the room and moved the furniture. Her father took the body to his wagon and dropped it in front of Tiffany's house in the rain and the mud. There was no blood because Bernard had already bled out in this room.

His death had been caused in self-defense.

An accident.

It was a fairy tale turned in on itself: Little Red Riding Hood had slayed the Big Bad Wolf.

No one should hang for his death. Bernard Coram had not been murdered. If only Tiffany could get out of this room, she believed that she could convince Judge Faulkner and the jury not to find Mr. Day or his daughter guilty. Especially if Miss Anstey gave her own testimony of Bernard's history of violating women. Mr. Anstey would have to support his daughter's version of what happened. According to the legal system, it was the male and father who was the victim of a crime. Women were nothing to the law.

Tiffany rubbed the sleep from her eyes. She didn't have time to rest. She needed to find a way out of this room. Samir's life depended on it.

CHAPTER 37

Tiffany awoke with her cheek against the floor—luckily, not the floorboards stained with blood, although they were inches from her face. She rubbed the sleep from her eyes and shuffled to her feet, out from underneath the blankets she had taken from the bed. The fire was out, but at least her clothing was mostly dry. She shrugged off the borrowed nightdress and slung it over the bottom of the bed. Piece by piece, she put on her mud-stained apparel. Touching her hair, Tiffany took out the remaining hairpins and allowed it to fall past her shoulders. All she could do without a brush was braid it.

After tying a lace to the end of her braid, she went to the window. The sun was up and shining. She guessed the time to be between nine and ten o'clock in the morning. The trial might have already started, or it could begin at any moment. Yanking open the window, she leaned her head out to see if there were any villagers about. But the alley was empty. Glancing down, she remembered her assessment from the night before. It was too far to jump.

She went to the door and knocked loudly. "Let me out! Please. Let me out!"

Pausing, she leaned her ear against the wood of the door. Either no one was home, or they were ignoring her. Tiffany grabbed her head and screamed in frustration. She finally knew the truth of what had happened to Bernard Coram. She could free Samir. They now had a fortune of over thirty thousand pounds! What a life they could live, and what a future they could offer their son together.

Tiffany bumped her head against the door. She felt like the character in the French fairy tale she'd told Beau. The ogre in the story was Mr. Day. Finette Cindron, or Cunning Cinders, would have asked her fairy godmother for help, but there was no such thing in real life. There was no ball of thread that would lead her out of this mess. There was no magical chest that produced new dresses for each ball.

But there was a chest in the room. Three of them. One trunk for each sister.

None of them contained red velvet slippers embroidered in pearls, but they had linens for each sister's dowry. Threads. Tiffany could tie them together to make a rope. She could secure it to the bed and climb out the window and down to the cobblestone ground. If she held on tight, she would be safe.

Taking a deep breath, Tiffany opened the chest and began to tie together the sheets. She took and used the linens from all three chests. She wrapped the end around the bedpost three times, then lowered the rest out of the window. The sheets were long enough to touch the cobblestone road. She dropped the yellow dress with the torn bodice and watched it flutter to the ground. Exhaling, Tiffany said a quick prayer before grabbing hold of the sheet-rope with one hand and using the other to help her climb backward through the window. When both of her feet were flailing in the air, Tiffany let go of the window ledge and grasped the sheet. She'd planned to climb down, but her arms would not hold her. Her fingers slipped down over the first knot . . . the second . . . the third . . . the fourth—until her stocking feet hit the hard stones of the pavement.

She gasped in pain, but she could not dally.

Unlike Cunning Cinders, she did not even have one red velvet slipper. Although one had been lost and found by a handsome prince. Tiffany's boots must have still been in the kitchen of the house, and she dared not go back for them in case Mr. or Mrs. Day was still there. Wincing, she picked up the gown and hobbled over the cobblestone alleyway and out to the front of the street. The Middlesex sessions house was over a block away. Tiffany gritted her teeth and carefully stepped on the bigger stones so that the pain would be less.

By the time she reached the doors of the sessions house, no one would have ever thought her a fairy-tale princess. She had no shoes. Her clothes were liberally splattered with dry mud, and her hair was falling out of the braid. Still, she opened the door and saw that the room was as full as it had been for Thomas's trial. Men, women, and even children. Thomas had been right. It was as if the trial and expected hanging had been set for their entertainment.

Samir was sitting on the front row of the room with Thomas, Mr. Sanger, and Mr. Giffin. Judge Faulkner sat behind his table, and the jury were discussing something among themselves. She concluded that the trial must already be over and they were deciding the verdict.

"Stop!" Tiffany called.

Clasping her side against the pain, she ran into the room and down the center aisle. "Please, stop! I know who truly killed Mr. Bernard Coram, and I have proof."

Judge Faulkner hit his gavel on the table. "Quiet, woman. You do not have permission to speak in my court."

"But I can prove Mr. Lathrop's innocence."

The judge hammered his gavel five times in a row. "Take her out of my courtroom."

Mr. Nix and Mr. Hadfield came toward her, as if to grab her arms. Tiffany moved closer to the jury.

"Please. You must listen to the truth."

Clack. Clack. Clack.

Tiffany turned. The sound had not come from the gavel, but from the Duchess of Beaufort's cane. Catharine was standing up, and every eye in the room was on her. She was in another sumptuously ornate gown of purple silk and an impressive white wig with matching violet ribbons.

"As the acting Lord Lieutenant of the area," she said, "in the place of my son, the Duke of Beaufort, who is a minor, I demand that Your Honor listen to Miss Woodall's evidence. I am sure that your highest aim, Judge Faulkner, is that justice be done. If there is new evidence in the case, it should be heard and evaluated thoroughly."

The room was quiet.

Tiffany turned to look at the villagers of Mapledown, gazing from face to face. They would not meet her eyes.

Then Mr. Wesley, the shop clerk, stood up. "The duchess done seen that all Sir Walter's debts were paid. Including his to me. If she wants me to listen to Miss Woodall's testimony, then I am willing to do so."

A few rows behind him, the wine seller also got to his feet. "Aye. Mr. Lathrop's been a fine constable and not paid so much as a farthing. Leastwise we can do in gratitude is listen to his defense."

One by one the other tradesmen to whom Catharine had promised payment stood and pledged their support. Four of them were members of the jury.

Judge Faulkner pounded his ever-ready gavel three more times. "Very well, Your Grace. Miss Woodall, you may speak."

Tiffany's hand slipped to her hot neck. She felt more nervous than she had when she was on trial. Then she saw Mr. Day and his family sitting in the back. On the other side of the room were the Ansteys; father, mother, daughter, and grandson. Sitting in front of them were Mr. and Mrs. Ford, Evie, and Mr. Tate.

Taking a deep breath, she began. "I am sorry that I do not know what has already been said. I would have arrived sooner, but I was locked in a room on the first floor."

Gasps and whistles followed her pronouncement.

"And who locked you in a room, Miss Woodall?"

Tiffany swallowed. "Mr. Day, Your Honor. I found the blood from the murder scene in his daughters' bedchamber."

The crowd began to murmur.

"Quiet!" the judge yelled, hitting his gavel to the table again. "Are you accusing Mr. Day of murdering Mr. Bernard Coram?"

She shook her head. "No, Your Honor. I am accusing him of moving the body to destroy the evidence. Mr. Bernard Coram was not murdered. He died from an accident."

"What accident, pray?"

"As I am sure Doctor Hudson has already told the jury and Your Honor, Mr. Bernard Coram's body was found in front of my cottage, but there was not any blood near it. Mr. Coram had a black eye, four scratches on his cheek, a bite mark on his thumb, a yellow thread stuck in the nail of his index finger, and a bash on the back of his head. In his pocket were three pennies and a packet of Queen Anne's lace—a common herb used to prevent pregnancies."

"Indecent!" a man yelled, shaking his fist at Tiffany.

She took another breath. "Since there was still money on him, the constable did not believe that the death was caused by a thief. And it was not. Mr. Coram did indeed threaten to blackmail Mr. Lathrop, but Mr. Lathrop did not attack his brother-in-law. Mr. Coram went to the Black Cauldon, where he drank too much and offended a young woman, Miss Anstey. She scratched his face and he called her a straw damsel. Mr. Hadfield took exception to his comments, and they got into a fight. Mr. Day threw both men out of the taproom.

"Mr. Bernard Coram was in dire need of funds, so he went to his mother's house. Mrs. Ludmilla Ford was married by auction to Mr. Ford. She is the natural mother of Mr. Bernard Coram. He demanded money, but she did not have any to give to him. He tried to strangle her and she bit his thumb. Her teeth marks will match the corpse. Her son might have succeeded, if his sister, Evie Lathrop, had not been there. She was able to force her brother out of the door. By this time, Mr. Hadfield had reached his farm on foot and decided to go back on his horse to confront Mr. Coram. When he arrived at the farm, Mr. Coram was not there. Mr. Hadfield waited for nearly two hours.

"Meanwhile, Mr. Coram went down the opposite road. He had no intention of going home yet. He met Miss Jessica Day, who let him inside of her cottage and up to the room that she shared with her two sisters. All of whom were still at the public house. I believe Miss Day changed her mind about intimacy, but Mr. Coram tried to force himself on her. She pushed him away as he tore at her dress, stumbling over the rug and hitting the back of his head on the fireplace."

Tiffany held up the ripped bodice of the bright yellow dress. "Mr. Coram's death was an accident. He was a ravisher and got what he deserved."

Farmer Coram stood up and pointed at her. "My son never forced no woman."

Tiffany's eyes turned to the Ansteys; she hoped that Caro would give her testimony. But the younger woman's eyes were focused on her lap.

Her father, Mr. Anstey, stood up. "Bernard Coram violently ravished my daughter and got her with child. This lad is not my son, but my grandson. If Bernard were still alive, I hope he'd have hung for what he done to my sweet and innocent girl."

Mr. Day got to his feet and walked to the front of the room, near to where Tiffany stood. Her pulse raged in her veins like thunder. He was such a large, muscular man, even if he was shorter than herself.

"If ye want to hang someone for Mr. Bernard Coram's murder, ye can hang me," he said. "I might not have killed him, but I wish I had. He had no right hitting my daughter or trying to force himself on her."

Judge Faulkner's nostrils flared. "Are you confessing to murder?"

"He's confessing to moving the body from the crime scene and protecting his family," Tiffany intervened. "Mr. Hadfield heard Mr. Day driving his wagon that night. Even though it was dark and in the rain. There was no murder, Your Honor. Only a young woman defending herself."

The crowd jeered and Farmer Coram sat back down on the bench.

Bang. Bang. Bang.

Judge Faulkner wielded his gavel again. "Mr. Hadfield, can you corroborate Miss Woodall's story?"

Mr. Hadfield was still standing on her side. He nodded his head. "Yes, Your Honor. I heard the sounds of someone driving a wagon near midnight."

"Is Mrs. Ford in attendance?" the judge asked.

Tiffany watched both Mr. Ford and Mrs. Ford stand up. Despite his limp, the butler held his wife's good hand and walked with her to the front of the room.

"Mrs. Ford, did you or did you not bite Mr. Coram, your son?"

She whimpered. "I did not know what else to do. He was choking me. Bernard was so angry that I wouldn't give him money, and the drink had made him violent."

Farmer Coram got back to his feet and rushed toward her. "Useless whore."

But before his fists reached Mrs. Ford, Mr. Ford swung his cane and hit Farmer Coram in the neck. The blow caused the man to fall back to the floor. Before Farmer Coram could get back to his feet, Mr. Hadfield and Mr. Phelps grabbed his arms to restrain him.

Judge Faulkner stood up and pointed to the door. "Remove Mr. Coram, Senior, from this courtroom. Let him cool his heels and his temper in the prison until the constable decides to release him."

Farmer Coram did not go quietly. He struggled against their hold and spit at Tiffany's stocking feet. "Spinster slut!"

Samir ran to stand between Tiffany and Farmer Coram. "Do not say another word, or I won't release you until the next assizes in six months."

Grimacing, Farmer Coram closed his mouth and was dragged from the room.

Samir turned and touched Tiffany's cheek. "Are you alright?"

Before Tiffany could answer, Judge Faulkner was hammering his gavel. "Mr. Lathrop, as the accused, you are not to speak during your trial. Back to your seat."

Tiffany nodded for him to obey, and Samir returned to the bench.

"Doctor Hudson," Judge Faulkner said, pointing his gavel at the young man, "does your examination match Miss Woodall's descriptions? Are you convinced of the truth of her words?"

The young man stood up on the jury's stand. "Yes, Your Honor. But I believe that myself and my fellow jurors should go and examine the Days' bedchamber."

The judge nodded his head, his wig moving slightly forward and back. "Myself and the jurors will accompany Mr. Day to his home. The rest of you may remain here until we return."

As usual, the women were told to stay behind. Tiffany saw Catharine poke Mr. Sanger in the back with her cane and gesture for him to follow. Mr. Giffin also shuffled to his feet and trailed behind Judge Faulkner and the jury members, like they were a parade going through town.

Thomas sprang up and went to meet her. "Good heavens, Tiffany. I had no idea that you were being held captive. Mary said you'd gone home. I should have stopped by your cottage and made sure you were alright."

Tiffany shook her head. "You had no reason not to believe Mary. I do not hold you at all accountable for last night's adventure. And in the end, perhaps it was for the best that I stayed the night, or I wouldn't have realized what had truly happened. I was certain that it was Mr. Day who had killed Bernard Coram. He seemed so much more likely with his size and strength."

She was then swept into the arms of a man who had both size and strength. Tiffany closed her eyes and held tightly to Samir. For the first time in a fortnight, there were no bars between them. No secrets.

Only love.

CHAPTER 38

"I knew there were something going on betwixt ye and m'husband," Evie said from behind them.

Tiffany and Samir broke apart. She could see a gentle flush in Samir's cheeks and knew that her own face had gone fiery.

Evie Lathrop tugged Mr. Tate beside her. "M'mother said that ye are taking care of the babe, Miss Woodall, and if ye are prepared to do that, then I shall let Sam sell me to Mr. Tate at the fair. Then ye two can get married proper-like. Ain't that right, Mr. Tate?"

The burly blacksmith seemed rather cowed by Evie, and he nodded. Tiffany was not certain that Mr. Tate was as thrilled by this arrangement as herself, but she was not about to look a gift horse in the mouth.

"When is the next fair?" Tiffany said, hoping it was soon.

Evie shrugged her shoulders. "May Day, I suppose. Mr. Tate and myself can come back then."

Clack. Clack. Clack.

Catharine came toward them and Mr. Tate and Evie broke apart to make way for her. Tiffany thought even the Queen of England would have moved.

"Mrs. Lathrop, go and fetch your mother and her husband."

Tiffany gasped at the duchess's audacity, but Evie merely nodded and turned back into the crowd to go and get them.

"Mr. Tate," Catharine said in her commanding voice. "Have you sufficient coins to purchase a wife?"

The blacksmith bowed his head, his beard nearly hitting his knees. "Two shillings, Your Grace."

The duchess shook her head. "Thomas, give the man ten guineas. Five to keep and five to pay for his bride with. A new wife should know she was worth a great deal of money. You would not want your wife to think she was purchased cheaply."

Mr. Tate nodded, apparently unable to speak.

Thomas pulled out a coin purse and counted ten gold guineas into the blacksmith's rough palm. "There you are, sir."

"I broughts them, Yer Grace," Evie said.

Mr. Ford executed a perfect bow, and Mrs. Ford curtsied.

"Ah, Mrs. Ford, you may safely remain in my company," Catharine said. "Ford, I require you to return to Astwell Palace in my carriage and bring back all of the servants and all the food that Bonne has prepared in the pantry and the larder. In the place of a hanging today, we shall have a fair. Request Wheatley and the maids to bring ribbons and whatnots. Beau and Drummond can be in charge of the games. I would suggest rounders and possibly quoits."

The butler bowed again. "Yes, Your Grace."

Catharine waved at him. "Off you go, Ford. Now, Thomas, I need you to go and speak to Mrs. Day and to the wine seller. I will pay for beer and wine for everyone in town for our fair today."

Thomas cleared his throat. "Perhaps Mrs. Day is already overwhelmed, Mother. Her daughter killed a man, and her husband tried to hide it."

"I do not doubt that she is. But nothing could help her custom or her place in the community more than free drinks for a day—especially when I am paying. I am sure it would be a boon to her, and not a burden."

Thomas glanced at the women in the Day family. Tiffany could see all four women clearly because everyone had scooted away from them on the benches, as if they were plagued instead of victims of an unfortunate circumstance and an evil young man.

He bowed to his mother. "Very well."

Evie smiled. "Wouldn't mind a pint or two meself."

"To celebrate the end of one marriage and the beginning of another," Catharine reminded. "But first, you must allow Mr. Lathrop to auction you to Mr. Tate."

Evie clapped the blacksmith on the back. "Aye."

Mr. Tate winced.

Tiffany felt her lips twitching into a smile.

Samir bowed his head to both Evie and Mr. Tate. "I wish you both all the happiness in the world."

Evie grinned. "We will be happy enough, I'm sure."

The blacksmith tugged at his black beard. He appeared decidedly less sure.

Thomas came back to the group. "Mrs. Day will open the Black Cauldron once the trial is over, Mother. And I saw Mr. Sanger and Mr. Griffin through the window. I believe we should all return to our seats."

The duchess gave him a regal nod and took Mrs. Ford's good arm and led her back to the bench. The second Mrs. Coram would not dare approach her when she was next to a duchess. Evie took Mr. Tate's hand and yanked him toward her. Even Thomas returned to his seat on the first row, leaving

Tiffany and Samir alone but surrounded by a courtroom of people.

"I cannot thank you enough, Tiffany."

Samir did not touch her, but she felt the warmth from his eyes.

Tiffany shook her head. "There is no need for any thanks. I would do anything for you. Samir—you are my entire world. My life story didn't begin until I met you."

"And you are the happily ever after that I no longer believed was possible for me."

She longed to touch him, but she knew it would be unseemly to do so in public. He was on trial for murder and married to another lady in the crowd—small details that Tiffany hoped would be cleared up by the end of the day.

Out of the corner of her eye, she saw Judge Faulkner leading the procession back into the Middlesex sessions room. Samir briefly touched her shoulder and took his seat next to Thomas. Tiffany, still in her stocking feet, without shoes, did not know where she was supposed to go. She had no seat, and the room was already full. Clasping her hands together, she stood awkwardly to the side as the judge and jury members returned to the front of the room. Mr. Sanger and Mr. Giffin sat beside Samir and Thomas. All of the twelve jurors took their place on the dais.

Judge Faulkner did not sit down, but stood behind the table. He picked up his favorite gavel and hit it three times.

"Mr. Samir Lathrop, bookseller and constable, you are found not guilty of the horrid crime of murdering Mr. Bernard Coram on March thirtieth, 1785. Mr. Bernard Coram's death has been ruled an accident, and no criminal charges will be levied against Miss Jessica Day. Nor for Mr. Frank Day for removing the body from the premises. The prosecution witnesses were Mrs. Ludmilla Ford, Doctor Hezekiah Hudson, Mr. Coram Senior, Mr. Lawrence Hadfield, Mr. Lucas Anstey, and Miss Tiffany Woodall. This assizes court session is dismissed."

A few people clapped, but most of the crowd appeared disappointed by the verdict. There were hisses and grumbling. There would be no hanging on the scaffold today. No body rotting at the crossroads in the gibbet.

Catharine stood up and hit her cane against the ground. "Good folks of Mapledown and Your Honor, it is my pleasure to announce that the new justice of the peace is Mr. Thomas Montague. He will be taking up residence at Maplehurst House. To celebrate this appointment, I mean to host a fair in the village square. All drinks and food will be paid for by myself. Please enjoy Mr. and Mrs. Day's custom at their public house and toast our new justice."

Her announcement was met with a standing ovation from the townsfolk in the back of the room. The sounds of clapping and cheers filled the court chambers.

CHAPTER 39

Shoeless, Tiffany clung to Samir as they walked from the sessions house to the town square. She could hardly believe her eyes. Mr. Ford and Mrs. Wheatley, the housekeeper, had worked a miracle. There were tables with foodstuffs. A maypole with ribbons. A makeshift instrument choir, consisting of six individuals and their fiddles, playing a lively jig. Beau and Miss Drummond had set up quoits and were currently playing a game of rounders with the other children from the village and Mrs. Able's son, Peter. Tiffany was quite surprised to see Miss Drummond swinging the bat. She was clearly a natural sportswoman.

Arm in arm, they watched the villagers swarm the food tables. Mr. Hadfield took Miss Anstey's arm, and they began to dance. They were followed by several other young couples and a few couples not so young.

"I am ready to be sold," Evie said from behind them.

Samir pressed a kiss to Tiffany's palm and then released it. "Where should I do the auction?"

Evie pointed to the wooden platform with the rope noose. "Everyone will be able to see me from there. Come, Mr. Tate—we's about to make our relationship legal-like."

Tugging the blacksmith, Evie pushed through the crowd to the scaffolding and scurried up the steps.

Samir followed behind her. He waited for the fiddlers to finish playing their song before he spoke. "May I have your attention, good people of Mapledown."

One by one, every eye turned to watch Samir and Evie on the hangman's platform. He pulled at his collar and appeared uncomfortable at all the people watching him. Evie, however, beamed at the attention. Clearly, she didn't mind being auctioned. She kept waving to different people in the crowd and smiling.

Samir gestured toward Evie. "Some of you may know my wife, Evie Lathrop."

She waved enthusiastically to the crowd.

He swallowed. "She and I have not been man and wife in nearly a decade. So today, I am auctioning my wife to the man she wishes to be married to. Mr. Tate, would you start the bidding?"

The blacksmith pulled at his beard with both of his hands. Tiffany had only heard the man speak once all day, and she feared he might lose his nerve now, with all the crowd watching.

Mr. Tate took off his hat. "I bid five guineas, although I knows my Evie is priceless."

Before Samir could speak, Judge Phineas Faulkner had joined them on the scaffolding. "Do I have any other bids on Mrs. Evie Lathrop?"

The crowd was silent.

Judge Faulkner hit his gavel against the wood (he must take it with him everywhere). "Mrs. Evie Lathrop has been sold to Mr. Tate. She will now be known as his legal wife and by the name Evie Tate."

His pronouncement was met with cheers. Mr. Tate held out the five guineas to Samir. He took them with a "Thank you."

Evie grabbed the lapels of Judge Faulkner's robes and kissed his cheeks. "Ye're a right one after all, Your Honor."

Then she kissed both of Samir's cheeks and nearly jumped off the wooden platform into her blacksmith's arms. She gave Mr. Tate a great smack of a kiss right on his lips in front of the crowd. Her enthusiasm warranted even more cheers from the villagers gathered around.

Samir pointed to the fiddlers, and they began playing another jig.

Evie pulled Mr. Tate to the center of the square to dance. "'Tis my wedding day afters all!"

Tiffany watched as the judge held out his hand to Samir. She waited with bated breath until Samir extended his own hand to shake it.

"The law should be without bias, Mr. Lathrop," he said. "From this day on, I will no longer assume a man's guilt and the color of his skin are the same thing. I hope you can forgive me, Constable."

Samir's jaw clenched, but he nodded. "I shall see you in six months for the next assizes, Your Honor."

Judge Faulkner dropped his hand, and one side of his mouth came up into what might have been a smile. "Try not to have any murders in Mapledown in the meantime, Constable Lathrop."

"I'll do my best."

They walked off the wooden platform together, side by side, for the first time as equals. Tiffany waited at the bottom, her hands held out to Samir. He took them into his own warm ones and pulled her against him into a tight embrace.

"You seem to have lost your boots, Miss Goody Two-Shoes."

He had read Mr. John Newberry's story! But Miss Goody had only one shoe. Tiffany kissed his cheek and whispered in his ear. "Even without two shoes, I still get to marry the rich widower or, rather, the previously married man."

He leaned his head back so that he could look her in the eyes. "Am I rich?"

Tiffany grinned. "I saw the contents of your desk. I should say you had a fortune! And that was before I sold your mortgage to the Duchess of Beaufort for thirty thousand pounds."

His brown eyes widened, and his jaw went slack. "That's three times what the note was worth."

She shrugged her shoulders, still smiling. "It is and it isn't. Catharine managed to purchase the house on the demesne with that mortgage. But now we have plenty of money to expand my cottage and our family. Shall we go and ask Mr. Shirley to read the wedding banns on Sunday?"

Samir shook his head. "Your new friend, the duchess, has already informed me and her solicitor that a special license is required, and he means to return within the week with one."

Grinning, Tiffany said, "It cannot be soon enough for me."

"Nor me," he said, brushing his lips gently against hers. "Will you dance with me, Tiffany?"

"I thought you'd never ask."

Taking her hand, he led her through the crowd to where the dancers were forming their sets. They bowed and he took her in his arms. Tiffany danced until there were holes in her stockings.

★ ★ ★

The sun was beginning to set, but the crowds continued to celebrate. Tiffany was about to ask Samir to walk her home, when Mary and Miss Jessica Day came toward them. Mary was carrying Tiffany's boots from the night before. They were freshly shined, and not a speck of mud could be seen on them. She set them on the ground in front of Tiffany.

Miss Jessica curtsied. "I owes both ye and Mr. Lathrop an impossible debt. If there is anything I can say or do to repay ye, I will."

Tiffany glanced at Samir.

He shook his head. "Miss Jessica, I am sorry that you were assaulted. As the constable and as a friend of your family, I can assure you that there will be no further unpleasantness caused by this accident."

Tiffany felt slightly less forgiving. The Days had locked her up in a room and would have let Samir take the blame for a murder he didn't commit. He'd spent a week in prison and had nearly been hung. She said nothing, for she was not sure if she'd ever fully forgive them.

Mary curtsied the way Tiffany had taught her, with her back straight, her head slightly lowered, and holding her gown out at the sides. "Miss Woodall, can ye forgive me? Will ye let me stay on?"

Despite being raised to be a Christian, Tiffany found that she could not. It was not simply that Mary had betrayed her, but it was her words about Samir's skin. She knew that he had faced prejudice his entire life, but he wouldn't in her home. *Their* home.

"I am sorry, Mary. I am a woman of my word and I will not break it. Even to forgive you."

Mary sniffed and rubbed at her eyes. "I can't go home, Miss Woodall. My Pa said never to come back."

Tiffany shook her head slowly. "I will not send you back home. I will help you find a new position or pay for your apprenticeship to a reputable milliner or modiste in Bath . . . I would also happily pay Miss Jessica's apprenticeship fees as well. Sometimes a young lady needs a new start."

Jessica lowered her head, staring at the cobblestone road. "I am not a lady, Miss Woodall."

Tiffany gently took Jessica's chin and tipped her head up. "You are a lady. Nothing that is done to you can take that away. Nor can a few poor choices of your own. Your worth as a woman does not change."

Tears fell from the young woman's eyes, and Tiffany released her hold.

Mary put her arm around Jessica. "I should like to be a milliner. Mayhap we can open our own shop in Mapledown in a few years after we've learned the trade. Imagine us as shop-keepers with our very own store."

Wiping at her eyes, Jessica smiled. "I have always been fond of remaking bonnets."

"I shall write at once to the milliners in Bath and see if they have openings for two apprenticeships."

Mary sniffed again, rubbing her nose with the back of her free hand. "I'll come and fetch m'things."

"Ye can stay at my house until it's time to go to Bath," Jessica said. "Papa can take us in his wagon."

Her former maid recovered quickly and giggled. "No one in my family's ever been to Bath."

Jessica wiped once more at her eyes, smiling. "Me neither. My mum says it's a very fashionable place."

Mary offered Jessica her elbow and said with exaggerated formality, "Allow me to escort ye, my fine lady."

Her friend intertwined her arm with Mary's, and they walked together toward the fair, where the musicians were playing and the villagers were still dancing and drinking.

Tiffany stooped down to put on her boots. She tied the laces slowly and stood back up, her eyes watery. "Am I a terrible person for not forgiving Mary? Miss Jessica did you a much greater wrong, and you frankly forgave her."

Samir pulled her into his arms. Tiffany rested her weary head on his broad shoulder.

"Forgiveness doesn't mean that you have to keep that person in your life or home," he whispered. "And forgiveness doesn't mean you allow them to hurt you again and again. True forgiveness is giving them an opportunity to change and grow, exactly what you offered both Mary Jones and Jessica Day."

Samir held her and they swayed gently together to the music. In each other's arms at last.

CHAPTER 40

Mrs. Able helped Tiffany dress for her wedding. She and her son, along with Nat, had moved into Bristle Cottage a week before. That same day, Mr. Day brought a rocking chair, but did not say a word. He simply placed it by her front door. Tiffany assumed gifting it to her was the Day family's way of making amends.

Yesterday, Mr. and Mrs. Anstey brought over a crib. The wood smelled fresh and newly cut. Mr. Anstey must have barely finished it. The coffin maker was clearly a talented woodworker. The crib was a work of art. The spindles looked like carved vines. And dear Nat would no longer need to sleep inside a drawer.

Tiffany's wedding dress was silk, a soft blue color with delicately painted flowers. The neckline was rather low, and Tiffany tucked a lace fichu around her collar. White lace adorned her quarter-length sleeves with matching ribbons.

Mrs. Able twined more white ribbon through Tiffany's barrel-like curls. She lifted the veil over Tiffany's face. "You look very fine, Miss Woodall. As pretty as a bride half your age."

Tiffany smiled and thanked her. She knew that she was old to be a bride and a new mother. But she believed in her Lord and trusted in his timing. And although she had forty years in her dish, she had earned each and every one of them. She had learned and grown and become the person she was today. A person that Samir could love. A mother to Nat. A friend to Thomas, Catharine, and Tess. A librarian to Beau.

No. She did not regret that she wasn't a blushing bride of seventeen or eighteen; or the life she might have known with Nathaniel Occom. Everything in her life had led her here. To this very moment.

"Thank you for your help, Mrs. Able," Tiffany said. "Dressing me is not one of your duties."

Mrs. Able bowed her head. "I know it isn't, Miss Woodall. But I was wondering . . . thinking perhaps that you might consider taking me on as your housekeeper after I'm done wet-nursing young Nat. I respect both you and Mr. Lathrop, and I should be glad for my son to have a steady home and not be moved every time I find a new client to nurse."

As a single, unmarried woman, Tiffany had had very few options when her half brother died. She had been willing to take his place rather than lose her home. She thought that Mrs. Able, as a widow with a child, had even fewer options than she had.

Tiffany held out her hand. "I should be pleased to hire you as our housekeeper, Mrs. Able, and I beg that you consider our home as your own for you and your son."

Mrs. Able smiled, reaching out her own shaking hand. "Thank you, Miss Woodall."

Together they walked carefully down the narrow stairs. Thomas was waiting for them at the bottom, in her front parlor. Since she had no father or half brother to give her away, as her friend he would fill that position.

"You look radiant, Tiffany," he said as he offered her his arm.

Grinning, she took it, and they walked to the carriage, where he passed her in and then waited for Mrs. Able to fetch Peter and Nat. Thomas helped all three of them inside the carriage, and they rode to Astwell Palace.

Catharine had planned for the wedding to take place in her ballroom, for she thought requesting Mr. Shirley to officiate the proceedings would have cast a damper on the entire affair. Tiffany couldn't have agreed with her more. But she had been surprised when Catharine invited Tiffany's old school friend Tess, the Duchess of Surrey, and her son, Lord Theophilus, who had recently taken orders, to officiate. She'd thought that Catharine hated Tess for having had an affair with her late husband.

When Tiffany asked her why, Catharine merely shrugged and said, "She is the only person who has responded to my letters, and I realized that I missed her as a friend. And since we both are being given the cold shoulder by the beau monde, we might as well endure it together."

It was Tess who had brought Tiffany the new dress for her wedding. Such a fine gown would have cost Tiffany a year's worth of wages.

The journey to Astwell Palace in a carriage was a short one. Tiffany's pulse was racing and her stomach churning. Not from fear, but anticipation. She could barely wait for Thomas to offer to help her out of the carriage. Impatiently, she stood until Mrs. Able, Nat, and her son left the vehicle. Tiffany wanted to pick up her son and carry him into the wedding, but she'd already been reminded three times by Catharine that a bride should not be carrying a baby.

Thomas offered Tiffany his arm again, and they slowly promenaded to the front entrance of the palace. Mr. Ford opened the door with all of his usual stateliness. They continued on to the ballroom, a place that Tiffany had only ever had a peek at before. Two footmen opened the double doors for them, and the large, austerely marble room was unrecognizable. If Tiffany hadn't known better, she would have thought that they were in a garden, there were so many fresh flowers. Catharine probably didn't have even one bud left in her greenhouse. Chairs had been set up in tidy rows, and in the front of the room, near the two pairs of French doors that led to the real gardens, was a wedding arch covered in white ribbons and flowers.

Samir stood underneath the arch and looked handsomer than ever in a new blue silk suit embroidered with silver thread, and matching shoes. His dark curly hair was pulled back into a low ponytail, but a few black curls escaped it and framed his strong jaw and handsome face. He took her breath away. He was like a prince in one of Comtesse D'Aulnoy's fairy tales. Yet, he was real, flesh and blood. And soon to be hers!

Mrs. Able and the two boys took chairs on the last row. Again, Tiffany was surprised to see so many people there, including her old school friend, Tess, a duchess, with only a row separating her from the housekeeper, Mrs. Wheatley; and Mr. Ford's wife, Ludmilla. Tiffany saw all the maids, footmen, and gardeners, spruced up in their Sunday best. It was a beautiful and humbling sight.

Catharine was standing, directing a footman to move a pedestal with a plant closer to the aisle. She was dressed in a silk sack gown the color of champagne, with flowing elbow-length lace sleeves, a square hoop, and the highest heeled shoes Tiffany had ever seen. Her eyes went up into her eyebrows when she saw them. She signaled to the local instrument choir to start their music. The first notes of the string instruments were sharp and sour, but soon they all harmoniously played her favorite hymn, "Amazing Grace." Then she hurried to the front row and took a seat next to Tess, who was also wearing a resplendent emerald-green silk gown more fitted for court than a country wedding.

Thomas patted Tiffany's hand on his arm. "Ready?"

She couldn't help but wish that her mother were there. She had died at a younger age than Tiffany was now. Sadly, she did not regret the absence of her father or her half brother. Both men were narrow-minded and would never have been able to see Samir's worth past the brown of his skin. Nor would they have forgiven Tiffany her mistakes and frailties, as Thomas had. Truly, there was no better person to escort her than a friend who would have given up everything to help her.

Nodding her head, Tiffany said, "Yes."

The audience stood for their wedding march. Tiffany smiled as she saw Mary sitting next to her elder sister Emily. Perhaps people could change. Slowly and often painfully, but change came.

Thomas gave Tiffany's hand to Samir, and Tiffany could not stop herself from smiling so widely at him that her cheeks hurt. Standing in front of them was Lord Theophilus, minister and soon-to-be missionary, holding a little black book. His expression was serious, but his countenance was overall pleasing. Tiffany could see Tess in the bright blue eyes of her son and in the dark color of his natural hair.

The musician's played their final note, and Lord Theophilus cleared his throat. "God is love, and those who live in love live in God, and God lives in them."

The young man's marriage sermon was short and focused entirely on God's love; Tiffany thought that the elderly Mr. Shirley could have taken a leaf from the young minister's book.

"In the presence of God, Father, Son, and Holy Spirit," Lord Theophilus said in a clear, loud voice, "we have come together to witness the marriage of Samir Lathrop and Tiffany Woodall, to pray for God's blessing on them, to share their joy, and to celebrate their love."

Samir sniffed and Tiffany saw a tear trickle down his cheek. He gave her a yearning look, and Tiffany knew that his tears were those of joy, not sadness. He was trying desperately to keep his emotions in check, but Tiffany did not bother trying. She smiled through her tears and said, "I will."

Lord Theophilus closed the little book he was holding. "You may now say your vows to one another."

Samir squeezed her hands. "I, Samir Lathrop, take thee, Tiffany Woodall, to be my wife, to have and to hold from this day forward; for better or worse, for richer or poorer, in sickness and in health, to love and to cherish, till death us do part, according to God's holy law. In the presence of God, I make this vow."

Tiffany repeated the same vow, each word a promise of the future they would have together.

Thomas gave Samir the diamond cluster ring. Samir had offered to buy her a new one, but this ring was a tie to everything she was and everything she hoped to become.

He slid it onto the fourth finger of her left hand. "With my body I honor thee, all that I am I give to thee, and all that I have I share with thee . . ."

These words may have been spoken thousands of times before at other weddings, but to Tiffany, they seemed new and full of hope. She slid a gold band onto Samir's finger and felt a thrill at seeing a symbol that he belonged to her now. And for forever.

The rest of the ceremony passed in a daze of light, happiness, and God's love. Lord Theophilus said his final prayer.

Mary stood up and called out, "Aren't ye going to kiss her?"

Tiffany couldn't help but grin, and she heard the audience laugh. Samir lifted the veil from her face and gently brushed his lips over hers before pulling her tightly into his arms and kissing her so deeply that she felt it all the way down to her toes.

When they at last broke apart, the musicians began to play a jig, and Samir took Tiffany's arm and led her back down the aisle. Beau had a basket full of petals, and he threw them directly into her face. Tiffany tossed back her head and laughed. Her favorite young charge would always be more of a pirate than a duke.

EPILOGUE

The afternoon of January 27, 1786, should have been cold, but it was not. Tiffany wiped the sweat from her brow with a handkerchief, but she still felt as if she were on fire.

"Push harder, Tiffany. I haven't got all day," Catharine said.

"Now, now, Your Grace," Mrs. Balogh said, squeezing out the water from a cloth and passing it over to Tiffany to put on her face. "The babe will come when it's ready."

The duchess sighed. "But I am ready now."

"As am I," Tess agreed, sitting in the chair next to her. "I'd quite forgotten how long it takes for a baby to be born. We should have come in the evening after dinner."

Tiffany rather wished that they had. Her two dearest female friends were excellent company in their own palaces, but they rather overwhelmed her small cottage. Catharine had Thomas bring in two chairs from the parlor to her bedchamber, so that she and Tess could watch the birthing like two queens' enjoying a play at court.

Catharine fanned herself. "I hope it is a girl."

"I always wanted a girl," Tess agreed. "Perhaps we should have your footmen bring us some tea?"

The pain began again, and it was so intense that it took Tiffany's breath away. Her entire body tensed and contracted. Squeezing her eyes closed, Tiffany groaned and then screamed out in agony. Then she felt each of her hands being held. She opened her eyes to see Catharine on one side and Tess on the other. They were here for her when she needed them most.

"Now, bear down with all that you have in you, Mrs. Lathrop," Mrs. Balogh said from the bottom of the bed.

Tiffany yelled again as she willed every part of her body to move her child out of the birth canal.

Mrs. Balogh smiled. "The babe is crowning. I can see its head. You must push even harder."

Tightening her hold on her friends' hands, Tiffany gasped as she spent the last of her energy pushing out her baby.

"I see the head. So much dark hair!" Tess said.

Catharine leaned her own head toward the bottom of the bed. "I see the shoulders. Ah! It is a girl! Well done, Tiffany."

A girl.

A daughter.

Tiffany smiled and wiped away the tears from her eyes as she heard her baby cry. Its first sounds in the world. Mrs. Balogh wrapped the babe in a linen cloth and presented the still bloody baby to her. Tiffany's arms brought her sweet daughter closer to her face, and she pressed kisses onto the dark curly hair. There was so much of it! Her face was round and babyish, but Tiffany could see that their daughter had inherited Samir's widely set eyes. She was perfect.

Mrs. Balogh shooed the two duchesses out of the room, so she could deliver the afterbirth and clean both Tiffany and her baby. Tiffany was grateful to feed her daughter for the first time without an audience.

"I'll go and fetch, Mr. Lathrop," Mrs. Balogh said. "Best let him in first, or the duchesses won't give him a turn holding the baby despite him being undeniably the father."

Exhausted, Tiffany's lips still quirked up at the truth of the midwife's words. The door closed behind her, and less than a minute later Samir came into their room, holding Nat in his arms. Their son looked enormous next to his little sister. His round head was mostly bald, and he was furiously sucking on one of his chubby fists.

When he saw his mama, he tried to dive out of his father's arms. Tiffany held her daughter with one arm, but opened her other for her son. Samir carefully laid Nat on her shoulder and her son cuddled up to her. Holding both of her children, Tiffany felt complete in a way she had never been before.

Samir smiled, sitting on the edge of the bed so that he could see their baby's face. "A girl. Just what our family was lacking. Oh, Tiffany. She is beautiful."

Tiffany pressed another kiss on her daughter's forehead and then her son's. "She looks like her papa."

Her husband gently caressed their baby's hair. "I forgot how little they are in the beginning. Have you decided on a name? You'd best do so before Catharine or Tess come in and demand that you call our daughter after one of them. Or both."

She laughed, shaking her head. "I thought we could name her after our mothers, Priya Elizabeth Lathrop."

Samir pressed a kiss to Tiffany's brow and then their daughter's. "Her life would be easier as an Elizabeth, then a Priya."

"Perhaps. But I want her to be proud of her Indian heritage. Proud of our family and who she is. If we try to hide it, we will be telling her that it is something to be ashamed of."

Flipping his hair back, Samir grinned. "My mother would have been honored to have a child named after her."

Tiffany glanced up at her handsome husband with his shoulders back, a look of pride in his face. Her eyes moved next to her son and then her daughter; and for the first time, Tiffany believed in fairy tales and happily ever afters.

AUTHOR'S NOTE

John Newberry (1713–1767) is considered to be the father of children's literature. The Newberry Medal for excellence in children's fiction was named after him in 1922. His first book for children, *A Little Pretty Pocket-Book* (1744), was aimed at simply *entertaining* children instead of teaching a moral. A novel thought indeed! The book was also small, perfect for a child's hands. He wrote and/or published, *The History of Little Goody Two-Shoes* (1765), which created the phrase "goody two-shoes" for its pious heroine.

"Fairy tale" was a term coined by Marie-Catharine Le Jumel de Barneville, Baroness d'Aulnoy. Also known as Comtesse d'Aulnoy. She published in French many fairy tales including "Finette Cindron," or "Cunning Cinders" (1697). Charles Perrault's famous *Tales and Stories of the Past with Morals: Tales of My Mother Goose* was published that same year in French. It included the stories "Cinderella, or the Little Glass Slipper," "The Sleeping Beauty in the Wood," "Little Thumb," "The Master Cat, or Puss in Boots," "Riquet of the Tuft," "Blue Beard," "The Fairy," and "Little Red Riding Hood."

Not all stories have a fairy-tale ending. Divorce in eighteenth century England was rare, expensive, and obtained only through the Church of England or an act of parliament. It was unrealistic for someone of the lower classes to receive one. I first read about a "wife-auction" in Thomas Hardy's *The Mayor of Casterbridge*. Hardy explains that the sold wife, "was by no means the first or last peasant woman who had religiously adhered to her purchaser." Daniel Pool notes that between 1750–1850, "there were some 380 of these do-it-yourself divorces effected in rural England." Records note that the wife was led to the auction with a rope around her neck, like an animal.

At trials, the accused was not allowed to speak in their own defense until 1898. Daniel Pool explains that the accused could not see 'the written record of evidence' against themselves until 1839. Tiffany and Thomas had no idea what proof Sir Walter Abney had against Samir before the trial. In the eighteenth century, trials were swift and sentencing swifter. A hanging could draw crowds of thousands. The executions of a husband and wife, who were murderers, drew over thirty thousand people in 1849. Public executions did not end until 1868.

Thomas Montague's appointment as the justice of the peace is based on a real Black person in Georgian England, Nathaniel Wells. He purchased Piercefield House in Chepstow and was appointed justice of the peace in 1803. In 1818, he became the deputy lieutenant of Monmouthshire.

A special license allowed a couple to be married at any place and anytime; but it was expensive and required someone to have connections with an archbishop. Luckily Catharine, the Duchess of Beaufort, had both the means and the connections to give Samir and Tiffany their happily-ever-after wedding.

SELECTED BIBLIOGRAPHY

Boreman, Thomas. *Curiosities in the Tower of London about his Majesties animals in the Tower Zoo.* Second edition. London: Tho. Boreman, 1741.

Boreman, Thomas. *Gigantick Histories.* [volume the second. Which completes the history of Guildhall, London. With other curious matters]. London: Tho. Boreman, 1741.

Boreman, Thomas. *Three Hundred Animals.* [A Description of Three Hundred Animals; viz. beasts, birds, fishes, serpents, and insects. With a particular account of the whale-fishery. Extracted out of the best authors, and adapted to the use of all capacities . . . Illustrated with copper plates, etc.]. London: R. Ware, 1753.

Cooper, Mary. *Tommy Thumb's Pretty Song Book.* Volumes I and II. London: Mary Cooper, 1744.

D'Aulnoy, Comtesse. Marie-Catharine Le Jumel de Barneville. "Finette Cindron" ["Cunning Cinders"]. In *Les Contes des Fées.* Paris: 1697.

Newberry, John. *A Little Pretty Pocket-Book, intended for the Amusement of Little Master Tommy and Pretty Miss Polly with Two Letters from Jack the Giant Killer.* London: J. Newberry, 1744.

Newberry, John. *The History of Little Goody Two-Shoes; otherwise called, Mrs. Margery Two-Shoes. With the means by which she acquired her learning, etc.* London: J. Newberry, 1765.

Perrault, Charles. "Englished by G. M., Gent." *Histories, or Tales of Past Times, told by Mother Goose, with morals.* London: 1719. [French publication in 1697].

Pool, Daniel. *What Jane Austen Ate and Charles Dickens Knew.* New York: Touchstone, 1994.

Sambler, Robert. *The Original Mother Goose's Melody* [To which are added the "Fairy Tales of Mother Goose," first collected by Perrault]. London: John Newberry: 1760. [Sambler's original translation is 1729.]

Swift, Jonathan. *Gulliver's Travels, or Travels into Several Remote Nations of the World. In Four Parts. By Lemuel Gulliver, First a Surgeon, and then a Captain of Several Ships.* London: Benj. Mott, 1727.

ACKNOWLEDGMENTS

Dear reader, I hope you enjoyed this cozy murder mystery that is part romance and part fairy tale. I am so grateful for your support! Thank you for leaving reviews, sharing my books on social media, and telling your friends. Word-of-mouth advertising is the best! A special shout-out to the members of my street team, who helped promote my book. Thank you to all the book bloggers, book TikTokers, Bookstagrammers, and more. I am blessed to be a part of your library.

If this were a fairy tale, Faith Black Ross would be my fairy godmother. She is an incredible editor with wonderful insight. I am so grateful to the cover illustrator, Sarah Horgan. The cover is truly magical. A shout-out to Dulce Botello and the incredible marketing team that spread the word about my books, without a wand. And a special thanks to Rebecca Nelson and Thai Fantauzzi Perez from Crooked Lane Books for all of their help.

A huge thank-you to my agent, Jen Nadol, and the Unter Agency, who do so much work behind the scenes.

I am so grateful for my dad, who read my sister Stacy and me bedtime stories every night. We even had a copy of *Tales of Mother Goose,* and I had no idea that they were three hundred years old! Growing up, we called my eldest sister "Cinder" Chelli because she did the most to help around the house. Fairy tales and characters are timeless. My mom took us to the public library so often that they offered her a job. Books have always been an important part of my life.

I adore fairy tales, and I have my very own Prince Charming! Jon, you might not be very helpful with dragons, but you're sure great with computer problems. Like the old woman who lived in a shoe, I have four incredible kids: Andrew, Alivia, Isaac, and Violet. Happily ever after has more laundry and dishes than I expected, but it's also better. Except for the new way to do math. It must have been invented by an evil witch or a bad fairy.

I am so thankful for my real-life friends who support me and my writing career, as well as for the incredible community of Utah authors. There are so many talented people who help build each other up. I am grateful for their words, their worlds, and the stories that fill them.

May the new pages of your story be the best ones yet.

DISCUSSION QUESTIONS

1. Why didn't Samir tell Tiffany the truth about his past? Would you forgive him for keeping it a secret?
2. Is Catharine, the Duchess of Beaufort, a good friend to Tiffany?
3. Caro Anstey is a victim of sexual assault; yet her own father doesn't believe that she is fully innocent. Do we believe victims today? Or do we put the blame on the victim for how they dressed, spoke, or behaved?
4. Is Evie Coram a sympathetic character?
5. Tiffany thinks, "One sometimes did terrible things to protect those they loved." Do you agree? Is a person justified in bad/criminal behavior if it is motivated by love?
6. Does Sir Walter Abney deserve his sentence?
7. Eighteenth-century divorces were difficult and expensive in England; making them impossible for the average person. What do you think of the wife-auction/do-it-yourself divorce? Would you condone or condemn it?
8. "Forgiveness doesn't mean that you have to keep that person in your life or home," Samir whispered. "And forgiveness doesn't mean you allow them to hurt you again and again. True forgiveness is giving them an opportunity to

change and grow." Do you agree? Should Tiffany have let Mary stay with her? What does forgiveness mean to you?

9. How is Tiffany's life similar to the characters Goody Two-Shoes and Finette Cindron? Does Tiffany get the ending that she deserves?

10. How is the death of Bernard Coram like the "Little Red Riding Hood" fairy tale? How is he like the *wolves* mentioned in the epigraph? Do you think that justice was served by the judge and the jury?